About the Author

Geoffrey Benson was born and grew up in Cheshire. After graduating from Cambridge with a degree in Economics, he qualified as a Chartered Accountant and spent many years in the profession. He is married with a grown-up son and divides his time between his homes in England and Spain.

Ben Jonson and a Matter of Grave Concern

Geoffrey Benson

Ben Jonson and a Matter of Grave Concern

Olympia Publishers
London

www.olympiapublishers.com
OLYMPIA PAPERBACK EDITION

A CIP catalogue record for this title is
available from the British Library.

ISBN: 978-1-80074-318-2

This is a work of fiction.
Names, characters, places and incidents originate from the writer's
imagination. Any resemblance to actual persons, living or dead, is
purely coincidental.

First Published in 2022

Olympia Publishers
Tallis House
2 Tallis Street
London
EC4Y 0AB
Printed in Great Britain

Dedication

To Pam, Dominic and Alexandra,
the wind beneath my wings.

Ben Jonson and a Matter of Grave Concern

I put down the latest copy of the Institute magazine as Janet, my mettlesome office manager, entered my room one afternoon.

'I see you're busy,' she said disapprovingly. She had recently rejigged her coiffure, and with her high forehead, her glasses and her stern air, the result was unnervingly similar to my primary school teacher, Miss Norbury, who had awed my early youth.

I tried to rise above the intemperate response which sprang to my mind and replied in an even tone, 'Yes, I was reading an interesting article about practice management. Now, Janet, what would you say my management style was?'

Janet narrowed her eyes and regarded me for a moment. 'How would *you* describe it?' she said finally.

I leant back in my chair and put my hands behind my head. 'Oh, I don't know,' I replied in a contemplative manner, 'perhaps benign dictatorship?'

Janet's lips went thin. 'Well, you can leave out the "benign" bit for starters.'

'Thanks very much, Janet,' I said, dryly. 'Anyway, can I help you? You look as though you came in here for some purpose.'

The lips went thinner still, if that were possible. 'Just to remind you that the management meeting is scheduled for five p.m.'

I cursed inwardly. I had of course totally forgotten, and had rather been looking forward to an early bath, so to speak, and a relaxing large glass of chardonnay with my old chum, Tom

Bremner, at our favourite watering-hole, the wine-bar 'Et Alia'. However, it wouldn't do to admit as much to my rottweiler of an office manager, so I looked her in the eye and said brightly, 'Yes, of course I've remembered. In any case,' I added, giving my laptop a light touch, 'with these automated calendars you get constant reminders.'

I hadn't actually noticed any such, but gambled, on there having been one.

Janet sniffed. 'Pity that the reminder didn't remind you to do an agenda then,' she said, 'so I've prepared one for you.' She dropped a piece of paper on my desk and steamed majestically out of the room.

I sighed. I have to admit that I find these meetings rather tiresome. I preferred my old way of doing things, by reviewing various reports — time costs, recovery rates, billings and so on — and hauling departmental mangers in from time to time if I thought they weren't performing as well as I would like. But I had been prevailed upon to be more 'inclusive' and 'open', and so we now have these regular meetings of the department heads. I soon discovered though that I had to be pretty rigid in keeping them short and to the point, and whereas I had tried the 'hard stop' approach, that is to say, an absolute deadline when the meeting would have to finish, I found that this was not wholly successful. I therefore decided to switch the time from first thing in the morning, to close of play, and discovered that this had a wonderfully stimulating effect on the participants, who were all anxious to slope off home.

I had also begun to find that if I was not careful, our new head of the tax department, Gary Lincoln, would try to take over proceedings. Now, I think on technical matters, Gary is actually very good, and we are lucky to have him on board, as it were.

However, he does have a very irritating habit of using 'office-speak' in his conversation, which tends to confuse and confound his audience.

At five p.m., I duly made my way to the Boardroom, where the company was assembled. Janet had enquired whether tea and coffee should be provided, but I had ruled out such niceties, on the grounds that it would only delay matters unnecessarily. 'Treat 'em mean, keep 'em keen,' I had added with a note of satisfaction.

Janet had pierced me with one of her looks. 'Treat 'em mean, watch 'em hand in their notice, more like,' she had retorted crisply.

We sat down, and I rattled through the agenda, so thoughtfully prepared by *la belle* Janet, at breakneck speed. By ten to six, I was just drawing matters to a close, when under 'any other business,' Gary stuck up a hand and asked, 'Chair, can I share a thought?'

Now if there is one thing I can't stand, it is referring to the Chairman of a meeting or enterprise as 'Chair'. I recall that on one occasion, I was involved with a local charity, and they were advertising for someone to do secretarial work for the Chairman of the Trustees. I happened to be shown the proof of the advert which was headed 'Part-time support required for Chair.' I had added the comment, 'Would suit unemployed stick of wood.' Satire, I felt, had had the last word.

Fighting back the impulse to make an ironic riposte, I said as neutrally as I could manage, 'Yes, of course, Gary, share away.'

'Good, thank you, Chair,' he began. I winced inwardly. 'Now, excuse me if I'm colouring outside the lines, but as the new kid on the block, it seems to me as a firm we are aiming for aggressive mediocrity. I think we need to re-evaluate the "bricks to clicks" agenda using our core competencies, involving the alpha-geeks naturally and the skills ecosystem, which, if we get all the aces in their places, when the rubber meets the road, we should be cooking on gas. I hope I'm not driving beyond the headlights here?'

A baffled silence met this little speech. Resisting the urge to enquire, 'And for the English speakers amongst us?' I said as smoothly as I could, 'Thank you, Gary. Perhaps you could put up a paper on that?'

I was fairly convinced that I heard my audit manager, old Alex 'Creepy' Crawley, say in a stage whisper, 'Put it up where?' but I decided it was best to ignore it and proceeded to dismiss the assembly and make a tactical withdrawal.

In a departure from our usual routine, and as my partner, Marcus was away, Tom had suggested we have a bite to eat in the new bistro, 'Chez Antoine' which had opened in the premises next to 'Et Alia'. After a couple of reviving glasses of vin very ordinaire at 'Et Alia', we duly trooped next door. An obsequious individual, who I took to be Antoine himself, duly guided us to a table in a discreet corner.

'May I present you with our menu,' he said in a hushed tone, and we solemnly took the proffered pieces of card. He bowed and retreated, leaving us to contemplate. After a brief glance, I sighed and said, 'God, I've had enough of jargon for one day!'

Tom raised an eyebrow. I managed to pretty much repeat Gary's little speech verbatim, and when I had finished, Tom looked as bewildered as the rest of us had done.

'What the blazes was he on about?' Tom asked, furrowing his brow. I had been able to think it over in the intervening time and thought I had grasped the essentials.

'I think what he meant is that my firm should try to devote more of its efforts and collective skills to online ways of doing our work, rather than relying on people actually coming to the office,' I replied, 'though I could be wrong!' I took a slurp of water and went on, 'But just look at this menu: "An infusion of water-bathed woodcock floated on mashed baby turnips", or how about this: "A suppression of hand-carved Monkfish entwined with sauteed celeriac". I mean, I ask you!'

Tom looked at me in a superior manner. 'Well, I think it all sounds terrific,' he said, 'I think I might go for the "Blade of salt-crusted Barramundi enrobed by marinated purple-sprouting broccoli".'

Antoine had at this juncture shimmied up to the table once more. 'A good choice if I may say so, sir,' he murmured, then turning to me added, 'and for sir?'

I hesitated, and my eye flickered over the menu once more. 'Actually,' I said, lowering my voice to match his, 'what I really fancy... you couldn't rustle up steak and chips, could you?'

For a frightful moment, I thought Antoine was going to keel over in shock. But then, in an accent which was pure cockney he said, 'Bleedin' hell! I go to the bother of dreamin' up this poncey menu and you want bleedin' steak and chips.' He paused, then grinned. 'Don't blame you,' he whispered, 'I have to put on this fancy stuff because that's what the punters expect. But I've got a nice piece of fillet I was going to have myself later I can do for you.'

He winked, then after taking our wine order, he moved off. Tom looked aghast.

'I can't believe you've just done that!' he cried, 'have you no finesse? What would Marcus say?'

'Marcus isn't here,' I said crisply, 'and anyway, it's what I want!'

Tom still looked askance but wisely changed the subject, and we talked about this and that until our meals were served.

I tucked in to my steak with gusto, but I noticed Tom rather toyed with his food. When we'd finished, I couldn't resist saying. 'Well, the steak was perfection! How was yours?' Tom just glared at me over the top of his glasses, but after a moment said,

'Oh, I know what I meant to say to you, Ben. Did you hear that old Willis Stanley has died?'

'Willis Stanley?' I thought for a moment, 'Oh, yes, I know who you mean. No, I hadn't heard. Must have been fairly ancient?'

Tom nodded, 'Yes, well into his eighties. He and his wife are clients of yours, aren't they?'

'Yes,' I agreed, 'have been for years. Not that I really know *him*. My tax guy deals with their stuff mostly. The wife I see from time to time — she's a member of CAOS. Do you act for them?'

Tom shrugged. 'Well, we didn't, but the widow — Gwen Stanley, is it? — asked us to help with the probate. She said your lot did their tax affairs, so we will need to get some stuff from you.'

'Sure,' I replied, 'speak to Gary Lincoln. If you can understand what he says of course! When's the funeral? I'd probably better make an appearance.'

'I'll let you know,' Tom said. We paid the bill and got up to leave. A thought struck me as I started to walk towards the door. 'Just a sec, Tom, you referred just now to "Old Willis Stanley" as though you knew him, but you said they weren't clients of yours?'

Tom looked mildly surprised. 'Yes, that's right, they weren't. But everyone around here has heard of Stanley. He had that chain of jewellers shops years ago, and he sold them to one of the big names for an absolute fortune apparently.'

'Mm, yes, I suppose so,' I replied, 'though I don't know the details. It was done, oh, twenty years or more ago, before I took over the business.'

Tom put a hand on my shoulder and said confidentially, 'Well, the story is that he got absolute millions for the deal, even all that time ago.'

'Really? Well, as I say, I don't know much about their affairs, but presumably the estate is going to be quite something. Nice fees for your lot, I should think. And easy money too, no doubt.'

Tom rubbed his hands, 'Piece of cake, I should think!'

But there we could not both have been more wrong...

I soon forgot about the late Willis Stanley, as I had other more pressing matters to deal with. The following day was a meeting of the Operatic Society to discuss our next blockbuster production, which was going to be "HMS Pinafore." However, before we got down to this, our director, Clive Pettit, was keen to talk about the Christmas concert which we were going to put on for one night only. Janet had co-opted me into doing a duet with her, and rather against my better judgement, suggested to Clive that we perform the classic Sonny and Cher song from the sixties, "I got you, babe." Clive's expression suggested that he was less than enthused, to put it mildly.

'I was thinking,' he began, 'of something perhaps more culturally enriching. After all, we are supposed to be an operatic society, aren't we?'

'Oh, nonsense,' Janet retorted briskly, 'we do operatic things all the time. This is a good opportunity to show our versatility.'

'And,' I chipped in, 'we thought we could spice it up a bit, and I could be Cher, and Janet could be Sonny.'

Clive's lips pursed into a thin line in a fair imitation of Janet's habitual look of disapproval.

'Frankly my dears, I'm not at all sure about that. I don't want this concert to turn into some sort of a frenetic drag-queen fest.'

At this point, I had to drag Janet away, as I seriously began to think she was going to land a punch on our director.

'Of all the ...' she began, 'I've never been so insulted in ...'

I had to use all my powers of persuasion to try to calm her, and she only subsided when Clive called the group together to announce the allocation of parts in "Pinafore". He handed out sheets with the proposed cast, and we all eagerly ran our eyes down to find what we had been given, if anything. She was somewhat mollified to see that she had indeed landed the role of "Buttercup" as she had hoped.

I was less satisfied with my part. 'Look,' I said, *sotto voce* to Janet, 'Ralph Rackstraw's been given to blasted Randall Barrett. I was hoping for that.'

'Oh, yes, well, look at the character notes,' Janet replied in an airy tone, 'it says for Ralph Rackstraw "a challenging tenor role that requires good acting skills".'

There was a pause. 'And your point is...?' I asked in an icy tone.

Janet was totally unfazed. 'My point is, Ben, for one thing, your acting skills aren't that great. Remember the review in the "Clarion"?'

It was my turn for a pursing of lips. How could I forget that appalling article?

'What was it they said? Oh yes, "his acting's so wooden, he's practically a fire risk".'

'OK, OK, Janet,' I replied testily, 'I remember perfectly well, thank you very much. Though I would point out that the review was actually written by that accountant who had a personal axe to grind as far as I was concerned.' Janet gave me one of her gimlet looks. 'Anyway, even if I didn't get Ralph Rackstraw, I thought I stood a chance as Captain Corcoran.'

Janet was leafing through her notes as I spoke. 'Oh yes, it says here, "Captain Corcoran… a bit stuffy and arrogant." Mm, yes, I could see that working.'

I wasn't entirely sure whether she was winding me up or not, but before I could speak, she went on,

'Oh, I see, you're Bill Bobstay, the Boson's Mate. Well, that's nice, isn't it? You've got a number of lines, and you sing in "A British Tar" trio. Perfect for you!' I was just formulating a suitable riposte when Janet dug me in the ribs and said, 'Look over there. There's Gwen Stanley. Had you heard that her husband has just died?'

I confirmed that I had. 'Tom Bremner mentioned it yesterday. Do you know when the funeral is?'

Janet nodded. 'Yes, the fifteenth. I found out today. I put it in your diary — I'm surprised you didn't notice. You're always going on about these automated calendars giving you reminders.'

I ignored this little dig and said smoothly, 'We'd better go over and give our condolences to Mrs Stanley, hadn't we?'

We duly made our way across the hall and murmured some words of commiseration to the widow Stanley. A slight woman, with a mane of grey hair and a vague manner, she looked considerably younger than her late husband must have been. She thanked us in a slightly distracted way, and we moved on.

'Right,' I said briskly, 'duty done! Now I've got an urgent appointment with a glass of vin-not-so-ordinaire! Care to join me, Janet?'

'Not on a week night, thank you,' came the firm reply, with a distinct tone of disapproval, and we parted company at the door.

Once again, the late Willis Stanley and his widow passed from my mind. In truth, I was preoccupied about the forthcoming weekend. My son, Sam, had asked me to come up to town for the weekend, and much to my surprise, had included Marcus in the invitation as well. Whilst I was naturally pleased about this, I was a little anxious about how it would all pan out. As I may have mentioned before, there is always a frisson in the atmosphere between Sam and Marcus when they meet, which can make social occasions something of a trial. I was heartened to hear that my daughter, Amy, and her boyfriend, together with Sam's new girlfriend, Holly, were also joining us for Saturday evening. I rashly suggested to Sam that we should all take in a show, and Marcus volunteered to get tickets. I blanched at the cost, and rather sarcastically said to Marcus that I hadn't intended him to put in an offer for the freehold of the theatre. Marcus had simply shrugged and said, 'You want this gig to be a success, don't you?' which I could not, of course, deny.

In fact, it all went swimmingly. Both Marcus and Sam were on their best behaviour, the latter prompted, I felt sure, by the new squeeze. I was the one who nearly caused a problem when we all met in Sam's apartment.

'Hi, I'm Holly,' the new girlfriend had said, then added, 'you know, just think of Christmas!'

Before I could stop myself, I had responded brightly, 'Oh, I'll probably end up calling you Carol, then.'

There had been a bit of an awkward pause, and Sam had scowled at me, before the fair Holly had suddenly grinned and said, 'Yeah, funny. Sam said you were a funny guy,' and we all relaxed.

We had a jolly supper before the theatre in a trendy and very noisy restaurant off Covent Garden, with copious amounts of wine. Marcus had insisted on picking up the tab for this, which he had done with great sangfroid, though he afterwards confessed, 'F--- me, I thought it was the friggin' phone number they'd written down!'

Later, after Amy and her companion, whose name I never quite established, had left us, we returned to Sam's apartment. I had suggested that Marcus and I book a room at the Oxford & Cambridge, but Sam had insisted on us staying with him. I felt foolishly self-conscious about sharing the spare room with Marcus, and fussed around after he and Sam had retired, clearing glasses and tidying the kitchen. Holly had stayed to help, although I would have preferred it if she had left me to it. She kept up a bright stream of chatter as we moved around, and I found myself liking her. At moments, she had a look of Julia about her...

She suddenly said, 'I do admire you. I think you're very brave.'

I looked at her quizzically. 'Brave?'

'Well,' she said, 'you know, you and Marcus. It can't have been easy to do.'

I shrugged. 'I don't know about that. What does Sam say?'

She didn't answer for a moment. 'He doesn't talk much about some things. Like his mother, for instance. Julia, isn't it?'

I said slowly, 'He was very close to her. He took it very hard when she died. I think he blames me...'

Holly cut in, 'No, no, he doesn't. But he misses her.'

I could feel the moisture in my eyes. 'Yes, I know. So do I. Every day.'

I was transported back to that impersonal hospital room. I

had held Julia's hand for some hours, and we had talked intermittently as the daylight slowly withdrew. She had said, 'I'm tired now, Ben, I think I'll sleep for a while.' And I had replied, 'Yes, my lovely, I'll be here when you wake up.' But she never had…

I said briskly, 'Well, better say good night,' and went into the spare room. I undressed in the dark and crept into bed, where the tears flowed down my cheeks, wetting the pillow…

It was some three or four weeks later that I was in my office one morning when I buzzed through to Janet to photocopy a document. There was no answer, so I sighed and made my way to the machine located further down the corridor. As I approached, I could see Gary Lincoln bending over it, looking harassed.

'Having trouble, Gary?' I asked.

'What? Oh, hi, Ben. Yes, I don't seem to have the knowledge density for this machine.'

I tutted sympathetically. 'Yes, it's never been quite the same since the office party last year. What it needs is a bit of percussive maintenance.'

'Percussive maintenance?' He looked puzzled.

'Yes,' I said, 'like this.' I proceeded to hit the copier sharply three times on its side. The machine burst into life and started to regurgitate sheets of paper. 'As I said,' I went on, whilst Gary looked on as if mesmerised, 'percussive maintenance. Or as I prefer to put it, hit the damned thing!'

As he collected his copies, he suddenly said, 'Actually, Ben, can I lay my silver on the table about something?'

'Please, feel free,' I replied solemnly, 'go to my office and I'll join you in a sec.'

I finished my copying, without having to resort to further percussion, and went back to my room, where Gary was already seated.

'Now, what can I do for you?' I enquired.

'I've been doing some work on the affairs of the late Willis Stanley,' Gary began, 'and if I may,' here he lowered his voice confidentially, 'I'd like to open my kimono.'

For a shocking moment, I thought Gary was making an indecent suggestion to me. Apart from anything else, it wouldn't do to dip my pen in the company's ink, as it were. But after half a second, I grasped that what he meant was that he wanted to reveal some confidential information.

'OK, open away!' I replied.

'Well, I was responding to Bremners, who are dealing with the probate for Mr Stanley, and they'd asked for various details of assets and so on. And of course, income and tax liabilities for the current year, up to the date of death.'

I nodded. 'The usual stuff. Yes, go on.'

'Well, that was all OK, but Alison just happened to be passing when I was on the phone, and mentioned Wallis Stanley's name.'

'And?' I prompted as Gary paused.

'Well, she said something like "oh, old Stanley must have been worth tens of millions by now, 'cos he sold his business for millions twenty years ago".'

'Yes,' I said, 'so I understand, although I don't know the details. I never had any involvement in the business. But what is your point?'

'My point is, that there doesn't seem to that much now,' said Gary, 'at a rough guess, about £2 million.'

'Well, perhaps he passed a lot over to his wife,' I suggested.

Gary shook his head. 'No, I've included her as well.'

'Children? Perhaps he's given away a lot to children and grandchildren?'

'No children that I can see,' Gary said with a shrug.

'Mm,' I mused, 'well, that's interesting, but there could be some perfectly simple explanation. Perhaps the Stanleys have given a lot to charity, or invested in non-income yielding stuff, like paintings or other art objects. Or perhaps they've had a riotous lifestyle, and it's all gone on wine, women and song?'

As I said this, a vision of the widow Stanley came into my mind. Whilst she certainly did a bit of singing, as a member of the chorus in CAOS, I doubted she spent much on wine, far less women.

Gary was speaking again. 'Well, it's not the long-pole in my tent right now, but I could look into it further if you want.'

'No, that's OK, Gary, let's leave it as it is for now,' I replied, frantically trying to work out what "long pole in my tent" meant. 'But tell you what, I'll mention it to Tom Bremner and see if there is anything we should investigate further.'

Gary nodded and took his leave. I leant back in my chair and toyed with the idea of speaking to Tom there and then. Before I could act, the phone trilled and other matters pushed the affairs of the Stanleys out of mind.

It was some days later that the little conundrum that Gary had posed came back to me. It was a Wednesday evening, and I was preparing to make my way up the High Street to 'Et Alia' for a reviving glass of their very reasonable New World chardonnay — 'the cup that inebriates, but does not cheer'— as Tom, who is a confirmed red wine drinker rather scathingly puts it. I had just cleared my desk when Janet put her head around the door and said brightly,

'Don't forget there's an extra rehearsal tonight.'

'Dammit!' I exclaimed, 'I was just on my way to an urgent meeting as well!'

Janet gave me one of her cutlass looks. 'And that would be with Tom Bremner at the wine-bar, no doubt,' she said in a tone of disapproval.

I could not demur. Janet continued with biting irony, 'I'm surprised you overlooked it in view of your faith in the computer reminders.'

I decided to ignore this jibe and said briskly, 'Right, well, I'll see you over there in a few minutes,' then quickly messaged Tom to say I would be somewhat later than envisaged.

I arrived at the church hall in the nick of time, just as our director, Clive Pettit, was clapping his hands together to bring the assembly to order. I was interested to see how the dynamics between the main characters would play out. Derek Hall, who was cast as the stuffy martinet, Sir Joseph Porter, was up against the egregious Randall Barrett as the 'hero,' Ralph Rackstraw. In real life, the two did not see eye to eye in a big way, and Randall's antics had even led to Derek storming off in the middle of rehearsals for 'The Gondoliers' and refusing to carry on as 'The Duke' until I had managed to mediate and persuade Derek to return.

Fortunately, things went fairly smoothly, although there was a slightly awkward moment in the break for refreshments. Derek was recounting to his group of chums a tale of how recently he had been obliged to go for medical tests, and found that the doctor involved was none other than Randall Barrett.

'And so, he says to me,' Derek related with a big grin, 'he says "I need to take some blood. Don't worry, it's just a little prick with a needle." And I says, "I can see that, but I'm just wondering what you're going to do with it"!' Derek and company fell about laughing at this (probably apocryphal) tale, but I could see Randall had overheard, and flushed a deep red. He looked as though he was about to say something, but I fixed him with a look, and he desisted. Meanwhile, Derek, who was obviously enjoying himself was carrying on.

'Then he says, "have you thought about becoming an organ donor?" and I says "No, but I once gave an old piano to the Salvation Army"!'

Fortunately, at this point, Clive, who had also overheard this conversation, called everyone to get back to work. As we trooped back into the main hall, I found myself alongside Gwen Stanley. 'How are things?' I asked.

She gave me a wary look. 'All right, I suppose,' she said, 'I'll be glad when the probate is through, though.'

It was then that Gary's comments came back to me. However, it did not seem an appropriate time or place to start making enquiries, so I confined myself to answering in a non-committal tone, 'Yes, I'm sure. Hopefully it will be soon done.'

We moved apart to take up our positions and did not come into contact for the rest of the rehearsal.

After we were dismissed, I hurried down the road to 'Et Alia' hoping to find Tom there. I was pleased to see he was in our usual corner and even more pleased to see that he had already lined up a drink.

'Phew, I'm ready for this,' I exclaimed, 'been a long day.'

Tom grinned. 'No Marcus again this evening?'

I shook my head. 'No, he's in Brussels for a couple of days. Probably having a wild time.'

We talked about this and that for a few minutes, then I remembered about the Stanleys.

'How's the probate coming along, Tom?' I asked.

'Oh, OK I think,' he said, 'I'm not directly involved in it. Why do you ask?'

I relayed the queries that Gary had raised a few days earlier. Tom looked thoughtful.

'That's an interesting point. As I said, I've not been directly involved, but I'll mention it to the team. Actually, now I think about it, one of them was saying that the widow Stanley was pestering them because there was a ring that she couldn't find, and did we have it in one of our security boxes.'

'Strange,' I said, 'I wonder what was so special about it?'

Tom shrugged. 'Don't know,' he said, 'hey, look at the time! I must go.'

It was a week or so later, and I was in my office giving a dressing down to a junior member of staff, who had taken a day's leave without the proper notice and authorisation.

'...and furthermore,' I said, winding myself up into a frenzy of self-righteousness, 'this is a place of business. It is not some sort of social club, where you can just drop in if you've nothing better to do! Now, don't let it happen again!' The unfortunate young man slunk off, and Janet appeared before me.

'Benign dictatorship indeed,' she said caustically.

I decided not to rise to that particular bait, but confined myself to asking, 'Was there something, Janet?'

'Tom Bremner was on whilst you were berating that poor boy,' she started, 'and wants you to call him back urgently. He said he tried your mobile, but you weren't answering.'

'OK, thanks, I'll call him now,' I replied, deciding to rise above trying to justify myself to her. She gave me one of her looks then vanished. I picked up my mobile from the desk and noticed the missed call from Tom, and quickly called him back.

'Oh Ben, thank goodness,' he exclaimed in his booming tones, 'you'll never guess what's happened.'

My mind quickly raced through a few unlikely scenarios, mostly involving a lottery win or an invitation to form the next government, but instead settled for the more mundane, 'No, haven't a clue, old chap.'

'Thought you wouldn't,' said Tom, 'I would never have thought it.'

'Thought what?' I asked impatiently.

'Gwen Stanley has applied for an exhumation order for the late Willis.'

I nearly dropped my mobile in surprise. 'You're kidding?' I cried.

'No, honestly, it's true,' Tom replied.

'But why?'

Tom gave a snort. 'All to do with that damned ring apparently. *La veuve* Stanley says she can't find it anywhere, and thinks it must have, by accident, been left on the finger of the deceased.'

'Good Lord,' I thought furiously, 'but would she be allowed to do that? I mean, just to look for a ring?'

Tom clicked his tongue. 'Well, it's certainly not one of the usual grounds for an exhumation. Normally they are only allowed if, for instance, you want to move the body from the original grave to a family plot in the same or a different cemetery, or perhaps repatriation overseas to be buried along with other family members. And, of course, if the court orders it for further forensic examination.'

'And none of those apply here, do they?' I paused for a second. 'Well, she must be pretty anxious to get hold of this ring. Did she say why particularly?'

'Only that it was made for her father, and he died when she was quite young, so she gave it to Willis to wear. It has great sentimental value for her, she says.'

'Well, keep me posted. Might see you later — depends when Marcus gets back from Brussels.' I rang off, and leaned back in my chair. *Quite a turn-up*, I thought, *I wonder if permission will be granted for the exhumation?*

I turned my attention back to more prosaic matters, and the strange affair of the Stanleys went from my mind.

As I walked up the path to my home that evening, I noticed with some dismay that there was an old Nissan in the driveway. This meant that our housekeeper, Freda, she of the mangled metaphors, was still around. It also probably meant that Marcus was back, and no doubt the two of them were gossiping over a reviving cup of tea in the kitchen. I could never entirely understand this cosy relationship, for whilst I admired Freda's housekeeping skills, I was not especially keen on social interaction. However, I braced myself and opened the door. Sure enough, I found the two of them side by side at the breakfast bar, deep in conversation.

'Well, it's all water under a duck's bridge as far as I'm concerned,' Freda was saying as I walked in, 'oh, hello, Mr J. Is that the time? Well, Mr Marcus, I'd better be making tracks whilst the sun shines. Now, make sure you don't go burning the midnight oil from both ends!'

She left the room and Marcus stood up from his stool and hugged me hard.

'Steady!' I protested, 'you'll break my ribs!'

He grinned, 'Well, I've missed you these last few days.'

'What were you and Freda talking about so earnestly?' I

asked.

He gave a rueful smile. 'I made the mistake of asking how Mr Bell was, and she said, "oh, he hit his head at work and he's suffering from a detached rectum"!'

'That must be a real pain in the backside!' I agreed dryly, 'What was that about burning the midnight oil?'

Marcus looked momentarily discomfited. 'Oh that!' he gave a shrug, 'just that I've got quite a pile of work to do tonight.'

'Oh,' I replied, feeling disappointed, 'I thought we could go out and celebrate the return of the prodigal. I'm quite fancying a bit of fatted calf!'

'At Chez Antoine?' Marcus queried with a wry look, 'Perhaps tomorrow night.'

I shook my head, 'Not tomorrow, I've got a rehearsal.'

'Well, then, the weekend,' Marcus sounded slightly impatient now, 'but in any case, before I start work, I need to talk to you. Here, let me get you a glass of wine.'

'This sounds ominous!' I said in a light tone, though I suddenly felt hollow in my stomach.

Marcus didn't reply but poured out two glasses of chardonnay. Instead of passing one to me, he put the glasses down and hugged me hard once more.

'I do love you, you know,' he said, holding me away slightly and gazing into my eyes. I could feel his warm breath on my face, and the heady smell of his aftershave filled my nostrils. 'Even though you are a grumpy old bastard half the time!' he added.

'Thanks a bunch!' I retorted, 'but all this is making me twitchy. What is it you want to talk to me about?'

Marcus pushed me gently onto a stool and passed me a glass. 'I've been offered a new role at work,' he began, 'it's a big promotion. Naturally with a big pay rise!'

'That's fantastic!' I replied, 'congratulations! I sense there is a "but" though?'

Marcus gave a rueful smile. 'Not much chance of getting anything past you, is there? Yes, you're right, there is a drawback. The post is based in Brussels.'

'So you'd be doing more travelling? But you're away quite a bit as it is, so I don't suppose I'd notice the difference.'

Marcus put a hand on my knee. 'Well, it would mean a bit more than that, Ben. There would be a lot of extra-curricular stuff involved — in the evenings and at weekends — so the firm want me to live in Brussels on a permanent basis.'

For a moment, the world seemed to stop on its axis. 'What was that?' I finally managed to say.

Marcus went on, 'and what I was thinking... why don't you come with me?'

I stared at him. 'You know that's a ridiculous suggestion,' I said coldly, 'what about my business? What about the family? And what would I do in Brussels whilst you are off working and doing your "extra-curricular" stuff?'

Marcus withdrew his hand from my knee as though it had suddenly become red-hot. 'I knew you'd be like this!' he said, a mulish look coming over his face.

We argued for some time, me pointing out, more than reasonably I felt, the difficulties of such a dramatic upheaval, and he trying to demolish every obstacle like a frenetic human steamroller. Finally, Marcus saw that even if I wanted to, I could not move with him any time soon. 'Well, you can come over at weekends and things,' he said, 'I mean, long-distance relationships can work perfectly well, can't they?'

'Of course!' I replied enthusiastically, whilst the hollow feeling in my stomach deepened.

A heavy mantle of depression hung over me the next day, though I tried to maintain a bright and breezy air with Marcus. I entered the office in a bad mood, and snapped at the staff all morning. Janet steamed into my room around midday and accosted me.

'What's biting you today?' she said accusingly, 'I've just had Alison come to me in tears because you've torn her off a strip.'

'Well, she's made a complete dog's breakfast, not to say a pig's ear, of a simple job I gave her the other day,' I replied in a frosty tone.

'Anything else to add to that bestiary of complaints?' Janet said, hands on hips.

'Yes,' I replied, 'I think the comments I wrote on her staff assessment are pretty apt — "works well when under constant supervision and cornered in a trap." That carries on the animal theme rather nicely, doesn't it?'

'Well, I hope you're satisfied, because the poor girl will probably now have a migraine and disappear home for the rest of the day.'

'More time costs then!' I retorted bitterly.

Janet regarded me with a not entirely sympathetic eye. 'Someone got out of bed on the wrong side, clearly.'

'My domestic arrangements are my own affair, I think,' I said in a pompous tone, 'and to misquote from "Pinafore":

"Bad language or abuse
I never, never use,
Whatever the emergency;
Though "B----r it" I may
Occasionally say…"
which is what I feel like saying now!'

'Well, then, I'll leave you to stew in your own ill-temper,' said Janet, with pursed lips, 'but since you brought up the subject of "Pinafore", don't forget the rehearsal later.' I was just about to make a sharp rejoinder when she added with undisguised sarcasm, 'Oh! I forgot! I don't need to remind you, because of all the automatic reminders you doubtless get from your automated diary!' And with that, she waltzed out of the room.

Needless to say, I had forgotten about the rehearsal, even though I had mentioned it to Marcus the previous evening, subsequent events having driven it from my mind. I had rather been envisaging a couple of glasses of reviving New World vino with Tom Bremner after close of play, when I could unburden myself to him of all my current woes.

As if by telepathy, my mobile started buzzing, and picking it up, I saw that it was none other than Tom himself.

'I was just about to call *you*,' I started, 'I need to talk to you, but I've got a rehearsal after work, so it will have to be later on.'

'Yes, OK then,' Tom said, 'perhaps Marcus can keep me company whilst we're waiting for you?'

'Oh, no, don't ask Marcus,' I said quickly.

'Why ever not?' asked Tom, puzzled by my vehemence.

I thought rapidly. 'Oh, just that he's got a pile of work to do and doesn't want to be distracted,' I said smoothly. I certainly didn't want to discuss the bombshell Marcus had dropped over the phone.

'Right you are,' Tom replied, though I thought I detected a doubting timbre in his voice.

I was so concerned with my own affairs that I was about to ring off, when I remembered that Tom had called me. 'Sorry, Tom,' I said, 'you rang. Was there something?'

'Oh, nothing really,' he said, 'I'll tell you later when I see you.' He hung up, but something in his manner left me wondering…

I tried to concentrate on work for the rest of the day, though I have to confess, with only limited success. I was relieved when it was time to close up the office, and although I would really have preferred to go straight to 'Et Alia' and unburden myself into Tom's ever sympathetic ear, I made my way down the High Street to the church hall. 'At least this will be a pleasant distraction,' I thought as I pushed open the heavy swing door. But there again, as with so many things, I was wrong…

Clive Pettit, our director, was already in full flow as I entered, hands fluttering in the air in his customary manner, one holding a spotted handkerchief with which he mopped his ever-moist brow from time to time.

'Right, now I want Captain Corcoran here please,' he pointed to a spot beside him, 'and Sir Joseph over here.' The two took up their positions. 'Oh, and Ralph Rackstraw, please as well.' There was a pause. 'Is Ralph Rackstraw here?' Clive asked in a querulous tone. There was a gentle murmur of 'no' from the ensemble.

'Oh really, it's too bad!' Clive complained, 'how can we get on when the company isn't present?' As this seemed an entirely rhetorical question, nobody replied. After a second, Clive went on, 'Well, as you're here, Ben, perhaps you could stand in for Randall for the time being?' I nodded assent and took up the position indicated by Clive. Fortunately, I was pretty well word perfect with all the main parts, though I did take the precaution of picking up the libretto from the table where I had left it. 'Right, from the top please, ladies and gentlemen,' went Clive.

We launched into the scene, and rattled through the dialogue for a minute or so. I did refer out of the corner of my eye to the libretto, in order to ensure I did not put off the other members of the cast, so I have to confess that I was not particularly paying attention to their faces, but I was vaguely aware that all was not well with Sir Joseph, otherwise known as our comic-baritone-in-chief, Derek Hall. At the point where he was about to break into song, he put his hand up and said, 'Can I have a moment, Clive, I'm suddenly feeling a bit out of breath.' The music stopped, and Janet rushed forward with a chair, onto which Derek sank with a grateful wave of acknowledgement. His face was now a peculiar shade of puce, and he was perspiring profusely. The remainder of the ensemble stood around hesitantly, not certain what to say or do, and then to our horror, Derek suddenly slumped sideways and slowly crumpled to the floor. For a few seconds, we were all frozen in disbelief, then the instructions for the first-aid course which Julia had insisted I do some years earlier, began to come back to my mind, and I sprang forward and knelt beside the prone figure of the burly Derek. Before I had a chance to check his pulse or begin CPR, I was roughly pushed aside by the athletic figure of Dr Randall Barrett.

'Someone call an ambulance, urgently,' he commanded, 'and you,' here he looked at me, 'get the defibrillator from by the front door.' I hurried off as instructed, and saw Janet already on her mobile, summoning the emergency services.

In the few seconds that it had taken me to run to the door and grab the machine, Randall had already unbuttoned Derek's shirt and was pushing rhythmically up and down on his chest. I opened the defibrillator and the disembodied, mechanical voice began its instructions. Randall called over his shoulder, 'Here, put the pads on him whilst I carry on.' I pulled the coverings off the pads and with Janet's assistance, stuck them on Derek's exposed flesh. The voice instructed that CPR cease whilst the machine assessed Derek's heartbeat. Randall rocked back on his haunches, and we all waited anxiously for the defibrillator's verdict. 'Shock advised,' it suddenly announced, and Randall ordered everyone to stand clear as he pressed the 'Shock' button. Derek gave a slight twitch, then the machine ordered CPR to recommence. Randall leaned forward again and pumped up and down. The ever-efficient Janet, meanwhile, was busily trying to track down the whereabouts of Derek's wife, whilst the rest of us looked on with a sense of helplessness. After what seemed like eons, but must have only been a very few minutes, the sound of a wailing siren could be heard, and I again ran to the door, this time to direct the paramedics to the patient. Within a short time, they had loaded Derek onto a stretcher and whisked him off, with Randall in attendance.

After the church hall doors had closed again, there was an excited babble from the remaining cast members, and Clive tried in vain to attract everyone's attention by clapping his hands and frantically waving the red-spotted handkerchief. Eventually, the hubbub died down and he was able to make himself heard.

'Ladies and gentlemen, in view of the recent — er — unfortunate events, perhaps we had better leave it there for this evening. Of course, we all are praying that our dear colleague will recover quickly, but it is likely that we may have to have a rethink about the production. I will send you all an e-mail as soon as I can. In the meantime, thank-you for your support.'

He gave a little bow at the end of this address, and I was tempted to burst into applause, but fortunately restrained myself, and we all trooped meekly out of the hall. I turned to Janet who had followed me and said, 'Well, I don't know about you, but I could use a drink!' Not entirely to my surprise, she demurred, and hurried off. I was not too sorry about this, as I wanted to talk to Tom unencumbered, as it were. I set off up the High Street and pushed open the door of 'Et Alia'. Although a lot earlier than I anticipated, I found Tom already inside, leaning up the bar, talking, as ever, to some of his cronies. His eyes lit up at my arrival, and he put an arm around my shoulder and drew me over to our usual corner. A quick nod of the head, and the barman rapidly appeared to take my order.

'I know I've said this before, but I don't know how you do that trick,' I complained, 'I could stand at the bar until Doomsday waiting to be served!'

He grinned. 'Just a knack I've acquired,' he said, 'but hey! You're here a lot sooner than expected!'

'I know,' I replied, 'the rehearsal was curtailed somewhat prematurely.' I quickly related the dramatic events in the church hall.

'Good Lord!' Tom exclaimed, 'is Derek going to be OK?'

I shrugged. 'I couldn't say. He certainly looked in a bad way. Lucky really that old Randy Randall happened to arrive at that moment, so that he could start the CPR and get the defibrillator going. If it had been left to the rest of us, we'd probably have taken a lot longer.'

I took a large gulp of wine. 'God! I needed that!' I had another swig. 'And that's not the only drama I've had in the last twenty-four hours, by the way.'

'Ah!' said Tom, sapiently, 'is this what you wanted to talk to me about?'

'Certainly is!' I confirmed.

'And would this have something to do with the fair Marcus, by any chance?'

'That obvious, is it?' I pulled a face. 'Sorry, I didn't realise I was so transparent.' I went on to tell Tom about Marcus' promotion and potential relocation. Tom looked sympathetic.

'I don't know what to suggest, to be honest. It's something you two will have to try to sort out.'

I sighed. 'I know, Tom. But long-distance relationships *can* work, can't they?'

'Of course they can!' Tom replied jovially, then added, 'Probably. Sometimes.'

'Thanks for that, Tom,' I said piquantly, 'you're a great comfort! Anyway, let's forget about all that for now. You had something to impart to me, didn't you? What is it?'

Tom put his glass down on the table. 'Oh yes! Well, two things really, one of which is a bit of a favour. Well, quite a lot of a favour, in fact.'

I wasn't entirely sure I liked the sound of this, but I said, 'Yes? Well, go on!'

'The exhumation request,' he started, then paused dramatically, 'it's been approved!'

'Good Lord!' I cried in astonishment, 'I can't believe it!'

'No, neither could we,' said Tom, 'you could have knocked me down with the old proverbial when I heard that. But anyway, that leads me on to the favour.'

I cocked an eyebrow, and Tom, after clearing his throat went on. 'Yes, it's a bit of an ask, I know, but…' he paused, then went on quickly, 'well, the thing is, I've got to be there at the exhumation, to make sure that, if the ring is there, it's kept safe and so on, and I thought it wouldn't be a bad idea if there were two sort of professional observers, so to speak, to…' He had started to gabble somewhat, but suddenly stopped, and said rapidly, 'Would you come with me please? Hold my hand?' He suddenly looked aghast. 'I don't mean literally, of course!'

'God, well, yes, of course I will,' I replied, 'when?'

Tom looked uncomfortable. 'Well, that's the thing. It's a bit of a bugger really. These things have to be done as discreetly as possible, so they tend to be done very early in the morning, before too many people are about. So, they're talking about four a.m., next Tuesday morning.'

'Oh, great!' I said, 'because that wipes out the day, doesn't it?'

Tom gave an apologetic smile. 'Yes, it's not great, I know. But we'll have plenty of company! There's all sorts going to be there: the vicar, of course, who is not entirely happy about it all, to say the least, two or three men to actually dig the coffin up, some council officials, including a health and safety guy would you believe, and God knows who else.'

'Cast of thousands in fact,' I said with a wry smile, 'oh well, it's all part of life's — or in this case, death's — rich tapestry, I suppose. Come on, we'll get some more drinks in, and let's hope this blasted ring is worth all the trouble!'

The next few days passed swiftly by. Later in the evening at 'Et Alia', after Tom and I had consumed more wine than was entirely wise, he had pointed out to me that Marcus had his career, just as I had mine, and that it was unfair of me to simply expect him to fit in with my needs and wants. And Tom had also pointed out that this move was probably not going to be permanent. 'You know how things are in their line of business,' Tom had expounded bibulously, 'they're always having these great ideas and rushing around, only to change their minds six weeks later and doing something completely different.' I had to acknowledge that there was some truth in this, and so had given myself a good talking to, and attempted to make the best of it. This had included agreeing to go with Marcus to Brussels on a trip to view apartments to rent before too long. We spent one evening looking at potential places on-line and I did my best to be enthusiastic.

As my home is within a few yards of the church and graveyard, I suggested to Tom that he might as well stay with me on Monday evening, and catch a few hours' sleep in our guest room. We had a simple supper, which Marcus had thoughtfully left for us, before he headed off to Brussels again, and retired early. Although convinced that I would not be able to sleep a wink, I fell into a deep slumber, and came to with a shock when I found a hand on my bare shoulder and Tom hissing in my ear, 'Time to get up, Ben!' I hastily washed and dressed, and we left the house about a quarter to four, walking the short distance to the churchyard. Although it was summer, it was still not light, and there was a distinct chill in the air.

Outside the church was a hive of activity, with several cars parked and their occupants gathered together, talking in hushed tones. A tall, thin individual with a clipboard, appeared to be in charge of operations, so Tom and I went up to him and introduced ourselves. He duly ticked our names off on a sheet on his clipboard, and bade us to follow him. We trooped along the path round the side of the church, described by Pevsner as 'one of the most convincing and impressive of its date in any county,' and stepped through the long grass to where a set of screens had been set up. Dodging around these, we came across the team of diggers, busily at work shovelling earth, to uncover the last mortal remains of the late Willis Stanley. Lights had been set up to assist the workers, for although the sky was now brightening rapidly, there were dark shadows still. A layer of mist, wreathing around the solemn tombstones, leant a spectral air to the scene. A robed figure just behind the diggers turned and revealed himself to be the vicar of All Saints.

'Shocking business,' he whispered in mournful tones, 'I've

never had anything like this in my life!' We nodded our heads in mute agreement.

After some while, the men digging managed to uncover the coffin, with brass handles still gleaming under a smear of grimy earth, and pass straps underneath. The coffin was hauled out of the ground and set down on the muddy grass alongside the now vacant grave. Two of the workers, closely monitored by the lugubrious council official, then proceeded to unscrew the lid. Tom and I watched in horrified fascination as the lid slid away, and the palely luminescent corpse was revealed. In spite of his protestations, I felt Tom's hand tightly grip my own, and had to admit that for once I was glad of his reassuring bulk next to me. Although I had secretly vowed to myself before proceedings began that I would not to look into the coffin, like the wedding guest in Coleridge's epic poem, 'I could not choose but hear,' or in this case, see. Braced as I was for some sight straight out of a horror movie, with cobwebs, spiders, worms and a rattling chain or two, the reality was somewhat anti-climactic. I could dimly make out the body of Willis Stanley, dressed in a dark suit, lying as though in a deep slumber, and with a slightly shiny finish on his balding pate.

The council man moved forward, and beckoned to Tom to come nearer to the open casket. I followed too, whilst the official knelt down and put on some protective gloves. He then peered in and scrutinised the body's hands, which were crossed, one on top of the other, on the stomach. 'No ring on any of the fingers that I can see,' he announced at last.

'Oh, well, that's that then!' Tom breathed, 'what an expensive waste of time this has all been!' He was about to turn away when I had a thought.

'Just a minute,' I said, 'isn't it possible the ring could have been put in one of the pockets?' Everyone swivelled round to look at me. 'I mean,' I went on, 'since we've got so far with this, isn't it worth just having a quick look?'

'I was about to suggest the same thing,' the council man said rather stiffly, and turned back to the coffin. He gingerly tried the side and breast pockets, but they were all sewn across.

'Inside pockets?' I suggested helpfully. The council man gave a slight snort, but whether at my impertinence, or with distaste at having to rummage around a dead person's clothing was hard to tell. His gloved hand probed the inside pocket on each side, but he shook his head. 'No go there,' he announced.

'How about the little ticket pocket lower down?' I persisted. Again, there was a muffled snort, but he carried on with his probing. After a few seconds, when he seemed about to withdraw his hand, he suddenly said, 'Here, just a mo! I think there is something in this one!' He reached slightly further in, then with a note of triumph said, 'Well, gentlemen, I think we've struck gold!'

'Quite literally!' I could not help remarking to Tom, *sotto voce*.

The man pulled the object out of the pocket and stood up. He opened his hand, and there in the palm, glinting now in the early morning rays, was a gold ring.

'Doesn't look much, does it?' commented Tom, and I was inclined to agree. A plain, thickish, gold band, with no decoration, it was hard to see, particularly at that ungodly time of day, what was so special. Tom took the ring from the council man, and was about to put it into a special, sealed envelope which had been brought along for the purpose, when I said,

'Just have a close look, Tom, in case there's anything engraved on it. May be needed for identification purposes, perhaps.'

Tom nodded, 'Yes, good point, Ben.' He held the ring up close to his eye. 'Can't really see too well without my readers! Here, you look,' and he passed the ring to me.

I turned it round and round in my hand. 'Can't make anything out,' I started, 'oh, wait a sec! There is something engraved on the inside!' I hurried over to one of the lights that had been used to assist the gravediggers. 'OK, I can see now. Some numbers, and a few letters.'

'What are they?' asked Tom impatiently.

I looked again. 'Well, they're slightly worn — not surprisingly, I suppose — but it looks like "10.30.15 L-R-L" I think.'

'Wonder what that is all about?' mused Tom, 'still, we've got what we came for!'

There was a considerable amount of paperwork to complete, so Tom, the council man and I retired to the vestry, which the vicar had made available to us, whilst the workmen commenced to seal the coffin and rebury it in the ground, and the vicar himself stayed behind to utter some appropriate words of prayer for the dear departed.

It was getting on for seven o'clock by the time Tom and I returned to my house. I put some coffee on to brew and asked Tom if he wanted something to eat.

'What have you got?' he asked. I suggested scrambled egg on toast, which was about the limit of my culinary expertise, and Tom readily agreed to this.

'I think it would be all right to ring the widow now, and tell her what we've got,' said Tom, and pulled out his mobile. I was busying myself preparing the eggs, which I find takes all my concentration, so I wasn't paying particular attention to the conversation, but I was aware of Tom saying 'Of course, as soon as I can,' and closing the phone.

'Well, she doesn't want to let the grass grow!' he exclaimed, putting a brawny hand on my shoulder as I was carefully stirring the pan on the hob.

'How's that?'

'She said come with it right away. So I said I would, as soon as poss.'

I served the breakfast before replying. As we sat and ate, I said, 'She must be pretty desperate for this thing. Doesn't that strike you as odd?'

Tom considered. 'I don't know. Perhaps a bit obsessive, but I suppose, as she's realised, she can't find the thing, better to do all this sooner rather than later.' He crashed his way through the toast, then said slightly indistinctly, 'Why don't you come with me? We'll be there and back before it's time to go to the office.'

'OK, then, why not?' I replied. We finished eating, and I hastily shoved plates in the dishwasher, then we went out to Tom's Merc, which was sitting in the drive.

On the way to the Stanley residence, I asked Tom where we were up to with regard to the probate on Willis Stanley's estate. 'I think the forms are all complete now, and it's ready to be submitted. Or it will be any time soon,' he replied, 'why do you ask?'

'Oh, just wondering,' I said casually. Tom drove on and we eventually pulled up outside a pleasant, though relatively modest house, in a quiet cul-de-sac.

'I thought it would be a bit swankier than this, considering all the millions he was supposed to have sold the business for,' I said as we were climbing out of the car.

Tom shrugged. 'I think they had one of those big places in

"The Avenue", but they sold that and moved here a few years ago. Easier to manage, I suppose, and quite new, so hardly any maintenance, and not much garden.' We went up the path to the front door, and he rang the bell. Gwen Stanley must have been waiting for us, as the door was opened within a microsecond. She ushered us in to the sitting room and bade us sit.

Tom, after explaining I was there as a witness to the handover, opened his briefcase and retrieved the envelope. 'I think this is what you were looking for!' he exclaimed and passed it to Gwen. She hesitated for a second, then opened it up and took out the ring. She held it in her hands and gazed at it wonderingly.

Tom cleared his throat. 'If you could just confirm that this is the ring in question, then I'll need a signature on this receipt,' he said, indicating a piece of paper he was holding, 'and then we can be on our way.'

'Yes, yes, of course,' she said, 'I can confirm that this is my late husband's ring.'

'Which I believe originally belonged to your father?' I chipped in.

Gwen looked at me startled, as though she had only just become aware of my presence. 'Oh, yes, well that's right of course, Ben. But I gave it to Willis to wear, so I think of it as his.' She paused and looked as though she was going to add something, but then closed her mouth tightly.

'I see,' I said brightly, then added, 'there's an inscription round the inside of the ring. It says "10.30.15 L-R-L" I think. I wondered what it meant?'.

Gwen peered at the inscription. It was a few seconds before she spoke. 'Yes, I see. I'd forgotten, to tell the truth. It's my father's date of birth — 30th October, 1915.'

'And the 'L-R-L'?' I prompted.

Gwen looked me in the eye. 'Liverpool,' she said firmly, 'my father was born in Liverpool.'

Before I could add anything, Tom pushed the receipt over to Gwen. 'If you could just sign this, Mrs Stanley, we'll get out of your way.' She took the paper and the pen Tom had proffered, and went over to a small side table where she duly signed her name.

'Thank you,' Tom said, putting the paper back in his case, then stood up and indicated to me to come as well. We made our farewells and were soon out in the drive again and heading back to the car.

'What was all the third degree about with the ring?' demanded Tom, as he engaged 'Drive' and the Mercedes took off down the road, 'it's none of your business!'

'Just making polite conversation,' I said a touch sulkily, 'what's the problem?'

'I know you, Ben,' said Tom, in his best magisterial manner, 'you've got some bee in your bonnet, haven't you?'

I shrugged, 'I wouldn't say that, exactly. But you have to admit that there are a few odd things here.' I paused for a second whilst Tom said,

'OK, go on.'

'Firstly,' I started putting my right forefinger on my left thumb, 'both my people and your people have expressed surprise that the Willis Stanley estate seems to be much less than everyone would have expected.' Tom nodded. 'Secondly,' I went on, sticking up my left forefinger, 'there was the fuss Gwen Stanley made with your people, going through strong boxes looking for this ring, then even going to the lengths of an exhumation to get hold of it. I mean, I ask you!'

'Anything else?' Tom asked as I paused.

'Yes,' I replied, with a note of triumph, 'the inscription on the ring!'

'What about it?' Tom snapped back, 'she said it was her father's date and place of birth.'

'I know she *said* that,' I replied, 'but she was lying. I don't know what the inscription *really* means, but you can bet your bottom dollar it isn't what she told us!'

Tom dropped me off outside my office, irritated because I had refused to explain why I was certain Gwen Stanley was being 'economical with the truth,' to coin a phrase. I in turn, was irritated with *him* because I hadn't had the opportunity to probe further the enigma of the ring, as I was coming to think of it.

I slumped down in my chair and thumped the desk in exasperation. What to do now? I looked at my watch. Only eight thirty, but there was a chance some of the staff were in. I buzzed through to Gary Lincoln only to get his voicemail. After leaving a curt message to come to see me ASAP, I slammed the receiver down. The strains of someone singing came to my ears.

'I'm called little Buttercup

Dear little Buttercup...'

Janet entered my room still singing, but abruptly stopped when she saw my face.

'Bad mood again, then?' she asked.

I felt nettled. 'I'm in a perfectly good mood, thank you. But perhaps if you could drag your mind away from light operetta for a moment or two, I've got something I want you to do.' I quickly issued some instructions. Janet became intrigued and forgot her waspishness.

'So why do you need this?' she asked.

'Just testing a little theory of mine,' I said, giving her a sly wink and trying to look mysterious. This obviously failed to work as Janet merely enquired,

'Have you got something in your eye?'

Before I had a chance to make a withering reply, Gary Lincoln appeared, and I barked out instructions to him as well. He too looked surprised, so I asked, 'Do you understand what I'm getting at?'

He nodded. 'Yes, sure, I just need to let it drip.'

'And ASAP,' I added.

Gary jumped up from the chair in which he had sprawled. 'Better start paddling on both sides then!'

Janet reappeared just as my phone started ringing. She rushed to answer it, like a dog after a rabbit, and snatched the receiver from me. She listened, then held it out for me.

'Clive Pettit for you. Oh, and don't forget the rehearsal later.'

'Thank you, but I do have my automated diary don't forget,' I responded pompously.

She snorted, 'Better safe than sorry, in my opinion,' and stalked off.

I turned my attention to the phone. 'Clive, good morning! To what do I owe this pleasure?'

Clive started speaking slightly nervously, and I could almost see him mopping his brow with his red-spotted handkerchief. 'Oh, yes, well, good morning to you too, my dear Ben.' I sensed an outbreak of mopping. After a moment, he continued, 'Well, you see, the thing is, Ben, we are in a bit of a fix, after Derek was taken ill.'

'Oh, yes,' I replied, 'How is he by the way? Any news?'

'Doing well,' said Clive, 'sitting up and taking notice. Should be home soon, but obviously he's not going to be fit to carry on as Sir Joseph. So, I was thinking, perhaps you...'

'You want me to be Sir Joseph?'

'Well, no,' Clive said a bit impatiently I felt, 'I don't think that would be appropriate. But I did wonder if we could move John from Captain Corcoran to do it, and then perhaps you could manage Captain Corcoran? With a lot of practice of course.' Another pause. 'And a bit of voice training, naturally.'

I thought for a moment. What was it Janet had said about Captain Corcoran? 'self-assured and a bit stuffy?' If I wanted to get on in CAOS this was my chance...

'How about me doing Ralph Rackstraw?' I suggested, 'You could move Randall to be the captain, perhaps?'

'Oh, I don't think that would work, Ben,' Clive began, 'after all, Ralph Rackstraw is a challenging tenor role which requires good acting skills.' I seemed to have heard that before, I thought indignantly, and was about to make an icy response when Clive, trying to pour oil on slightly choppy waters went on, 'what I mean is, there doesn't seem any point in making more disruption than necessary. No, I think you'll do splendidly as the captain.'

I relented. 'Well, what can I say but yes, Clive, of course. Anything to oblige.'

'Splendid! I knew I could rely on you, Ben. We can talk more at the rehearsal tonight.' He rang off, and I leant back in my chair, feeling rather pleased with myself. This was definitely a step up the operatic ladder, so to speak. Then a thought struck me. I was going to have to spend a great deal more time in rehearsal if I was to do myself and the role justice, but at the same time, I had said to Marcus that I would travel to Brussels with him when I could.

'Dammit!' I thought, 'when God opens a window, he's certain to slam a door in your face!'

I struggled on through the business of the day. At the back of my mind, the Willis Stanley affair was gnawing at me. And then

I had a vague feeling that something Janet had said was important, but I couldn't for the life of me think what it was.

Around lunchtime, Janet came in with a piece of paper in her hand.

'Here's the information you asked for,' she said pushing the paper across my desk. I read for a moment. 'Interesting, isn't it?'

'Interesting isn't the word!' I said, 'in part, it confirms what I thought. But it also explains something I couldn't quite understand.'

Janet had barely left the room when Gary poked his head round the door.

'I've got some dope for you,' he began, 'it's a bit of a complicated report, so should I just hum a few bars? Then I'll give you the dead tree edition.'

It took me a few seconds to work out that he was firstly going to give me a verbal report, followed by a printed version, but I nodded anyway.

When he had finished and left me with the hard copy, I leant back in my chair again. It was all falling into place, but I was still missing something: what was the meaning of the inscription on the ring which Gwen Stanley had been so eager to locate? And what was it that Janet had said which had struck a chord somewhere in the recesses of my brain? I went back over the scene earlier that morning. Janet had come in, the phone had rung, she had said something about the rehearsal, and then...

It came to me in a flash! Of course! I quickly opened my laptop and did a search. Yes, as I thought! There was no time to lose. I reached out for the desk-phone, then changed my mind and pulled out my mobile. I called Tom, and when he answered said, 'I think we'd better get back to Gwen Stanley's house PDQ!'

For the second time that day, Tom's Mercedes pulled up outside my office. I had been watching out for him, and jerked open the passenger door almost before the car had stopped rolling. 'OK, step on it!' I exclaimed.

'Would you like me to turn on the blue lights and the siren?' Tom asked with a hefty dose of irony.

'No, that won't be necessary,' I replied crisply, 'as I assume you've already arranged the motorbike outriders for us?' Two can play at being sarcastic, I thought.

Tom gave a grin. 'All right then, I give up! Now are you going to explain what this cloak and dagger stuff is all about?' I quickly outlined my thinking and the results of the exercises I had given to Janet and Gary. Tom sighed and said, 'Well, I suppose we better confront her with this and see what she says.'

Once again, we stopped outside the Stanley residence. Tom's PA had thoughtfully taken the precaution of ringing Gwen Stanley to make sure she was in, and making up some story about an extra form that needed her signature.

She must have been on the look-out for Tom, as the door opened before he had time to ring the bell. Gwen looked slightly agitated, I thought, and even more so when she spotted me. 'I wasn't expecting you as well, Ben,' she said, with an edge in her tone.

'Can we come in, please, Mrs Stanley?' asked Tom in his most unctuous manner, 'this shouldn't take a moment.'

'If it's just something to sign, can't we do it here?' said Gwen, with a touch of irritation, 'I'm just about to go out.'

'Easier if we can sit down and I can find the right papers in here,' Tom replied smoothly, tapping his briefcase.

Reluctantly, Gwen let us in. I noticed in the hallway a small airline-style, carry-on bag, tucked just out of sight of the front-door. 'Going away?' I asked brightly.

Gwen, following my line of sight, muttered, 'Just to a friend's for the weekend.'

'Oh, how nice,' I gushed, 'whereabouts? London, by any chance? Hatton Garden, say?'

Gwen looked at me with some disfavour. 'Why should I be going there? And what are you doing here, by the way? Do you always follow Mr Bremner around?'

'No, not always,' I replied cheerfully, 'only when I'm trying to prevent a crime being committed.'

Gwen's eyes widened. 'Crime? What crime?'

Tom said, 'I think Ben is referring to tax evasion, Mrs Stanley. In particular, inheritance tax evasion.'

If Tom and I had any doubts about our suspicions, they were now dispelled. Gwen sank slowly into a chair. 'I didn't want any part of it, but Willis was so insistent. He went ahead without telling me, then after he died, I found the letter giving me his instructions, so I felt obliged to carry on.'

'Yes, I'm not sure that would be an adequate defence in a court of law,' said Tom dryly, 'but I suppose I can understand the dilemma you were in.'

'But how did you know?' Gwen asked helplessly.

'Well, it was Ben here, of course,' said Tom generously, 'he worked it out.'

'It was the ring,' I said gently.

Gwen gave a mirthless laugh. 'Yes, of course! The ring. And I thought I'd covered that up so well!'

'It was a good try,' I replied, 'and whilst your acting skills are fine for the chorus in HMS Pinafore, I don't think you have a natural flair for deceit, Gwen. And I would take that as a compliment!'

'But how did you work it out?' Gwen was still puzzled.

'Ah, that would be telling,' I said, giving what I thought was a mysterious wink. Wrong again.

'I say, Ben, have you got something in your eye?' asked Tom in a tone of concern, then turning to Gwen added, 'anyway, Mrs Stanley, I think we had better tear up these probate forms and start again, don't you?'

It was late in the afternoon by the time Tom and I returned to our respective offices. Tom had suggested we have an early shower, as it were, and go for a reviving glass in 'Et Alia'. I was about to agree when I remembered the rehearsal. 'Dammit, I'll have to go to it,' I told him, 'but how about later?' We agreed on that and I whizzed off down the High Street.

There was a rather moving moment when, just before we began the rehearsal, Derek Hall had shown up. 'Just out of hospital,' he said, 'so I thought I'd look in and see how you were coping without me.' We all assured him that we were trying to make the best of it, and Clive outlined the cast changes he was proposing.

'Yes, so Ben here is going to take over the role of Captain Corcoran,' he began. Derek's complexion changed so rapidly that for a moment I thought he was going to have another coronary.

'Ben?' he spluttered, 'Ben's going to be the captain?'

Pleased as I was to see that Derek was making a good recovery from his heart attack, I couldn't stop myself saying in an icy tone, 'And what's wrong with that? Perhaps you think I'd be more suitable as Ralph Rackstraw?'

Derek's complexion immediately improved and he gave a loud guffaw. 'Well, clearly not, Ben old chap. You see, Ralph Rackstraw is a challenging tenor role...'

'...which requires good acting skills. Yes, yes, so everyone keeps telling me!' I cut in, irritated.

Luckily, at that moment Ralph himself, in the form of Randall Barrett appeared. Derek turned to him and giving a slightly embarrassed clearing of the throat said, 'Oh, hello Randall, I'm glad you're here. I just wanted to thank you properly in person. I understand that your quick action probably saved my life. I know we've had one or two little differences of opinion, in the past,' there was a stifled laugh from the onlookers at this point, but Derek carried on, 'but I'm obviously very grateful that didn't stop you helping me that night.'

He stuck a hand out toward Randall, who took it and said, 'Just being professional and doing my job.' Perhaps aware that this sounded a little ungracious, Randall added, 'But I'm pleased you're doing so well. And of course, I did have help from Ben here and the others.' We all shifted slightly uncomfortably on our feet and looked at the ground until Derek's wife tugged at his sleeve and they made their farewells.

'Actually, Clive, I wanted a little word with you,' I said to our director after Derek had left. The red-spotted handkerchief came out and mopping operations commenced.

'Oh dear,' he said, wiping furiously, 'somehow I have a feeling I'm not going to like this!'

It was a lively little group that finally met in 'Et Alia' later that evening. Janet had been curious to know what had happened in the 'Stanley Affair' as we all called it, and Gary too was sufficiently intrigued that he came to join us as well.

As expected, Tom was already ensconced as we entered the wine-bar, and before long, we were sitting in our usual corner with a couple of bottles of wine. Before we could get started on these, to my surprise, Marcus appeared as well. 'I didn't expect you back this week,' I exclaimed, 'I thought the idea was I would join you in Brussels at the weekend.'

'Ah, well, I thought I'd surprise you,' he said, with a knowing wink, 'Good surprise? Or bad surprise?'

'Oh, good surprise,' I said, 'probably!' I received an indignant poke in the ribs for this, but he grinned and went on, 'So what's been going on here?'

'Yes, that's what I'd like to know,' said Janet impatiently 'come on, Ben, spill the beans.'

I leant back in my chair. 'Well, there's not much to it really,' I started, 'I mean, I suppose Gary here first pointed out there was something odd, when he said how relatively small Willis Stanley's estate was. Then Tom and his crowd made the same sort of comment. And to cap it all, there was this business of the exhumation.'

'But that was to get Gwen Stanley's father's ring back, wasn't it?' said Janet.

Tom intervened. 'Well, that was the story she told us, yes. But as Ben and I thought, it was a lot of fuss to go to for a fairly simple ring, no matter what the sentimental value.'

I continued, 'And then when we did find the ring, there was the inscription.'

Marcus interrupted, 'I haven't heard this bit. What did it say?'

'It was very simple,' I replied, 'it was just some numbers and letters: 10.30.15. L-R-L.'

'And what did it mean?' Gary this time.

'Well, when we asked the widow Stanley, she said it was the birth date of her father: 30th October, 1915.'

'That's the numbers part I suppose,' Gary mused, 'what

about the letters?'

'She said that it was an abbreviation of Liverpool, where her father was born.'

'And you didn't buy that?' Janet gave me one of her looks.

'Yes, why didn't you? You haven't explained that to me yet,' said Tom in a reproachful tone.

I took a slurp of wine and gave a deprecating little laugh. 'Well, it seemed obvious to me that Gwen was lying. For a start, if her father's date of birth was 30th October, then surely the numbers would have read '30.10' not '10.30.' The latter would have been an American way of writing it.'

'Which of course as she claimed her father was born in Liverpool, would not stack up,' Tom said triumphantly.

'Exactly,' I nodded, 'plus, the normal contraction for Liverpool you would expect to be "LPL", not "LRL".' I took another drink. 'So I was fairly sure that her explanation was false. I think she just made it up on the spur of the moment. Which actually was pretty smart of her.'

'But not smart enough for Inspector Ben Jonson of the Yard,' Marcus grinned, giving my shoulder an affectionate, if painful, squeeze. 'So what did it mean, and how did you get to the real meaning?'

'Well, I did some basic detective work,' I said, 'or rather, I asked Janet to do it.'

'So that was why you asked me to look up Gwen Stanley's marriage certificate details,' said Janet.

'Yes,' I said, 'and of course, once we had that, you could find her father's name, and once we had *that,* you could find *his* birth certificate information.'

Janet interrupted, 'which of course showed that not only was he *not* born on 30th October, 1915, but also that his place of birth was Birmingham.'

I nodded again. 'Quite. But that just confirmed what I'd suspected. It also turned up something even more intriguing, and the answer to another puzzle. But I'll come to that later. Now Gary's work was also interesting, and again confirmed what I thought. By looking back over many years tax return information, he was able to work out that one way or another, the Stanley's had divested themselves apparently of millions in assets.'

'OK,' said Marcus slowly, 'and so?'

'And so, my dear boy,' I explained, giving him an equally affectionate and painful squeeze back, 'and so, it was obvious that what they, or at least Willis, was trying to do was to hide money away so that when the time came, the survivor wouldn't have to pay Inheritance Tax.'

'But just a minute,' Gary broke in, 'that doesn't make sense. There wouldn't be any inheritance tax payable on Willis Stanley's death if he left everything to his widow. Transfers between husband and wife are exempt.'

'You're right of course,' I said, 'and that puzzled me for a while. That Gwen was up to something fishy was quite obvious, as I said to you, Tom, in the car this morning. But the motive wasn't clear at all, was it Janet?'

Janet took up the story. 'Yes, well, as Ben said, I traced Gwen's marriage certificate so that we could find her father's name. But the certificate also gave her husband's name.'

'Yes,' said Marcus impatiently, 'Willis Stanley.'

'Actually, no,' I said, 'the point is, Gwen and Willis weren't married. Gwen was married to someone else.' I paused dramatically to let that information sink in. Marcus and Gary looked suitably stunned. I carried on, 'After we put that to Gwen, she admitted it. She and her actual husband are Catholics, and don't believe in divorce. So when she left her husband for Willis, she didn't bother to divorce.'

'But when they realised about the inheritance tax problem, why didn't they get a divorce then? Surely they would have been apart for a long time, so that Gwen could have got one more or less automatically?' asked Marcus, puzzled.

Tom chipped in, 'Yes, I asked that. But apparently Gwen and Willis were concerned that Gwen's husband would contest it. Willis in particular had become something of a miser, and he didn't want to risk the costs of a messy court case. Plus of course, they didn't want everyone to know they weren't married.'

'OK, OK,' said Marcus, 'but you still haven't explained the inscription on the ring.'

I gave a modest smile. 'Yes, that was quite a puzzle. Actually, it was Janet who gave me the answer.'

'Did I? How?'

'Yes, you said something about "better safe than sorry", and that was it of course.'

The others looked at me expectantly.

'It was the code for the combination lock of the safe!' I said triumphantly. 'The numbers are obvious of course. And the L-R-L was simply a reminder of the direction to turn the dial: left, right, left.' I stopped, waiting for the round of applause, which regrettably did not materialise. After a moment I went on, 'And in the safe was apparently a stash of diamonds, which Willis had gradually built up over the years. He of course had the connections with the jewellery trade, so he could buy them easily enough — and quite legitimately — and if necessary, Gwen could dispose of them, again quite legitimately. The only criminal part was to try to avoid a big tax bill.'

'But why the exhumation and all that fuss?' Marcus was still puzzled.

Tom took up the reins. 'Willis did all this and deliberately kept Gwen in the dark about the ins and outs. Which was fine, but unfortunately, he forgot to tell her where the code for the safe was kept. She only discovered it was inscribed on the ring when she came across a letter he had left. Unluckily for her, she didn't find it until after the funeral. That was why she was so anxious to get the ring.'

'Couldn't she have got a locksmith? That might have been easier?' Janet asked.

'She says she was worried that the locksmith would find out what was in the safe, so she didn't want to do that,' Tom replied, 'though personally, I think that would have been a better option.'

'So what happens now?' asked Marcus.

'Well,' said Tom, 'as the probate papers haven't been submitted yet, we will simply update them to include the value of the diamonds, then deal with the Inland Revenue and the tax. So no harm done as far as all that is concerned. It'll cost Gwen quite a bit though, but we can't help that.'

'So all's well that ends well,' said Janet raising a glass.

'Yes, thanks to Ben,' said Tom generously, and they all raised their glasses in salute.

'Well, thank you, though I'm not sure the widow Stanley, if I can still call her that, would share your sentiments.' I too raised my glass.

It had been a long day, and my eyes were starting to droop, so the party broke up and Marcus and I strolled up the High Street back home.

'I'm glad you made it tonight,' I said, 'there was something I wanted to say. Clive this morning offered me the role of Captain

Corcoran in 'Pinafore'. He's had to jiggle things around because of Derek's heart attack. It's a major role, so it would involve a lot of extra rehearsal and training. Particularly for me, apparently, as my acting skills seem to be questionable!'

Marcus was silent. 'So you wouldn't be free to come to Brussels at the weekends?'

'No, I wouldn't,' I said simply. He gave a snort of exasperation. 'Which is why,' I continued in an even tone, 'I told Clive this evening, that honoured as I was by the request, I wouldn't be able to accept after all. I will probably give up the minor part I've got as well, so I will be free to come over. Whenever you want.'

'Oh Ben,' Marcus draped an arm over my shoulder and gave a laugh, 'you'd really do that? For me?'

'For us,' I corrected him, 'yes of course. No question really. I mean I can't easily move there, lock, stock and barrel, but I can do that much.' He laughed again. 'What's so funny?' I asked.

He stopped. 'Nothing. Nothing at all. It's just that I wasn't sure you'd be prepared to sacrifice your acting and singing for me. For us.' I was about to speak and tell him not to be so silly, but he went on, 'You see, the thing is, I was missing you when I was away, even though you are a...'

'...grumpy old bastard. Yes, I think you *may* have mentioned that before!' I interrupted.

'...as I was saying, I missed you, so I thought 'what the hell am I doing this for? Brussels is actually pretty tedious, and the Belgians are so ugly! I used to think Bruegel's paintings of the peasants exaggerated their ugliness, but I understand now that he just painted what he saw!' He paused as we reached our front door, and I fumbled with the key. We went into the kitchen, and he poured us two glasses of wine. 'Anyway,' he went on, 'I went to the European Director and said, "Can I stir fry an idea in your think-wok"?'

'Good God!' I exclaimed, 'he's not related to Gary Lincoln, is he? Or are you?'

Marcus grinned, and gave me a playful cuff around the head. 'Not that I know of! He does go on though, doesn't he? No, actually, I said that I thought I could save them the time and expense of setting up a permanent Brussels base, and could do it all just as effectively from over here. And in the end, he agreed. So I'm afraid you're stuck with me here permanently.'

The effects of a very early start, an eventful day, and a few glasses of wine were beginning to take their toll. I managed to say how glad I was, and give him a hug, then my eyes began to droop even more. I vaguely remember Marcus saying that the Stanley affair and the inheritance tax implications had given him pause for thought, before I fell into a deep, deep slumber...

Ben Jonson and a Question of Trust

I looked at my watch and gave a start. Nearly six thirty. Just about time to sprint home to collect my things and whizz up the road to the tennis club. This tennis league thing was becoming a bit of a nuisance, but I had committed to playing, and I didn't like to back out of it.

I tidied my desk quickly and went down the corridor, calling to Janet, my Pit Bull of an office manager as I went. No reply. Then I remembered that she had put her head around my office door an hour or so earlier, saying she was leaving promptly as her sister Trudi was due to arrive for a visit. 'Blast it!' I thought, 'that means I'll have to check round and lock up before I go.'

I was as a result in a less than equable humour by the time I turned in the driveway of my house, and my mood was not enhanced by finding that there was an old Nissan parked to the side. This belonged to our housekeeper, Freda Bell — she of the malapropisms and mangled metaphors — and meant of course that she was still in occupation. I thought it odd that she was still there, as generally she likes to leave punctually at five o'clock, so she can hurry home to prepare supper for her 'hubby', Mr Bell.

'He likes something hot on the kitchen table when he comes in,' she once explained to Marcus and I, to which comment we had some difficulty in maintaining straight faces, though Freda herself seemed blissfully unaware of the *risqué* overtones of the remark.

If I do run across Freda these days, it is generally because she and Marcus are sitting down with a cup of tea at the breakfast bar, nattering away. Though, to be strictly accurate, it is Freda who does the nattering, and Marcus listens, apparently spellbound by her tales of family squabbles and disputes with neighbours, not to mention the various medical problems that appear to afflict the whole lot of them. Whilst I appreciate Freda's talents as a *femme du maison* as it were, I am less than enthralled by these stories of people I do not know, and most likely do not wish to know. However, today she could not have been detained by chatting to Marcus, as he was away in Brussels yet again, and had been for some days.

I let myself in through the front door and hurried upstairs to collect my gear. I called out as I went past the kitchen door, 'Only me Freda, sorry, in a bit of a hurry.' A minute or two later as I dashed down again, Freda was waiting for me at the foot of the stairs.

'You're here late today,' I remarked, fumbling in my pocket to check I had my keys.

Freda nodded, 'Yes, I know, Mr J. But I was late getting here today. It was my hubby, Mr Bell. Having terrible trouble with his prostrate.'

'Dear me,' I said gravely, 'well, you don't want to take that lying down, do you?'

I edged around her in an effort to get to the front door.

'Mr Marcus still away?' Freda had a cloth out now and was busy polishing away at the hall table.

'Er, yes,' I replied, 'he'll be away a few more days yet.'

'Ah well,' Freda said sapiently, whilst turning her attention to the bannisters, 'you can't change the spots on an old dog!'

I was rather baffled by this response, but said lightly, 'True, true. And a leopard can't change his stripes, either.' I made my excuses and exited the house.

I trotted along the High Street to the far end, past a pub colloquially called the 'Wonk', a contraction for the 'Wonky Donkey', and more formally known as the 'Black Horse', and into the grounds of the tennis club. Truth to tell, I had joined the club after Julia had died more as a means of therapy rather than because I have a great love of the sport. I had though felt I needed some reason to get out of the house and away from the office and engage in physical exercise, to try to stop my mind from being overwhelmed with the sheer burden of living. Not that I had a huge amount of time to spare: running a business and a home, and trying to deal with two teenage offspring was more than a full-time occupation. Still, some friends had suggested, firmly but kindly, that it was essential for my own well-being, as well as for the family.

The friends in question were Ewan and Rose McBride, the latter being Julia's closest friend. I too had found Rose to be a wonderfully sympathetic yet practical person, and she was a tower of strength in the dreadful period of my early widowhood. She had encouraged me to try all sorts of activities, and had persuaded Ewan, a somewhat dour Scot, to take me with him to play golf. I had a few lessons first with the golf pro at our local club, then set out with Ewan one fine Saturday morning for a proper round. After struggling with a few holes, Ewan had watched me hit off the sixth tee. He looked thoughtful for a moment then said in his dry Midlothian accent, 'You know the trouble with you, Ben, is that you're standing too near the ball,' there was a short pause, then he added, '…after you've hit it!'

Thus ended my ignominious and short-lived golfing career, although I occasionally, if forced, go to a corporate golfing day, where if possible, I avoid actually playing. I have tried a bit of squash in my time, though since meeting Marcus, that has rather gone by the board as well. I found that on the occasions when we did play, as he is taller and faster around the court, and overall, just so much better, matches became boringly one-sided. Eventually, we agreed not to play each other any more, as it was not helping our relationship: I would end up frustrated and angry, and the more Marcus tried to be emollient and encouraging, the more I felt he was just being condescending. We do occasionally play tennis together, though here again, Marcus is undoubtedly the superior player. The trouble is, he is not really interested in the game. He did manage to get us tickets for Wimbledon one year, via his firm's corporate hospitality budget, and I began to think he was developing a taste for the game. But he admitted after we had been there a while, that the only reason he came to Wimbledon was to eat strawberries, drink Pimms, and ogle the more muscular male players when they changed their shirts between games.

So, I plough a somewhat lonely furrow in the tennis club 'ladder', whilst Marcus devotes his sporting energies to squash. Tonight, I was drawn to play Jonty Moore, a man I knew only slightly from occasional meetings at the club. He was already in his tennis gear as I hurried into the changing room, apologising for my tardiness.

'Think nothing of it,' he said casually,' I know you're a busy man. Take your time. I'll go and warm up a bit.'

I thanked him and changed as quickly as I could and joined him on the court. A good-looking man of around forty, with short dark hair and deep brown eyes, he had an easy manner and a ready smile. We were reasonably well-matched playing-wise, but he had the advantage of relative youth over me and his superior stamina won the day, though I was quite pleased to make it 6–4,

6–3, so it was by no means a walk-over for him.

We shook hands at the end and he said in apparent earnestness, 'Well played. That backhand of yours is certainly a stroke to reckon with!' I gave a little shrug of acknowledgement at the compliment, and was about to make some equally flattering remark about his serve, when he carried on, 'Look, I've nothing on for the rest of the evening. How about a drink?'

I readily agreed. Marcus was away, and my old chum Tom had already said he was otherwise occupied that night, so I only had an empty house to look forward to.

'Sure,' I replied, 'that would be good. Do you want a beer in the bar here?' I gave a nod in the direction of the clubhouse.

Jonty pulled a face. 'Not really,' he said, 'it's a bit basic in there isn't it? I mean, all right if you're in a hurry, or absolutely desperate, but it's not great.'

I was forced to agree. 'Well, I usually haunt the wine-bar up the High Street, "Et Alia". How about there?'

Jonty happily agreed to this, so after quickly showering and dressing, we left the club and starting walking back along the High Street.

'What about your car?' I asked, but Jonty said he'd leave it in the tennis club car park, and walk back to it later. Passing the 'Wonk' once more, Jonty asked if I ever went in there. 'Only if forced,' I replied crisply, recalling some earlier exploits.

We entered the hollowed portals of 'Et Alia,' and I made my way to the usual corner. I tried Tom's trick of effortlessly summoning one of the bar staff to come to take our order, but failed lamentably. I was just on the point of giving up and heading for the bar, when Jonty, apparently with only the slightest gesture, made one appear, in a manner not unlike a stage magician. 'How do you do that?' I asked, exasperated, 'I could die of thirst before anyone takes any notice!'

Jonty shrugged and gave a self-deprecating smile. We ordered some drinks and fell into conversation. He was easy to talk to, being obviously intelligent and well-informed, with an engaging manner and wry sense of humour. I found myself relaxing and enjoying his company.

I asked him what he did for a living and he replied that he was an engineer by training, and a few years ago had joined a local firm as their technical director.

'Yes, we specialise in high quality pumps,' he said, 'it's slightly niche, but pretty profitable.'

Something rang a bell with me at this point. 'Do you mean Anglo Pumps?' I asked.

Jonty looked surprised, but nodded. 'Yes. Do you know us?'

I shrugged. 'Not well, but I've heard of you. But you're now a client of my firm. As of last week, actually.'

Jonty looked surprised. 'Really? I didn't know that. Our accounts and what have you were always done by Huxleys.'

I gave a grimace. 'So I understand. But after that business with Keith Huxley...'

I paused, whist Jonty nodded, 'Yes, but I thought people had been put in to take over the firm?'

'True,' I said, 'but even so, not surprisingly, quite a few of the old clients have upped sticks and gone elsewhere, so to speak. But presumably you weren't party to all that?'

Jonty shook his head. 'No, not really. I mean, even though I'm nominally the CEO these days, I'm only a small shareholder. The family, well the old man and his son, have seventy-six per cent of the shares, and they tend to take some of these decisions unilaterally. I will raise it with them though, because I should have been kept in the loop.'

'Sure,' I said, 'well, I'm sorry if it has come as a surprise, and I hope I haven't broken any confidences. In fact, it is really one of my people, Alex Crawley who has been involved in all this.'

'Don't worry about it,' Jonty reassured me, then glancing at his watch, he went on, 'good lord, is that the time? I must be getting along.' He rose to go, and I stood up. We shook hands and he murmured, 'It's been great, to talk to you, Ben.' He started to move away, then turned back and said, 'I don't know if you're busy tomorrow, but how about a bite to eat so we can carry on our conversation?'

I was slightly taken aback, but thought rapidly that as Marcus was still going to be away, it would be good to have some company, so replied, 'Yes, great, why not? I do have a rehearsal early on, but I should be free a bit later. How about "Chez Antoine" next door to here?'

Jonty grinned, 'It's a date,' then strode off out of the bar.

I too decided it was time to make a move, and walked the two hundred yards or so back home. I suddenly realised that I hadn't eaten, and was just preparing a sandwich, that and scrambled eggs being about the limit of my culinary expertise, when my mobile started vibrating. I flicked it on and saw that it was Marcus. Feeling suddenly guilty as I hadn't really given him a thought all evening, I answered it by saying, 'Hi there, you just beat me to it! I was about to call *you*.'

'Oh, yeah, right,' he said, 'just as well you didn't earlier, 'cos I've been tied up all evening.'

'Sounds like fun!' I said jocularly.

'No, I mean seriously, I've been working.' Marcus sounded a little huffy.

'Oh, yes? What were you up to?'

'As I said, work things. You know, this and that. Working on a presentation.' He sounded a little evasive. I wished we were skyping, as I can always tell if Marcus is not being straightforward. He develops what I call his 'shifty look', by which I mean he looks you full in the face with a slightly defiant air. He continued quickly, 'How about you? What have you been doing?'

'Oh, just work, then a tennis match in the ladder.' Somehow, I didn't quite want to admit to having gone to 'Et Alia' with Jonty. We chatted about this and that for a few minutes, then I could hear Marcus yawning, so I said, 'Sounds as if it was time you went to bed, old lad,' and we ended our conversation.

I went to bed myself a little while later with a vague sense of unease but found it hard to go to sleep. Snippets of conversations I'd had that day kept whirling around in my head, like autumn leaves in a sudden squall, though I couldn't quite pin any of them down.

I woke with a start at about three in the morning, with two sentences echoing in my brain. One was Freda saying, 'You can't change the spots on an old dog,' and the other was from Jonty: 'It's a date!'

I arrived at my desk the next morning feeling less than fully refreshed. I had lain awake for some time pondering the significance of Freda's comment about Marcus, but had come to no very firm conclusion. Then there was Jonty's throwaway comment about a date, which had caused me some heart-searching. 'Of course, it's not a date in *that* sense,' I had told myself brusquely at about four am, 'it was just a jokey comment…' I had eventually gone back to sleep, although to quote the Lord Chancellor in one of my favourite G&S songs, my slumbering teemed with such terrible dreams that I'd very much better be waking.

I had barely sat down when Janet pounced into my room, like a jaguar after its prey.

'Morning Jag — er — I mean Janet,' I mumbled.

'What do you think about winter snow?' Janet began, without wasting time on pleasantries.

I looked at her in blank incomprehension. 'Well,' I said, 'it's all very well in the winter, I suppose, and it can make the landscape look most appealing, though it's a bit disruptive as far as efficient working is concerned.'

Janet gave her usual look of barely concealed impatience, and rolled her eyes heavenwards.

'I mean,' she said with exaggerated emphasis, 'the colour I marked on the colour charts I left for you yesterday. "Winter Snow" it's called.'

Light began to dawn. 'Oh, right, I see,' I replied, 'I wondered what they were.' I had a vague recollection of picking up some pieces of paper and thrusting them in my case as I had hurried out of my office the previous evening. 'In fact,' I went on, 'why did you leave them there?'

'It's so we can decide on a colour for the offices when we decorate, of course.' Janet had her arms folded.

'*We* decide?' I asked in a heavily ironic tone. Janet regarded me with some disfavour. 'Anyway,' I went on, 'I don't remember giving instructions for the office to be redecorated.'

Janet snorted. 'Well, of course *you* wouldn't. If you had your way, you'd only paint it every twenty-five years or so.' I was about to interrupt at this unsolicited slur, but Janet pressed ruthlessly on. 'Anyway, I did mention a fortnight ago that it needed doing, and you told me to go ahead, so I've had three quotations done and selected the best. All *you* have to do is agree the choice of colour.' All this vaguely rang a bell, though in truth, Janet had caught me at the end of the day just as I had an urgent appointment with a glass of chardonnay in the wine-bar, and I had blithely told her to carry on so that I wouldn't waste valuable drinking-time arguing about it.

'Well, let me see the quotations before we go any further,' I said sharply. Janet produced some sheets from a folder she was carrying and passed them over.

I read for a moment. 'Good Grief!' I exploded, 'did these people think they were quoting to redecorate the Sistine Chapel? What sort of materials were they thinking of using, gold-leaf?'

'Well, in any case, they're starting next week, so we, that is *you*, better choose a colour ASAP,' Janet retorted, arms furled once more and foot tapping a syncopated tarantella.

'Mm,' I said, through gritted teeth, retrieving the colour charts from the depths of my case and spreading them out on my desk, 'I suppose I'd better have a look then.' I gazed at the sheets for a minute or two, looking rapidly from one to another.

The tarantella slowed somewhat, and Janet spoke. 'If you don't like "Winter Snow", how about "Misty Morning"? Or "Evening Lily"?'

I looked at her. 'Janet,' I said as patiently as I could, 'no matter what fanciful names the manufacturer has dreamed up, there are sixty different samples here, and they are all *white*!'

'Oh, men!' she said crossly, 'it's all because you haven't got as many receptors in your retina as women, so you can't see colours properly. Of course, there's a huge variation in colour in these samples.'

'I don't see what's wrong with magnolia,' I said mulishly. Janet didn't dignify this comment with a response, but I noticed the eyes roll upwards once more. Eventually, I said, 'Well, I'll take these home again and discuss it with Marcus when he gets back. Now was there anything else?'

'No,' said Janet shortly and turned to go, 'oh, just a minute, yes, there was a message from a Jonathan Moore. Could you call him back, please. Here's his number.' She banged a post-it down on my desk with some force, and exited the room.

I stared after her, musing that her talents were somewhat underutilised as 'Buttercup' in HMS Pinafore. 'She's more suited to the Valkyrie, or perhaps Lady Macbeth!' I thought viciously. Coming back to the here and now, I reached for my mobile and tapped in the number Janet had given me. 'Wonder what Jonty wants?' I pondered. The phone was answered almost immediately. 'Ah, Ben, good morning, thanks for calling back,' said Jonty.

'No problem,' I replied, 'what can I do for you?'

'Just wanted to check you were still OK for tonight.'

'Sure! Looking forward to it. I'll book a table for us.'

'Good! See you later then,' Jonty went, 'and now of course I've got your mobile number, it'll be easier to keep in touch. Ciao!'

'Yes, indeed, ciao,' I replied, and rang off. I sat for a moment, then buzzed through to Alex 'Creepy' Crawley. 'Could you spare me a few minutes, please Alex? And could you bring the file on Anglo Pumps with you?'

Some minutes later, a knock on my door, even though, as usual, it was open, heralded the arrival of old Creepy Crawley. To be fair, he was not at all creepy, but I couldn't resist the alliteration of this soubriquet, though I had to keep reminding myself *not* to call him that to his face. I had on one occasion, in a moment of caprice, written a less than enthusiastic staff report on him, but I had been most unfair. He was an able, astute and very diligent guy, and I in fact relied upon his judgement a great deal. He did though have a rather unfortunate squint, so when engaged in conversation, he would disconcertingly appear to be addressing something or somebody over your left shoulder, and I often had to restrain myself from squirming in my chair to move into his apparent field of vision.

'Alex, this new client firm, Anglo Pumps, just fill me in on them will you, please?'

I motioned Alex to take a seat, and he settled himself down, before replying apparently to the air-conditioning unit mounted on the wall behind me. 'Well, Ben, they are a manufacturer and supplier of specialist pumps, and the company was started about twenty years ago by Terry Murphy, who everyone calls "Spud".'

'Spud?' I queried.

Alex nodded. 'Yes. Apparently because where he grew up, Murphy was a dialect name for potatoes, so his friends called him 'spud.'

'Ah, I see,' I replied, although I wasn't altogether sure that I did.

Alex went on, 'Well, as I was saying, he, that is "Spud" Murphy, together with his wife and son, Lance, hold seventy-six per cent of the shares with the remainder held by the other directors.'

'Do Terry and Lance have executive roles in the company?' I chipped in.

Alex nodded. 'Yes, they do, although Terry is part-time these days. Lance is nominally there full-time, although his role is a bit difficult to define. It seems to be somewhere between general admin and sales and purchase liaison.'

'So he's not a technical guy then?'

Alex shook his head. 'No, no they've got someone who is

the technical director, and a couple of lower tier managers and so on. Plus, the CEO is on the technical side as well. Terry Murphy himself was an engineer of course, but now he mainly acts as Chairman.'

'What about the finance director?'

Alex shrugged his shoulders. 'They don't have one now. There was one, but he left, oh, two or three years ago, and he wasn't replaced. The accounts side is done mainly by a youngish guy who has been with the firm since he left school. Craig Morgan. He's got some accountancy qualifications, and seems to do a reasonable job, but for some things, they rely on the external accountants.'

'Like Huxleys,' I said, with a wry smile, 'and now us. But the firm doesn't require an audit, does it?'

'No,' Alex confirmed, shifting his gaze from the air-conditioner to a low coffee-table, 'no, it's technically a small company, though actually, pretty close to the threshold limits.'

'Profitable?' I asked.

Alex nodded, 'Quite profitable. Though Terry feels they could be more so. Their year-end was three weeks ago, and wants us to come in fairly soon, and give the accounts lad a hand with a few things, then try to finalise the accounts pretty smartish.'

'Right,' I said, then went on, 'by chance, I was talking to the CEO the other day, and he didn't know that we were taking over from Huxleys.'

Alex shrugged again. 'I don't know about that. I've not actually been introduced to him, that's true, but I got the impression from Terry that it was discussed by the Board as a whole.'

'Mm,' I mused, 'still, I suppose if you've got seventy-six per cent of the votes in the family, you probably don't have to worry too much about the rest of the Board! OK, well thanks, Alex, that's been useful.'

Alex got up and went out of the room, leaving me the Anglo Pumps file which I flipped through quickly, then leant back in my chair. It looked as though this could be a good and profitable client. Just then, my phone went, and I got swept up in the other activities of the day.

Around six, Janet appeared and said, 'I'm just off to the rehearsal. Are you coming?'

Looking up from my desk, I replied, 'Yes, go ahead if you like, I'll be across in a few minutes.'

Janet departed, and I finished what I was doing, then followed her the few yards down the High Street to the church hall where CAOS held its rehearsals. I made a beeline for our director, Clive Pettit, as soon as I arrived.

'Clive, could I have a word, please?' I asked when I encountered him talking to Betty, our stalwart accompanist.

Clive threw up his hands in his usual manner. 'Yes, my dear Ben, of course!'

I plunged straight in. 'Well, you see, the thing is Clive, you know you asked me the other day if I would consider taking on the role of Captain Corcoran, now that Derek has had to drop out, and I said "yes", and then I said I couldn't do it because of Marcus' job?'

Clive nodded, and produced a handkerchief to mop his brow, which he frequently did as soon as he started feeling stressed.

'Well, I wonder if I could change my mind?' Clive looked at me blankly. 'You see,' I continued, 'Marcus isn't going to be permanently in Brussels as it happens, so I will have the time to come to rehearsals and so on after all.'

The mopping became more vigorous. 'Oh dear, well, you

see, Ben,' Clive began, 'you see, I've already filled the vacancy, as it were. I decided to move Dick Deadeye to Captain Corcoran and I've put that new guy in as Dick. I suppose though that I could switch it round, and you could be Dick, and he could be Bill Bobstay.'

'Just a sec, Clive,' I said, and thumbed through my character notes which I had thoughtfully remembered to bring with me, 'Ah yes, here we are, "Dick Deadeye — somewhere between panto villain and Richard III... a lumpen figure...physically repellent... halitosis..." yes, thanks, but no thanks, Clive.'

'It's a great character part,' Clive protested, 'but in fact, vocally it's quite demanding, so perhaps you're right to say no.' With this he turned on his heel and strode into the middle of the hall, clapping his hands for attention.

'Dammit,' I thought to myself, 'perhaps I shouldn't have been so hasty. Oh, well, back to Bill Bobstay then.' I was about to follow Clive when I felt a tap on my shoulder and turned to find Janet standing behind me.

'Gooseberry fool,' she said.

'I beg your pardon!' I responded.

'Gooseberry fool,' she repeated, then noting my look of incomprehension added, 'the colour for the office. Gooseberry Fool. It's a very subtle soft white with a hint of green, to give a cool, fresh feeling.'

'Oh, that!' I said, 'I thought you were insulting me. Just leave it for now please, Janet, and I'll have a look at some colours over the weekend when Marcus is back.' Noting Janet's pursed lips and look of rebellion, I quickly moved to change the subject by asking, 'How is your dear sister, Trudi? You said the other day that she is staying with you.'

If anything, the lips pursed tighter still. 'Trudi is very low.

She's come to stay with me for a while because she found out her husband was having relations with the Avon lady.'

I was just trying to formulate a suitable response to this shocking information, along the lines of, 'So now she's the Barred of Avon,' or some such, when we were told to get to our positions for the rehearsal. Clive was giving a little pep talk as we were doing this.

'Now we've had to make some changes as you are all aware,' he started, 'due to the unfortunate indisposition of Derek, so I just want to remind everyone that the character notes I've given you are just possible interpretations but whilst I welcome suggestions, bear in mind that characterisation in this operetta is crucial, so please try to make them convincing, consistent and above all, comic. OK, from the top, please, Betty!'

The rehearsal went fairly smoothly, particularly bearing in mind all the changes in casting that had taken place. I was glad though when I was finished and I scuttled out of the hall and across the road to Chez Antoine. I found Jonty already seated at a table in a discreet corner, with a large glass of what looked like sauvignon blanc in front of him.

'Evening, Jonty, sorry to keep you,' I apologised as I slid into a seat opposite.

'No worries!' He gave an easy smile and pointing at his glass looked quizzically at me.

'Yes, please, I'll have the same,' I confirmed and Jonty poured out a glass from the bottle resting in its cooler beside him.

'Cheers!' We clinked glasses in salutation and brought each other up to date on the events of the day. I did not admit to having spent some time quizzing Alex and going through the files on Anglo Pumps, as it might have sounded as though I was checking up on him. After a few minutes, Antoine himself, oozed up and proffered menus, and made suggestions. I eschewed the more whimsical dishes on offer, such as 'Sauteed Oysters topped with spiced German sausage and a fume of gorgonzola,' and my companion agreed. 'I'm not keen on German sausage,' he admitted.

'Is that because you fear the Wurst?' I shot back, and Jonty laughed loudly.

'Very good, Ben. Very quick. I think I would like something plainer, to be honest.'

'OK, then. How about steak and chips twice?' I said to Antoine, who I suspected was in reality better known as Tony from the East End. Antoine, probably Tony, gave a resigned shrug and scuttled off.

Our conversation moved on from the general of the previous evening to more personal matters. I told him about Julia and the children, and Julia's untimely death seven years earlier, and then of course Marcus. After a while, I realised that I had been talking about my affairs, but had not asked about Jonty. 'So, are you married or anything?' I asked.

Jonty looked at me with a wry smile. 'Not sure I quite know what you mean when you say "or anything" but, no, I'm not married. Never have been.'

'Girlfriend?' I tried, but he shook his head, 'or...?'

'Let's just say I've been around,' he said evenly, 'but anyway, I want to know what makes you tick?'

'Me?' I thought for a moment, then said, 'I am poor in the essence of happiness, rich only in never-ending unrest. In me there meet a combination of antithetical elements which are at eternal war with one another. Driven hither by objective influences — thither by subjective emotions, wafted one moment into blazing day, by mocking hope, plunged next into the

Cimmerian darkness of tangible despair, I am but a living ganglion of irredeemable antagonisms. I hope I make myself clear?'

Jonty looked startled. 'Jesus!' he said, 'I wasn't expecting a complete psychological profile.'

'It's OK,' I reassured him, 'I was just quoting from Ralph Rackstraw in HMS Pinafore. Those are the words of W. S. Gilbert, not B. Jonson. Although there are elements of that speech which are not totally off the mark.'

Jonty looked relieved. 'Well, thank God for that!'

We talked for some considerable time, until we found we were the last ones in the restaurant, and Antoine was making not so subtle efforts to make us pay the bill and leave.

'I'll get this,' Jonty snatched the bill as I reached to pick it up, and passed a credit card over to Antoine. I made a token effort at protest, but he waved this aside. 'You can pay next time,' he said with a sly wink, 'assuming you want a next time?'

We left 'Chez Antoine' and in the street made our farewells. I toyed with the idea of asking him back to my house for a nightcap, but decided against it. 'Too late and too complicated,' I thought as I trudged off down the High Street. We had a tentative arrangement to meet the following week, when Marcus was going to be away again.

The next day was Friday, and Marcus was due home that evening. I wondered about attempting to prepare a meal for him, though I was somewhat doubtful about my ability to do so. I had once in a fit of enthusiasm in our early days together decided to make chilli con carne for us. I remembered watching Julia do it countless times, and in a folder where she had compiled her favourite recipes, and which I had wittily (so I thought) labelled 'Of Mince and Men', I found one for chilli, and set to.

Unfortunately, I made two rather fundamental errors whilst I was doing this. The first was to overlook the fact that I had not bought 'easy-cook' rice, and therefore had not bothered to rinse it thoroughly in cold water before cooking. When I came to serve it, the resulting sticky mess could have been used to resurface the M1. The second major blunder was to confuse paprika and cayenne pepper. Picking up the cayenne and thinking to myself, 'Ah, this is quite mild, I must remember to add plenty,' I had liberally poured it in on top of the meat. I dished the mixture out on top of the rather unappealing glutinous pile of rice, and set the plate before Marcus. He had bravely taken a couple of mouthfuls before coughing and reaching for a glass of water. The whole lot had gone in the bin, and we had resorted to a takeaway pizza. As far as I was concerned, it did have the benefit that I was never expected to cook after that fiasco, though I have an idea Marcus suspected I did it on purpose to achieve that end.

Before I had a chance to do anything further, a message popped up from Marcus himself, instructing me *not* to attempt to prepare anything, and that he would pick up some stuff on his way back from the airport. He did however suggest meeting him in 'Et Alia' straight after work.

The day seemed to drag on, but eventually six o'clock approached, and I felt free to leave for the weekend. As I walked down the corridor, I noticed Janet still at her desk.

'Haven't you got a home to go to, Janet?' I enquired jovially. She muttered something in return, but I did not pause to respond, and exited the building, then made my way the few yards along the High Street to the wine-bar. I headed for our usual corner, but there was no one there. I spent a few moments vainly trying to attract the attention of one of the bar staff, but eventually gave up and was about to go to the bar myself when Marcus appeared and enveloped me in a rib-crushing hug.

'God, it's good to be back!' he breathed in my ear, then releasing me, gave a flick of his finger, and, to my irritation, a barman immediately appeared to take our order. 'I thought you would have got them in already,' Marcus said casually, sitting down at the table. I was about to explain when Tom Bremner came up and greeted us.

'Mind if I join you two?' he asked and sat down without waiting for a reply.

We had a lively conversation for some while, catching up on each other's news, when Tom suddenly said to me, 'How was Chez Antoine last night? Don't tell me you had the steak and chips again!'

I was momentarily taken off guard. 'How did you know I was there?' I asked, 'I didn't see you?'

Tom replied, 'Oh, one of my colleagues was in there and mentioned he'd seen you. You were with the same chap you were having a drink with in here the night before, apparently.'

I felt two pairs of eyes looking at me closely, and tried desperately to stop the flush which I was sure was rising up my face. I tried to keep my voice cool and level as I said,

'Don't tell me, same colleague?' Tom nodded and I went on with a careless laugh, 'Anyone would think he was following me!'

'So who was this mystery man, then?' Marcus asked, with a slight edge to his voice.

'Oh, just a new client,' I said in a casual way, 'thought I'd better make a bit of an effort to get to know him and the company. Actually, by chance, he belongs to the tennis club as well.'

'Funny you didn't mention it on the phone.' Marcus looked at me with narrowed eyes.

'Well, it was only work. I didn't think it was important.' In an effort to change the subject, I reached in my case and brought out the colour charts that Janet had foisted on me. 'That reminds me,' I went on smoothly, 'what do you think of these? Janet has been badgering me to choose a colour for the office, when the decorators start next week.'

Tom, who had started to look a bit uncomfortable at the exchanges between Marcus and me, as if he wished he had not brought the matter up, glanced at the charts.

'They all look white to me!' he exclaimed in disgust.

Marcus reached out for them and studied them closely for several minutes, whilst Tom and I started talking about an accident case he had referred to me. Eventually he put then down and said, 'I think it would have to be "Clair de Lune" for you. Or possibly "Moon Dance".'

'Definitely a heavenly body theme going on there,' I replied, 'but why those? They're still white.'

Marcus rolled his eyes upwards in a fair imitation of Janet's reaction to this. 'Oh, rubbish!' he said, 'they're all quite different. As to "Clair de Lune", well, it's fresh and bright with a cool, efficient ambience which would be very suitable for an office environment.' Tom and I exchanged wry glances at this, as Marcus went on, 'but seeing these colour samples does put it in my mind that our house could do with decorating, couldn't it?' He flashed me a look.

I tried to ignore this remark, as it opened up another uncomfortable area between us. Since my wife, Julia, had died, I have been reluctant to make any changes to the house, including doing any decoration. I did however have to admit that certain areas were beginning to need some attention, but I was wary of giving the green light, so to speak, in case Marcus pushed for a more radical overhaul. Although I could understand, and sympathise with, his wish to put his own mark on the house, which was now his home, I was nervous of so doing partly through fear of offending my children, and also out of a vague feeling that it would somehow be disrespectful to the memory of my late wife. Marcus had on occasion made some pointed comments about how he felt things should be altered, but he had so far not pushed this too much.

Luckily Tom at this point distracted us by ordering some more drinks and asking Marcus if he needed any more suggestions for product names. Tom rather fancies himself as a creative spirit in this line, though in fact it was a chance remark of mine which had given Marcus his most recent idea. Marcus had absent-mindedly plonked his mobile down on the table, and I was by chance just looking at it when it suddenly lit up as an incoming call came in. The muted vibration caused Marcus to glance down and hurriedly snatch it up and put it in his pocket whilst simultaneously declining the call. He was very quick, but not quite quick enough. I had just time to read the name of the caller: Alan Lowe.

'You're very quiet,' Marcus said half an hour or so later as we made our way back home from the wine bar.

'Am I?' I tried to sound casual, though in fact I was acutely aware of having been silent ever since I had seen the caller's name. I had instantly recognised it, although we had never actually met. Alan was a man with whom Marcus had had a brief relationship, admittedly a while before we had got together, but Marcus had always assured me that they were no longer in contact. So why the call? I was uncertain whether to bring the subject up, but decided that now was not the time. 'Sorry,' I went on, 'just getting tired, end of the week and all that, you know?'

Marcus laid an arm around my shoulder, 'Sure!' he said, 'me too.'

He made us a pasta dish, and after, whilst I was clearing up, he pulled out the colour charts once again, and started prowling around, holding them up in different places and regarding them thoughtfully. I affected not to notice, but after a while he said, 'I know you're studiously ignoring me, Ben, but I do think it's time we had the decorators in.' He must have seen my face because he put his hands up in mock surrender. 'OK, OK, Ben, I'm not suggesting we do anything radical, here. I do understand, you know, how you feel about the kids and — er — Julia.'

I forced myself to become reasonable. 'Yes, yes, perhaps you're right. What were you thinking of?'

Marcus had the bit between his teeth now, and led me from room to room, reeling off suggested colours. After a while, my head began to spin with it all and I interrupted his flow to say, 'Look, tell you what, Marcus, I'll speak to the decorators at the office when they appear, and ask them to come over and give us an estimate for all this. It sounds as if it's going to cost me a fortune!'

'I'll pay my share if that's what's eating you,' Marcus snapped back, 'typical bloody accountant, always thinking of money!'

Before I could stop myself, I shot back, 'Well, someone's got too!' and instantly regretted it. Marcus is used to a generous expense account at work, and sometimes carries this over into domestic life, which has been the cause of some tensions in the past.

'Is this why you've been so moody tonight?' Marcus glared at me.

I was about to reply that I hadn't, but I had to admit to myself that I probably had. Instead, I said coolly, 'And how is Alan?'

Marcus looked startled for a moment, then remembered the call on his mobile. 'Oh, yeah, didn't I mention it? Alan is working in Brussels now and we bumped into each other at a reception the other night.' He gave me one of those looks which, as I may have mentioned before, I call "shifty". That is, he looked me full in the face without blinking. I was about to reply in a withering tone, 'Oh, how cosy,' but he carried on. 'Anyway, what are all these candlelit dinners with this chap Tom's colleague saw you with.'

I bridled. 'That was work!'

'So was this!'

I opened my mouth to reply, but thought better of it. If I was not careful, this could descend into a full-blown argument, and I suddenly felt that I didn't have the energy for it. Instead, I said in a more emollient tone, 'I'll get us both a drink,' and padded off to the kitchen. When I had filled our glasses, I found Marcus in the sitting room. I handed him a glass, then said softly, 'Here's to us, eh?'

The rest of the weekend passed peacefully enough, though I had the feeling we were both being a bit careful with each other. I brooded about Marcus and Alan. Was it just a chance encounter as Marcus had intimated, or was there more to it? I tried to be stern with myself and say, 'Don't be ridiculous: don't you trust Marcus?' Unfortunately, there was a part deep inside my brain that kept replying, 'Not entirely!' I couldn't help but recall how Marcus behaved around my erstwhile operatic rival, Randall Barrett, which was not totally reassuring.

Monday morning. I was at my desk promptly, having risen early as Marcus had a seven-thirty flight to Brussels, and for once I was ahead of Janet. I was concentrating on reviewing a report when she entered my room, and stood in front of my desk.

Without looking up, I could feel her glowering at me, and for a few seconds pretended not to notice her, then finally raised my eyes and bade her a good morning.

In response, ignoring my pleasantries, she merely said, 'Satin soufflé!'

I blinked. 'Thanks for the offer, Janet, but I've already breakfasted,' I replied politely.

'No, no!' Janet pursed her already thin lips even more than normal, 'I mean the colour for the decorators.'

'Oh, that old thing!' I affected a tone of nonchalance, 'actually, I have decided on "Clair de Lune".' Perhaps you could tell the painters that, please.' Janet looked as though she was about to demur, but I quickly went on, 'oh, and by the way, could you arrange with the head honcho to come over to my place to do a quotation for some work there?'

She gave a small toss of the head, and disappeared. Something about her demeanour made me wonder for a while if everything was all right. She was often — in fact, when I think about it, was *usually* — curt to the point of discomfort, but today she seemed especially so. Before I could ponder any more, a 'ping' indicated the arrival of an e-mail on my mobile, and I could not help but notice that it was from the Tennis Club. I opened it up and found it was from the fixtures' secretary in charge of the ladder.

'Ben,' it read, 'Could I remind you please that if you need to alter a game you must do it through me. If players start making their own amendments to the roster, it disrupts the whole match system. Regards, Mike.'

Puzzled, I read it again, then started to smart with the injustice of it. I had never altered any arrangements that I could recall, and certainly, none recently. I was just about to concoct an indignant response when the phone went. It was Janet.

'You said the other day to make an appointment to see Terry Murphy of Anglo Pumps, if you recall,' she began, 'so I've made one for later today.' There was a short pause, then she added, 'though I expect you've already noted it because it's on your automated diary.' This was a bit of a nasty one, as I had on previous occasions been somewhat hubristic about this piece of kit.

I decided not to rise to the bait, but simply replied, 'Yes, thank you, Janet.' I was about to put the phone down when something made me ask, 'Everything all right with you, Janet?'

There was a snort from the other end. 'Of course. Why wouldn't it be?'

I felt rebuffed. 'Why indeed?' I said and replaced the receiver firmly on its holder.

The appointment had been scheduled for midday, so around eleven thirty I whizzed up the High Street to my house to collect the car. I was irritated to find that Freda's old Nissan was inconveniently parked in the drive in such a way that I could not get my BMW out of the garage. Cursing, I let myself in by the kitchen door and shouted to her, 'Freda! Could I trouble you to move your car, please. I need to use mine.'

A voice came from on high. 'Oh, there you are, Mr J. We're like two ships that go bump in the night, aren't we? I'll be right down.'

She was as good as her word, and after a further exchange of pleasantries, she coaxed the Nissan into life and moved a few yards. I reversed smartly out of the garage and with some difficulty, managed to turn the car around and head out of town towards Anglo Pumps' premises.

I swung the car into the parking area of Anglo Pumps'

factory and came to a halt in a bay marked 'Visitor.' Trotting across the tarmac, I entered a modern and clinically-sleek reception area, where a nice-looking girl in a top emblazoned with 'Anglo Pumps' enquired in what way she could help me.

'I've an appointment with Mr Terry Murphy,' I responded, 'the name's Jonson, Ben Jonson.'

'Of course,' the girl confirmed, 'I'll let him know you're here.' She spoke into a phone, then said to me, 'go straight in, second door on the left.'

I did as requested, and entered Terry Murphy's office. He rose from his chair as I entered and we shook hands. A stocky man of medium height, and around the age of seventy, he had black-rimmed glasses behind which were a pair of small yet shrewd-looking eyes. He waved me into a chair, and I started my spiel about how good it was to meet him and how privileged we were to have his company as a client.

When I had finished, he leant back in his chair and looked at me thoughtfully. 'Yes, well, you've come highly recommended.' I raised a quizzical eyebrow, and correctly interpreting me, Terry said, 'Oh, Tom Bremner, from Bremners solicitors. Good chap.'

I nodded in agreement, as Terry went on, 'You see the thing is, Ben, we are paying far too much tax. I was just looking at my tax return the other day and it's ridiculous. Plus, God knows how much VAT and PAYE and what have you. It's absurd.'

I sighed. I could just see that Terry was the sort of client who seems to think that somehow, we accountants get a share from the government of the amount of tax they pay. Terry was in his stride now. '…not to mention Capital Gains Tax on a few shares. Quite ridiculous.'

I began to come out with my usual line that the thing to remember about Capital Gains Tax was that at least you had made a *gain*, not a loss, but I had a feeling it was going to be an uphill struggle. Fortunately, we were interrupted by the door opening and a thirty-ish something man wandered in with a bunch of papers in his hand.

'Could you sign these, Dad?' he said, without apology for the intrusion. Terry looked slightly put out, but with a wave of his hand said, 'Ben, this is my son, Lance. Lance, Ben Jonson, from the new accountants.'

We shook hands and I murmured some greeting. Lance was good-looking enough in a slightly nondescript way, but what struck me most was the dullness of his eyes and expression generally. As I tried to explain afterwards to Marcus and the others, the phrases that went around my mind were those such as 'The lift doesn't quite make it to the top floor', 'the wheel is spinning but the hamster is dead', 'the gates are down, the lights are flashing, but the train isn't coming', or 'one pork-pie short of a picnic'.

Lance left. 'Quite a chip off the old 'spud' — er, block!' I remarked brightly.

Terry threw me a sharp look, but replied in a level tone, 'Yes, well, Lance has a sort of liaison role here. Does a splendid job.'

'I'm sure,' I murmured. We talked for a few minutes about the business in general, with Terry giving me a potted history as to how it started and his own background. He took me on a tour of the factory, explaining the various processes and products as we went, and finally around the offices, introducing key members of staff as we went. Amongst these was Craig who had assumed the role of financial controller following the departure of the finance director two or three years earlier. A fresh-faced and seemingly very youthful lad, I had to restrain myself from enquiring whether his mother knew he was out on his own. Of course, he also introduced me to Jonty, and we both admitted that we had already met at the Tennis Club, although neither of us mentioned the drinks and dinner at Chez Antoine we had shared so recently.

Back in his office, Terry commented on Jonty, 'Good man there. We're lucky to have him running the show now that I've taken a back seat.'

I made some anodyne reply, expressing agreement, then Terry leaned forward in his seat and said in a confidential tone, 'Ben, although the company does fairly well, I think it could do better. One of the things I'd like you to do is see if we can be more efficient. And profitable. Whatever that shows up.' He paused and before I could reply, he added, 'And report to me, eh? Not anyone else.'

I was slightly taken aback, but replied, 'Well, Terry, we will do what we can, but obviously we are not management consultants, and we are certainly not qualified to advise on technical matters relating to production and so on. But of course, if we come across anything, we will let you know.'

We talked for a few minutes more, then I took my leave. I had to walk past Jonty's office, but he was talking to Craig and didn't look up as I went by.

I drove back to the office thinking hard. What was it Terry was hinting at? I was still pondering on this as I sat at my desk an hour later, and dashed off an e-mail to Alex with a brief resume of my talk with Terry Murphy. Just as I was pressing 'Send', Janet appeared before me with a sheaf of paper.

'Sign these,' she said.

'And good afternoon to you too,' I replied, feeling irked by her peremptory tone. I looked up in some irritation and was struck by her extreme pallor, and the undoubted signs of moisture around her eyes.

'Good Lord, Janet, are you all right?' I exclaimed.

'Never better!' she replied, lips thinning, but the involuntary sob that followed gave her away.

I was alarmed. I had never seen Janet so obviously upset before, not even when she had discovered that her putative date, Randall Barrett, was married, a fact he had somehow omitted to mention to her. 'Come on, you'd better sit down,' I went on in a more ameliorative tone, 'tell me what's the problem. If you want to,' I added as she hesitated.

'It's Trudi,' Janet began as she sank down on the chair opposite my desk.

'Trudi?' I put my head on one side. A vision of pouting lips and staring eyes came to me. 'Oh, yes, your sister. She's staying with you at the moment, isn't she?'

'Not any more!' came the abrupt reply, 'she went last night.' I raised an eyebrow, and then the whole story came out. Trudi, who had come to stay with Janet after discovering her husband was having a fling with the Avon lady, had owned up after rather too many glasses of merlot, to having had a fling herself with the builder who had done her extension. Janet had been horrified, and there had followed a fierce argument at the end of which Trudi had stormed out and presumably returned to the errant husband, who had, it seemed, been dumped by the licentious cosmetic Queen.

'And I trusted her!' Janet wailed, tears flowing unchecked down her cheeks by now, 'I feel so disillusioned with her. I trusted her implicitly.'

I muttered some platitudes, feeling totally out of my depth in all this display of emotion. I gave her a glass of water, which she drank, then standing up and dabbing at her tear-stained cheeks with a handkerchief I had fished out of my desk drawer, she said, 'Thanks, Ben, I'm feeling better now. It's just the disappointment. I thought I'd never have to go through it again after the way my "ex" behaved. But there you go.' She turned to leave the room, then stopping, handed me the by now rather damp handkerchief and added in a soft tone, 'You've been kind, thank you.' I was quite touched, though the effect was somewhat undermined when I heard her say to herself in something more approximating her normal *timbre*, 'Quite surprising really.' Before I could protest, she had gone, only to reappear a moment later to say, 'Rehearsal tonight don't forget,' and disappeared once more.

'At least she didn't make some crack about the automated diary this time,' I thought to myself, wryly.

All of this, plus the need to catch up with what I had been doing, drove thoughts of Terry Murphy and Anglo Pumps from my mind for the rest of the afternoon. At six thirty, I tidied my desk, then headed out of the office and along the High Street to the Church Hall, which served as the rehearsal rooms for the Operatic Society. I pushed open the door to find the company talking in excited whispers in little groups, whilst Clive, our director, was wandering around, wringing his hands and mopping his brow, which had a colour nearer to shamrock than chartreuse.

'Oh, thank goodness you're here, Ben,' he gasped, clutching hold of my arm tightly.

'Why, whatever's the matter, Clive?' I asked whilst delicately trying to extricate my arm from the vice-like grip he had on it.

'Disaster!' Clive exclaimed putting one hand against his forehead in a dramatic gesture. 'It's Captain Corcoran.'

'What's he done?' I said, rubbing my biceps where Clive had

dug his fingernails in.

'Only been having a bit of "hanky-panky" with one of the *soi-disant* ladies of the chorus,' Clive intoned primly.

'Well, whilst perhaps not the sort of conduct we expect from a noble Captain, I don't see what all the fuss is about,' I said.

'Oh, you don't understand at all,' Clive pursed his lips in displeasure, 'you see, *Mrs* Corcoran, if I can call her that, found out about the goings-on, and gave the captain an ultimatum: give up the fair maiden *and* of course the Operatic Society, or don't bother coming home. As she's the one with all the lolly, it was not something he wanted to argue about. You know the woman — she's turns up at rehearsals sometimes — the rather glamorous one with the expensive frocks.'

I thought for a second. 'Ah, I think I know her. So I suppose it was a case of do what I say, or never darken my *Dior* again!'

'This is no laughing matter, Ben,' Clive admonished me with a finger aimed at my midriff, 'as I see it, there's only one course of action now.'

'Which is?'

'You'll have to play Captain Corcoran, of course,' Clive exclaimed. I was flattered.

'Desperate times call for desperate measures,' he added after a pause, which was rather less flattering.

'Well, Clive, I don't know,' I started, thinking that I wouldn't want to seem too eager. 'Why me? Why not promote Dick Deadeye instead?'

'Of course, I could do that. Then you could take over Dick Deadeye's part...' Clive began thoughtfully. A vision of the character notes for Dick Deadeye floated before my eyes, "Richard III... a lurching lumpen figure... physically repellent..." and I hastily said to Clive,

'All right, of course I'll do it, Clive. Anything to oblige, you know me.'

'Oh, Ben, thank you. I knew I could rely on you,' Clive cried, and dug his fingers once more into my arm until I nearly cried out in pain.

Although naturally rather pleased to have this opportunity for a leading role thrust into my hands, I did have a few qualms. For a start, I had some doubts about my voice. Captain Corcoran was written for a baritone, and I am nearer a tenor, if anything. It is true that Bill Bobstay is also technically a baritone, but it is of course a pretty small role and easier to get away with. In particular, the captain's second act opener 'Fair Moon, to thee I sing' although lovely, is a bit challenging to carry off well.

Then there was the matter of time. It was going to take me a while to memorise the part, and a great deal more rehearsal would be required. I had once before turned down the role on those grounds, though admittedly that was when I thought Marcus was going to be permanently in Brussels, and I would be spending every weekend travelling over there. That was no longer the case, but still, it would be a big commitment of my time. How would Marcus react? And did I care? The thought, unbidden, struck me with the force of an electric shock. Before I had time to think, my mobile vibrated in my pocket. Taking it out, I saw there was a message from Jonty: 'Time for a drink later?'

Without pausing I replied, 'Great! In rehearsal, but come to my house at 22.00. See you.'

I didn't have time for further consideration as Clive was rounding us up to start, and I had to find my script...

It was just after ten, when I scurried up the drive and inserted my key in the door. A movement by the side of the house made me look round, and I gave an involuntary jump as the figure of Jonty appeared, silhouetted against the light.

'Gosh, Jonty, you gave me a fright,' I exclaimed, 'I didn't realise you were there. Where's the car?'

He put a reassuring hand on my shoulder. 'Sorry about that, Ben. I was a bit early, so I sat on the bench round the side there to wait for you. I left the car at the tennis club — I was there earlier, so there didn't seem a lot of point moving it.'

'Right,' I replied, 'well, come on in then.'

We went through to the kitchen, and I motioned for him to sit at the breakfast bar, whilst I went to the fridge and took out a bottle.

'Glass of chardonnay?'

He nodded, and I poured out two fairly generous measures. 'Cheers!'

We clinked glasses. 'How did you get on with Terry today?' Jonty began, 'sorry I didn't have much chance to see you.'

'Oh, it went fine,' I said, 'I had a tour of the place and met a few people, including son-and-heir, Lance.'

'Oh, yeah, you mean "Chinese brunch".' Jonty laughed.

'Chinese brunch?'

'Yeah, the original "Dim Son".'

I grinned. 'Yes, he didn't strike me as the sharpest blade in the drawer, that's true.'

'Terry say anything in particular?' Jonty asked.

I was about to tell him of Terry's comments about the profitability, but my professional instincts kicked in, and so instead I replied, 'Oh, he said some nice things about you, and how invaluable you were, if you're fishing for compliments.'

Jonty gave a wry smile. 'That's something, I suppose.' He had a mouthful of wine then went on, 'What did he say about

Lance?'

I was slightly surprised by this question and didn't answer for a moment. I flicked a glance in Jonty's direction. He had on a white shirt which was open perhaps a little too low to be entirely proper, and rather tight dark trousers which stretched somewhat over muscular thighs... I cleared my throat and replied, 'Oh, erm, not a lot really. Just that Lance did a good job in a sort of liaison role, I think.'

Jonty pulled a face and gave a snort, but before I could say anything he suddenly said, 'Is your partner — Marcus, isn't it? — is he coming back tonight?'

I could feel my face reddening as I stammered, 'No, no, actually he's back in Brussels until the end of the week.'

'So home alone then?' Jonty gave a sort of mocking smile.

'Looks that way,' I said, in as breezy a tone as I could manage.

'Good,' he murmured and I felt his hand lightly brush the hairs on my forearm where I had rolled my sleeve back.

A sudden clanging from the front-door bell made us both pull away as if we had touched a live wire.

'Who the hell can that be at this time?' I cried, leaping down from my stool and heading for the door. I could still feel my cheeks burning and my arm seared as if it had been touched with a branding iron.

I could see a dark figure through the glass of the door and for a second thought it was the police with some devasting news about a terrible accident. I wrenched open the door, only to discover the reassuring bulk of none other than my old friend, Tom Bremner.

'Sorry to disturb,' he began, 'but I saw your lights were on, so I thought I'd come across for a nightcap.'

'Bloody hell, Tom, you nearly gave me a heart attack! I thought it was going to be the coppers with some bad news.'

'Nice to see you too!' Tom said with a wry smile.

I laughed. 'Oh, yes, well sorry, Tom, but you gave me a bit of a turn. Come along in.'

He pushed past me and headed for the kitchen before I had a chance to explain that I had company. I hurried after him saying, 'Actually, Tom, funnily enough...'

Jonty was standing up by the time we got to the kitchen, and although I felt I detected a slight annoyance at the interruption, he answered civilly enough when I did the introductions. Tom said, 'Sorry, I didn't realise you were entertaining, Ben. Have I interrupted something?' He gave me a curious look as he said this, and I could feel the colour rising in my cheeks once more.

'No, not at all,' I replied, in what I hoped would pass as a casual tone, 'Jonty here, like your good self, saw my light on and popped in for a nightcap. Isn't that right, Jonty?'

Jonty nodded in acquiescence, and I busied myself getting Tom a drink. He took the glass and raised it in salutation, then said, 'Actually, Ben. I've got a bit of a favour to ask. Could I crash down here for the night? I've got an early start in the morning and it's a bit late, so there doesn't seem a lot of point going back home now.'

Later, I wondered if Tom had really intended to ask that, or whether he had just made it up on the spur of the moment. Of course, what could I say other than 'yes, no problem at all'. After a few minutes of rather stilted conversation, Jonty yawned ostentatiously and announced that he had better be making tracks. He said goodbye to Tom, and I saw him to the front door.

'Thanks for the drink, Ben,' he said, 'I'll be in touch, eh?' He walked down the gravel a few yards before half turning and putting a hand up in salutation. Then he was gone, swallowed up in the deep shadows of the rhododendrons bordering the gateway.

I returned to the kitchen. 'Nice chap,' Tom said, but there was an edge to his voice which I found unnerving.

I slept badly that night, and taking Tom at his word that he had an early start, woke him promptly at seven with a cup of tea. He sat up in bed, wearing a set of Marcus's night wear, the tee-shirt top of which stretched rather dangerously tight over Tom's not inconsiderable girth, and looked at me through bleary eyes. Taking the cup from me he said,

'Now listen, Ben, I will say only this and then no more: just remember and be thankful for what you *have* got, not hanker after what you haven't got.' With this somewhat gnomic comment, he took a gulp of tea, then flinging back the duvet, leapt out of bed and headed for the bathroom.

At the office, for once I kept my office door firmly shut, and settled down to work. After an hour or so, I fetched myself a coffee and turned my attention to something that had been worrying away at my subconscious from the previous day. It was Anglo Pumps of course, or more particularly, Lance Murphy. Why was it that Terry Murphy had sounded rather odd when he had mentioned him, as had Jonty late last night. Terry had gone on, in a rather vague way, to imply that the profits of the company were not what they ought to be, and then exhorted me, or more strictly, my firm, to explore this, 'whatever that shows up'. Was this a veiled hint that Terry suspected his son of something? Certainly, the exhortation to report only to Terry himself lent credence to this theory. I wondered also if that was what Jonty was trying to get around to saying as well. Of course, Jonty had also implied that Lance was not overburdened in the brain department, but I had come across cases in the past where individuals, whilst not clever in the usual sense, had a certain low cunning which enabled them to get up to all sorts of illicit misappropriations.

My mind drifted on from that to Tom's words that morning. Tom had presumably detected some frisson between Jonty and me, and was issuing a warning, that was plain...

I buzzed through to Alex, and asked him to come through to my office with the Anglo files. He duly arrived about ten minutes later, putting his head around the door and solemnly addressing the window to the right of me.

'Ah, Alex, thanks for popping in,' I started, 'come on, take a pew.' I indicated a seat opposite and Alex gingerly lowered himself onto the chair, almost as if he expected it to collapse beneath him.

'Right, now Anglo,' I continued, 'how are we getting on?'

Alex opened a file in front of him and looked down. 'We're pretty much there, I think,' he said, 'I've just got a few things to tidy up, then I can pass it through to Gary to do the tax work.'

'OK,' I nodded, 'have you got some draft accounts there?' Alex nodded and passed me a copy. I flicked through them, and as I was doing so said, 'Anything out of the ordinary show up?'

'Not really, Ben,' Alex replied, 'why, did you think there might be?'

I hesitated. I didn't want to start casting aspersions, even though I knew I could trust Alex' discretion. Still, if there was something to find, we needed to be on the ball, so to speak. 'I'm not sure, Alex, to be honest. It's just a gut feeling if you like. Now I know this is not an audit, but I think I would sleep easier in my bed if in this case we applied a few more tests and checks than normal. What about running the data through that new software we've got for the forensic side?'

Alex shrugged. 'OK, if you think it's necessary. How far do you want to go back?'

I thought quickly. 'Five or six years if we can, please Alex.'

Alex addressed a point over my left shoulder. 'Right, Ben, I'll get on to it. Might take a little while, and it's going to blow the time budget.'

It was my turn to shrug. 'I suppose so, but I'll take it on the chin and authorise the write-off.'

Alex stood up, and giving a brief nod, exited the room. I sat for a while after he left, staring into space. I was running over the events of the previous day, or more specifically, the evening. I realised with a pang of guilt, that I had not spoken or communicated with Marcus at all for two days. Then, some little devil in my head suddenly made me want to look at Marcus' mobile account. I had all the passwords necessary to access this information as indeed he had for my account, and I quickly entered the site. I found the call history and looked down. With a lurch of my heart, I saw a number of calls and texts in the last fortnight to one particular name: Alan Lowe.

I am not sure how I got through the rest of that day. Somehow, one half of my brain was able to function perfectly normally and deal with work, whilst the other was frozen. Tom messaged me halfway through the afternoon suggesting a session in 'Et Alia', but I made an excuse that I needed to learn my part for the rehearsals of 'Pinafore' later that week. I felt that I could not cope with even Tom's reassuring presence that evening. Around half six, I left the office and walked home, noting with relief that Freda's car was not there: I felt I could not have coped with her either that night. I heated up some ready-meal from the freezer, and pulling out the script for 'Pinafore' did as I had told Tom, and settled down to learn my lines.

Around nine, my mobile rang, and picking it up, I saw it was Marcus. I toyed with the idea of not answering, but then told myself sternly that it would be immature not to. I wasn't sure whether to act coolly or try to be normal, but in the event, I need not have worried. Marcus was brief, saying that he was in a plenary session that was likely to carry on for some time, and that he would call me the next day for a proper talk. I felt relief, though I knew it was only postponing the problem.

I slept surprisingly well in view of the state of mental turmoil I was in, and awoke the next morning feeling much more alert. I opened the front door of the office to find a variety of men in overalls, moving furniture and laying down dustsheets. I had of course completely forgotten that the painters were starting that morning on the redecoration of the building. I tried to enter my room, but as I put my hand on the door handle, Janet rushed up to me, clipboard in hand and barred the way.

'No, you can't go in there,' she began, then consulting her clipboard added, 'let me see, I've put you in that little room next to me for the moment. Now off you go!' I started to protest, but she cut me off by saying, 'Your stuff has all been put in there, and there's a screen and terminal, so you should have all you want. Now, let me get on!'

I made my way rather disconsolately to the little room Janet had indicated and threw my case down. The room had no window, and only a small desk and chair. Efficient as ever, Janet had put that morning's correspondence and matters for my attention on the desk ready, so I sighed and started ploughing through it. After an hour, feeling in need of refreshment, I wandered down to the kitchen, only to find that too under siege from decorators, with the coffee machine nowhere to be seen. I was standing in the corridor rather helplessly, wondering what to do, when Alison from Business Services, better known to me as 'Alice in Ledgerland' came by.

'Looking for a coffee, Ben?' she asked brightly, and seeing my nod I she went on, 'We've manged to find a kettle in the stationery cupboard, so I'll bring you one if you like. Milk and no sugar, isn't it?'

I accepted gratefully and went back to my temporary cubbyhole. 'Not sure how much longer I can stand this,' I thought and started considering which clients I could visit to get away from the office. After a couple of minutes, Alison bustled in with my drink and as she was putting it on the desk, Alex arrived.

'Got a minute, Ben?' he started, then stopped when he saw Alison. A flush slowly spread over his face. 'Oh, er, hello, Alison,' he stammered, 'I didn't see you there.' There had been an awkwardness between the two of them ever since the office Christmas party the previous year. Fuelled by too many glasses of vino collapso, Alison had launched herself at the hapless Alex, who, attempting to sidestep the attack, had tripped heavily over a decorative planter and ended up on the floor. In the meantime, the unfortunate Alison had ricocheted off and collided with the stationery cupboard door, causing it to come away from its hinges. Alison too flushed, and muttered something about leaving us to it. The two of them then performed a rather uncomfortable quadrille, as Alison, who is, shall we say, of comfortable proportions, attempted to sidle past Alex to the door in the confined space which was now my lot.

I attempted to keep a straight face as I said to Alex, 'Yes, of course, what can I do for you?'

'Anglo Pumps,' he began, 'I did as you suggested, and ran the data with that new program.'

'Gosh, that was quick!' I exclaimed, 'I thought it would be a while yet before you could do it.'

'Yes, well the accounts guy at Anglo was very helpful, and e-mailed all the data I needed straightaway, so I was able to get cracking.'

'Anything interesting?'

'Possibly.' Alex wasn't giving much away, I thought. 'Look, I've done a brief report and summary, which you'd better have a look through.'

I took the file which he was proffering from him, and absent-mindedly waved him into a seat, forgetting that there was no spare chair in the little room, so that he was obliged to lean rather awkwardly against the door-jamb. I skimmed through the report. In essence, Alex had found a number of interesting factors. Firstly, and actually quite obviously from a scan of the accounts over the last few years, the cash and other liquid assets of the firm were quite markedly down. This appeared largely due to an increase in the stock and work-in-progress at the year-ends. The overall gross profit percentage of the company had stayed remarkably constant, although the net profit, not surprisingly, had fluctuated over the term.

I put the file down and looked up at Alex. 'Just remind me, Alex,' I said, 'when did the former finance director leave?'

'About three years ago,' Alex replied, addressing a coat-hook on the wall behind me.

'And these ratios started going awry before that?'

'Yes,' Alex agreed, 'but apparently this chap had some sort of nervous breakdown, so he was missing for quite a lot of the year before he actually left.'

'Mmm,' I mused, 'Anything else show up? How about the analysis of the cost of sales?'

Alex took the file from me, and pulled out a sheet. 'The

analytical review threw up this item,' he said, pointing with a finger to an item headed "GW Services". It looked innocuous enough, although the totals invoiced to Anglo were quite considerable — about £200,000 per year.

'So that needs looking at further?' I thought for a moment. 'OK, Alex, it looks as though there might be something odd. Tell you what,' I scribbled some notes on a piece of paper and passing it to him said, 'just find the answers to those few points, will you, and we'll take it from there.'

Alex looked at the sheet and raised his eyebrows, then nodded and left.

I pondered on what Alex had shown me. On the face of it, there could well have been some defalcations, to use a splendidly euphemistic expression. It could be that someone was slipping false, or at least, inflated, invoices from this supplier, GW Services, into the accounting system. Presumably the payments for these were ultimately going into the hands of the perpetrator, who was somehow manipulating the year end stock and work in progress figures to disguise the fraud. The fact that the fraud, if any, had increased since the departure of the finance director was also of interest. This would presumably preclude him from any fiddling, but it unfortunately made the obvious suspect his assistant, Craig, who had now taken on the function of Chief Financial Officer. Or of course, it could be someone more senior, such as Lance Murphy...

Whilst I was still mulling this over, my mobile vibrated. It was Marcus. I was tempted for a brief moment not to answer, but then thought better of it.

'Hello stranger!' he began. I ignored this and just replied 'Hi.'

'I'm on my way home,' Marcus continued, 'just thought I'd

let you know.'

'OK,' I replied in a cool tone. I should just have left it at that, but some little devil inside prompted me to add, 'Can you bear to tear yourself away from Alan?'

I instantly regretted saying it, but it was too late. I could hear Marcus' sharp intake of breath. 'I don't know what you mean!' he began.

'Oh, come on, don't treat me like an idiot,' I cried, 'I've seen a list of all the calls and texts you've had with him these last few days.'

There was a silence. 'You've been checking up on me?'

'Just as well I did!'

Marcus gave a snort. 'I thought you knew you could trust me, Ben. But as you don't appear to, I'll tell you what I said. He kept pestering me, and I told him that whatever it was between us was over, and that I didn't want to see him again, except of course, I may have to because of work. But outside work, nothing. I said that I was with you now, and I wouldn't let him come between us. I'll show you the messages if you don't believe me. Now I have to go. I'll see you later.' The line went dead before I could respond.

Did I believe him? Did I even *want* to believe him? As I sat contemplating my innermost feelings, my phone vibrated again. It was a message from Marcus. 'As promised, here are the messages. On the way to airport, back later— if you want me back.' I skimmed through the correspondence between Marcus and Alan, which I had to concede, verified what Marcus had said. Feeling contrite, I sent a quick reply: 'Course I do.'

The day wore on, and I did my best to concentrate in the confines of the temporary office. Not long after lunch, which consisted of a sandwich eaten at my desk, Alex poked his head around the door once more, and solemnly addressing the filing cabinet in the corner, said, 'I've got some answers for you, Ben.' He handed me some sheets of paper, and I quickly read his notes.

'I see,' I said gravely, putting them down on the desk, 'and you're sure about this?'

Alex nodded, and I added, 'Well, leave this with me. Oh, and could you find Janet for me and ask her to come through, please?'

Alex left, and a minute or two later, Janet came in, clipboard still in hand and lips pursed. 'I hope this is important,' she began, 'I'm up to my eyes today!'

'I'm sure you are, as always,' I replied, 'but could you spare a few minutes. Please. I want you to phone Terry Murphy and ask if I can come and see him this afternoon. Oh, and I want these other people to be on hand as well.' I scribbled on a piece of paper and passed it to Janet. She looked at it briefly, said, 'I'm on to it now,' and departed.

I finished the report I was writing, then gathered up my papers, put them in my case and headed out of the office. I met Janet in the reception area, where we had to shimmy past each other because of all the furniture which had been piled together under dust-sheets. 'All arranged,' she said with a confirmatory nod as I went.

I hurried down the High Street and collected the car from home, then once more set off in the direction of Anglo Pumps' offices. At reception I was ushered quickly in to Terry 'Spud' Murphy's room, where I revealed what we had uncovered. He listened without speaking, and when I had finished said, 'Right, Ben, thank you. I've got the others waiting in the Board Room, so let's go through, and you can tell them what you've just told me.'

We entered the Board Room, where we found Lance Murphy

and Craig Morgan sitting around the table, looking rather ill at ease. Terry waved a hand at me and asked me to begin. I cleared my throat and standing at the head of the table, started to speak.

It was two hours later that I got back to my office, just as Janet was about to lock up. 'Good heavens, Ben, you look dreadful!' she exclaimed, 'whatever have you been up to?'

'Thanks, Janet, I love you too!' I retorted. 'Anyway,' I continued, 'tell you what, come over to "Et Alia" with me, and I'll reveal all. It's all right,' I added, seeing her startled look, 'I messaged Tom Bremner on my way back, and he will be there as well to act as chaperone!'

Janet considered for a moment. 'Well, I suppose I haven't got anything pressing tonight, now that Trudi has gone and there's no rehearsal, so why not?'

We locked the door and set off the few yards to 'Et Alia'. I headed for our usual corner and sat down whilst Janet said she would just go to the Ladies to freshen up. Tom, had not yet arrived, so I beckoned a barman to take our drink order. Five minutes later, he had still not come and Janet reappeared.

'Not got any drinks yet, Ben. Honestly!' and with a peremptory wave of her hand, she summoned the recalcitrant *camarero* who whizzed over in the flash of an eye.

I resisted the urge to enquire how she had managed that and was about to launch in to an account of the events of the last few hours when Tom came in and greeted us. He plonked himself down, and I began again.

'Well, it's all been a bit traumatic really. You know this new client, Anglo Pumps?' The others nodded, and Tom cut in, 'Yes, we act for them as you may know.' I nodded, and said, 'Yes, so I believe, which is why I don't mind telling you all this.'

I went over the issues that Alex had discovered earlier.

'So these GW Services invoices are phoney?' Tom asked.

'Yes,' I replied, 'well, to be accurate, those for the last three or four years are. There *was* a legitimate supplier with a similar name a few years earlier, but they went out of business. The neat trick here was the culprit used a similar name so people would not think much of it.'

Janet said thoughtfully, 'Alex was telling me something about this whilst you were out. I can see how the computer program might pick up these things, but how did you find out so quickly who was doing it?'

I tried to look modest, but I suspect I failed. 'Well, actually, that was my hunch. I got Alex to check the bank details of GW Services, and then cross check with the employees' bank details. A bit of a gamble, but I reckoned it was possible that the perpetrator would use the same bank as he used personally.'

'And you found a match?' Tom cut in.

'Indeed, we did,' I confirmed.

'So was it the son — what's his name? — Lance — or the accountant?' Janet asked eagerly.

I gave a rueful smile. 'In the event, neither,' I said.

'What?' Tom and Janet exclaimed together. 'Well, who then?' Tom asked impatiently.

'Jonty Moore,' I said, sucking my lips as I did so.

'You mean that chap you've been hanging around with these last few weeks?' Tom sounded a little censorious, 'though I can't say I'm altogether surprised. Didn't like the look of him.' He turned and leant towards my ear. 'Unlike you!' he whispered.

'I don't know what you mean!' I said, feeling slightly uncomfortable.

'OK, OK,' Tom put his hands up in mock surrender, 'anyway, tell us the full story. How did you get on to all this?'

I was about to start when I happened to look up and there was Marcus just coming through the door of the wine-bar. Muttering an excuse to the others, I stood up and made my way through the crowded bar and we met face to face. For once I was oblivious to the people around us and flung my arms around him. 'Thank God, you're back,' I murmured. Marcus was taken aback, I could feel, but returned the embrace with enthusiasm.

'Not sure what that was all about, but I don't mind you carrying on!' he said, with a sardonic grin.

'Come over here and sit down,' I commanded pulling him by one wrist over to where the rest of the party were gathered. 'Tom, get this man a drink before he dies of thirst,' I instructed, and Tom, with his usual air of effortless efficiency summoned a barman before I had time to sit.

'I was just about to enlighten everyone,' I started, and quickly filled Marcus in with the events of the afternoon.

'OK, Sherlock,' Marcus said when I had finished, 'so tell us how you did it?'

'Well, of course, it wasn't easy,' I began, 'because for a start we weren't doing an audit.'

'Ah yes,' said Tom, 'if you were doing an audit, you would be looking for fraud.'

'Well, no, not exactly,' I replied, 'you see, to quote Lord Justice Lopes in the 1896 Kingston Cotton Mills Case, an auditor is "a watchdog, not a bloodhound". In other words, the auditor is keeping an eye on things generally, not specifically sniffing around for evidence of wrongdoing. No, it's when we're doing the *forensic* stuff that I consider myself a bloodhound...'

'Yeah, right down to the long floppy ears and the drooling!' cut in Marcus, to hoots of laughter all round. I gave him my best withering look.

'Yes, thanks for that Marcus. No, what I mean is, we wouldn't necessarily have been looking in any detail at the accounts and so on in this instance. But two things prompted us to look for something fishy. Firstly, of course, it was the old man, "Spud" Murphy. He obviously had an inkling something was up, from the way he behaved when we met. I think he suspected in the first instance that it was something to do with Keith Huxley, but I think he was also worried that Lance was somehow involved.'

'That was the first thing,' Tom interjected, 'what was the second?'

I could feel the colour rising in my cheeks, and had to pick my words carefully. 'Well, the other thing was the way Jonty Moore suddenly appeared and — er — well, I suppose, started chatting me up, for want of a better phrase. I mean, I know that sometimes I perhaps have quite a good opinion of myself...' here I paused, awaiting the exclamations of indignant denial. However, I was sadly wrong there, so I ploughed on. 'Anyway, I thought it was all a bit strange, but I couldn't understand at first. Then, I thought that perhaps Jonty suspected something as well, and was for some reason trying to either warn me, or simply pump me for information. You see, I made discreet enquiries at the tennis club, and it turned out that it was Jonty who had altered the tennis fixtures, presumably in order to engineer a so-called casual meeting with me.'

'And that was with the intention of keeping tabs on you to see if you found anything?' Marcus looked me in the eye as he asked this.

'Er, well, no, not entirely,' I stammered, 'well, I suppose that was part of it. No, it was more brazen than that. You see, I think it is entirely possible that Keith Huxley *did* know what he was up to, but Jonty paid him to keep quiet. But I'm only guessing. Whatever it was, once of course Keith had disappeared off the scene, so to speak, and we had been appointed, then Jonty became worried that we might find out what he had been up to. Which explains why he was so put out when Spud and the family decided to move the accounts to us. Incidentally, he did of course know perfectly well what had been decided before we played tennis and had dinner — it was minuted in a Board meeting at which he was present. That was one of the things that I got Alex to check.' I paused and gulped down some wine. 'No, what he had in mind, I think,' I continued, 'was to — er — put me in a compromising position, so to speak, and then either blackmail me into keeping *shtum* if I discovered anything, or perhaps just rely on my — er — *goodwill* towards him to stay quiet.'

'And were there any other suspects?' Janet put in.

'Well, I wondered if the old finance director could have been on the fiddle, which is why he went a bit off the rails,' I said, 'but it seemed that in fact it was *after* he left that the fraud really started. Of course, that was because there was no one to prevent it. And again, it could have been the young lad, Craig, who then became the financial controller, without a great deal of scrutiny from the directors. And finally, there was Lance. Could anyone really be that dim?'

'And the answer was "yes"!' Tom laughed.

'Well, that's a bit unkind,' I said, 'and he's not dim really.'

'And what other pointers were there?' asked Marcus.

'Well, the credit card for example.'

The others looked puzzled. I went on, 'You see, Jonty paid for our meal with his company card, so I got Alex to check how it had been dealt with in the accounts. Alex found it had been put down as "travel" whereas it should of course have been a purely private expense. Not conclusive, I know, but it was another indicator.' I took another mouthful of wine. 'But most crucially, it was Jonty who was able to manipulate the stock figures. He did the calculations, and fiddled around with overheads and other factors, then gave the results to Craig, who just accepted them at face value. Not surprisingly, of course.'

'Anyway, well done Ben. You weren't taken in by this Jonty Moore,' Tom gave me a literal as well as metaphorical pat on the back.

'Well, thank you, Tom, but I have to give credit to Spud Murphy of course, who evidently felt something was adrift and put me on my guard. And of course, Clive Pettit.'

'Clive?' Janet cried, 'Whatever has he got to do with it?'

I grinned. 'Well, he put me back as Captain Corcoran, and it was whilst going through the script, a line of his struck me:

"Though to catch your drift I'm striving
It is shady — it is shady."

And that made me wonder what old Jonty was *really* up to!'

It was a little later that evening. Janet had left, saying she had a meeting to go to (no doubt her feminist group, I thought) leaving Tom, Marcus and me. The other two were in earnest discussion and as I sipped my wine, I studied Marcus. Clever, funny, sensitive, caring, and I had to admit, not bad-looking. And a tall, muscular frame to boot. What had I been thinking? Tom's words came to me: *just be thankful for what you have got, not hanker after what you haven't.*

Marcus must have felt my gaze on him, as he suddenly looked at me and said, 'Penny for them, Ben? What are you thinking about?'

I smiled at him. 'Oh, nothing at all, Marcus. Nothing at all. Trust me!'

Ben Jonson and a Lack of Internal Control

I was leaning back in my chair one afternoon with a hefty tome on my lap when Janet, my termagant of an office manager, presented herself before my desk. As so often happened, I cursed the 'open-door' policy which results in these appearances without warning, leaving no time to strike a pose of earnest endeavour. No words were spoken, but I could sense the waves of disapproval as Janet's eyes fell upon the book I was reading.

'It's called "Interview Techniques for Financial Witnesses", and I'm reading it as part of my continuing professional education.' I laid the book on the desk, wondering why I should feel the need to explain myself. It was in part because in certain lights, Janet bore an extraordinary resemblance to my former primary school teacher, Miss Norbury, who had so blighted my early years. Fortunately, I have got past the bed-wetting these days…

'Oh, yes?' Janet seemed less than impressed by my explanation.

'Yes,' I went on in an enthusiastic tone, 'it says a lot about ways to empathise with the interviewee, and how to get the most out of them.'

'For instance,' I picked the book up and thumbed through it, 'where is it, oh, yes, here we are: "Use cognitive behavioural and kinetic techniques together with a neurolinguistic programme for the most effective interrogative ambience".'

Janet regarded me stony-faced. 'Have you been talking to

Gary Lincoln again?' she asked, with to my mind, more than a hint of irony. Gary, of course, is our tax manager, and has a penchant for using absurd office jargon whenever he speaks. He rather floored me on one occasion when he asked me 'Can I open my kimono to you?' I thought for one horrible moment that he was making an obscene suggestion, but I gathered that in fact all he meant was that he wanted to reveal some confidential information to me.

I withered Janet with a look. 'Leaving all that aside, Janet, did you want me for something?'

Janet plonked a hefty file on my desk. 'These are this month's invoices that need your approval for payment.'

I gave a sigh. 'All right, just leave them with me and I'll go through them in the morning.'

Janet's hands went to her hips: always a dangerous sign, I have observed. 'No way! I need them today, so you better get on with it before you slope off to the wine-bar with your chums.'

I opened my mouth to protest about this unwarranted insinuation, but before I could do so, Janet continued, 'And it's no good saying you're not, because, if you recall, I was here earlier when Tom Bremner was on the phone to you. And you definitely ended by saying "I'll see you there at about six". Isn't that so?' The arms were folded now.

I toyed with the idea of flatly denying this, and saying that we were having a meeting in Tom's office, but the expression on Janet's face, so redolent of Miss Norbury, the primary school teacher, made me think better of it. Instead, I suddenly recalled a chapter from the book I had just been engrossed in, where it talked in enthusiastic tones of the benefits of copying your interlocutor's body language. 'Kinetic mirroring' it was termed. *'When an interviewer adopts similar body positions and mirrors the interviewee's movements, a greater chance for rapport is realized.'* I folded my arms to match Janet's, and was about to reply in a soothing fashion, but before I could speak, Janet was off again.

'And don't you fold your arms at me in that passive-aggressive way! I could probably have you for sexual harassment!'

I hurriedly unfolded my arms. *So much for establishing empathy,* I thought, *she's probably been to another of her feminist group meetings.* 'All right, all right, Janet, let's calm down, should we?' I said.

'I'm perfectly calm, thank you!' came the retort, 'but whilst we're on the subject of invoices, if you find it so much trouble to go through them, why don't you just leave it to me? I'm quite capable of dealing with it all, you know.'

The kinetic mirroring technique kicked in unbidden, and I found my lips thinning in a fair imitation of Janet's habitual expression. Making a conscious effort to relax them in order to avoid another intemperate outburst, I replied in as even a tone as I could muster, 'I am sure that is quite true, Janet. But the thing is, businesses need to have systems of internal control, particularly businesses such as this where we are often investigating other enterprises. We need to set a good example, if nothing else.'

'Internal control?'

I leaned back in the chair once again and put the fingers of my two hands together in my best didactical manner. 'Internal control,' I began, 'as defined in accounting circles, is a process for ensuring an organization can achieve its objectives in operational effectiveness and efficiency, reliable financial reporting, and compliance with laws, regulations and policies.

More particularly, an internal control is a procedure or policy put in place by management to safeguard assets, promote accountability, increase efficiency, and stop fraudulent behaviour. In other words, an internal control is a process to prevent employees from stealing assets or committing fraud.'

The hands once again moved dangerously onto the hips. 'And you think I would do that?'

'Well, of course not, Janet. But,' I went on pompously, 'controls protect weak people from temptation, strong people from opportunity, and innocent people from suspicion.'

'But surely you can trust me to deal with the invoices?'

'Blind trust is *not* an internal control, I'm afraid,' I retorted crisply, 'and in this particular instance, the control *I* am relying on is that I approve *all* invoices before payment. Do I make myself clear?'

'Crystal,' came the terse response, as Janet started to leave the room, 'but I still need those invoices back before you leave to go and play!'

Miss Norbury herself could have learned a thing or two from my office manager…

For the sake of the orderly running of the office, and if I am honest, a quiet life as far as I was concerned *vis-à-vis* Janet, I applied myself to the wad of paper that Janet had so unceremoniously flung down on my desk. As ever, all was in perfect order, and try as I might, I could not find anything to query. When I finished, I again leaned back in my chair, pondering on whether Janet might in fact have a point. I *could* have spent the last hour doing some productive work, rather than tedious administration. But, on the other hand, as I had pointed out to Janet, controls are put in place just as much to protect the employee, and it might not be fair to her to simply sweep them aside. I was still mulling this over when my mobile beeped, and I looked down to see there was a message from my old friend, Tom Bremner, to the effect that I was wasting good drinking time, and to get myself over to Et Alia *tout de suite,* as it were. I quickly gathered my things together and hurried out of the office, making a great show of dropping the pile of approved invoices on Janet's desk as I went. 'Don't stay too long, Janet,' I advised her cheerily as I left. The response was muted, and the resemblance to Miss Norbury grew even more marked...

Entering the wine-bar, I found Tom at the bar, talking as ever to a group of colleagues and acquaintances. At my appearance, he put an arm around my shoulders, and ushered me off to our usual corner table. Without apparent movement on his part, a barman appeared to take our order. 'I don't know how you manage that, Tom,' I complained, 'I could write "War and Peace" waiting to be served.'

Tom merely gave a laugh. 'Well, you've either got it or you haven't, eh?'

'And I definitely haven't,' I retorted.

'Oh, well, you've got other talents, eh?' Tom gave me a knowing wink. 'By the way,' he carried on, his arm removing itself from my shoulder, 'did you have a chance to look at that case I sent over to you this afternoon?'

'The two old-folks' home workers you mean?' I responded.

'Yes, that's the one,' Tom affirmed, 'looks a bit hopeless to me, to be honest. What do you think?'

'On the face of it, you may be right,' I agreed, 'but you never know, we may be able to come up with something. But I need to go through it in more detail first.'

In truth, I had barely skimmed the file, but as Tom had indicated, it was not encouraging. The case concerned two men in their late twenties, Kenny Mitchell and Noah Kirby, who were employed by a local care home. Part of their role was to take residents on trips out to local shops and attractions where they could spend their own funds, withdrawn for the purpose from safe custody at the home. The old folk could of course purchase items for themselves and even spend small amounts on gifts for the staff such as a cup of coffee, for example. After each trip Kenny and Noah had to account for the residents' monies. But then one day an allegation was made that Kenny had been stealing cash from the old folk. After a local authority investigation, a report was prepared which alleged that, as well as stealing their cash, Kenny had been spending excessive amounts on trips out. In other words, Kenny was alleged to have been treating himself and Noah on these trips, taking improper advantage of the residents' vulnerability by using their money inappropriately.

Kenny and Noah were interviewed by council staff, and Kenny immediately admitted that he had taken some money. Following those interviews, the matter was referred to the police and both Kenny and Noah were arrested and interviewed under caution by a Detective Constable Sparkes. The latter looked into the personal bank accounts of the two men, and also a schedule of money withdrawn by Kenny from the old folk's home. He concluded that there were suspicious deposits into Kenny's bank account, which more or less matched the sums taken from the home, and that there were also in the same period transfers from Kenny's account to Noah's. Prima facie, it seemed as though Kenny had stolen money from the residents of the home, and given part of the proceeds to Noah as his 'share'.

I recounted some of this to Tom. 'Oh yes, I remember,' he said, 'this DC Sparkes seems to have nailed them well and truly!'

Tempted as I was to comment that DC Sparkes was obviously a bit of a live wire, I merely replied, 'Well, you never know. Perhaps there's some other explanation for it all.' Though for the life of me, I couldn't think what it could be…

Other matters intervened for most of the next day, so that I did not give the case of Kenny and Noah much thought. Returning home the next evening, I found the house in a state of some disorder, with dust sheets everywhere, and ladders and tins of paint strewn around. I had of course completely forgotten that the decorators were scheduled to start that day. It could be that I had deliberately blanked it from my consciousness, as the original, fairly modest proposal for a mild refreshment of the décor by Marcus had escalated into a total revamp of the whole house. In white, of course, although no doubt there would be some rather fanciful names on the paint tins themselves. I had put my foot down over the kitchen, though, and ruled out Marcus' idea of ripping out all the units and appliances and replacing them with a design rather akin to an American diner, as seen on all those US television shows from my youth.

'It's like stepping back to the 1950s!' I had exclaimed, having studied the computer-generated images from the kitchen design shop.

'Some people *like* the 1950s!' Marcus had riposted with a mulish look.

'Regrettably, I'm not one of them!' I had retaliated, with an equally obdurate countenance.

Picking my way gingerly across the hall, I entered the kitchen. I had noted an ancient Nissan in the drive, so was not surprised to find Freda, our redoubtable *femme de menage* ensconced at the breakfast bar, nursing a cup containing liquid of a dubious origin, but which was probably intended to be tea.

Amongst Freda's many foibles was her complete inability to prepare a palatable hot drink of any variety, with her attempts at tea being particularly execrable: Marcus and I used to joke that Freda merely waved a tea-bag at a mug of hot water before drinking it. Freda's other most notable attribute was her penchant for using mixed metaphors and mangled sayings to an almost stratospheric degree, as I may have mentioned before. She is, however, a very efficient and reliable housekeeper, and invariably relentlessly cheerful. I was therefore taken aback, to say the least, to find her dabbing her eyes with a handkerchief, whilst tears streamed down her cheeks. Although I normally eschew too much conversation, I could not help but be moved by her distress to enquire, 'Freda! Whatever is the matter? Can I help in some way?'

'Oh, Mr J! Whatever are we going to do?'

'Do? About what?'

'About our Noah!'

'Sorry, Freda, I think you'll have to be little more explicit!'

'My nephew, Noah. He's in trouble with the police. Now all his dirty laundry is coming home to roost.'

Trying to ignore the rather startling image that this conjured up, I responded, 'I'm sorry to hear that, Freda. What is he supposed to have done?'

Freda blew her nose loudly and looked at me through dew-filled eyes. 'He hasn't done anything, really, Mr J. It's that friend of his, pinching money from the old folks' home and saying he'd given it to our Noah.'

Something rang a bell with me here. 'Just a sec, Freda. Does your Noah work at the "Riverview Residential Care Home" by any chance?'

Freda nodded.

'And would the "friend" be one Kenny Mitchell?'

Freda stared back at me. 'How do you know that, Mr J?'

'Well, by one of those strange coincidences my pal, Tom Bremner, asked me to look into the matter for him. Apparently, his firm is representing your nephew, Noah.'

'Oh, Mr J! Can you really help our Noah?'

I shrugged. 'I don't know, Freda, I haven't had a chance to go through the papers in any detail as yet.' Freda looked downcast, so I hurried on, 'But we will certainly give it our best shot.'

'Oh, Mr J, I'm sure you will. I know you'll take the bull by the horns and run with it!'

'Certainly, though I suppose we have to be careful not to open a Pandora's Box and find a can of worms,' I replied sagely, giving the side of my nose a knowing tap.

Freda left soon afterwards, looking a great deal more cheerful than when I had arrived. I felt some disquiet, since I normally do not care to act in those cases where the client is connected to me, however remote that connection might be. Although I had been rather flippant in mentioning Pandora's box to Freda, I was always aware that it was entirely possible that my findings might just confirm young Noah's guilt…

As Marcus was away again, I rooted in the freezer for something to eat, and found a bag marked 'Chilli con carne'. Fortunately, it was one that Marcus had prepared, so it was therefore in all likelihood edible, in contrast to my own efforts. I was just heating it up when I glanced down at my phone and saw an e-mail had arrived from my son Sam. This was something of a novelty: Sam is to say the least sparing with his communications, to the extent that once or twice I have made some sarcastic comment along the lines of that perhaps he had not realised you didn't need to go and buy a stamp before sending e-mails to family members.

'*Dad,*' I read, '*As it's your birthday this coming Saturday, why don't you come up to town? Going out to a gig in the evening, but we could do a pub lunch say, with Amy and the bf. Love, Sam.*'

To be honest, I'd not really thought about my birthday very much, so I was about to agree, when I had an idea.

'*Hi Sam,*' I replied, '*thanks for your note. How about you and Holly (and Amy and the bf of course) coming down here for lunch? You should have plenty of time to get back for your 'gig' and it would be great to see you here. Love, Dad.*'

I had two motives for this suggestion. Firstly, the kids (as I still like to call them) had not actually been home for some months. Secondly, I noticed that Sam's e-mail was a little vague as to whether he was including Marcus in the invitation. This is one of the curses of the English language: the lack of a distinct plural form of the word 'you'. Of course, to be fair, Marcus had been included when Sam had asked me up for the weekend a little while ago, and in fact, it had all gone rather well, with Sam seeming much more relaxed about Marcus. But I was still a little hesitant about relations between them, so that at least if Sam came to me, then he would be aware that Marcus would be present, and it would not come as a surprise. Also, Sam's current girlfriend, Holly, was a good sort, and Amy and the 'bf' (whose name I could never remember) would be there too. Of course, there was the slight drawback that there was a lunch to prepare, and bearing in mind my culinary skills, or rather, lack of them, I would have to hope that Marcus would be prepared to come to the rescue.

An hour later, it was all sorted. Sam, prompted I suspected by the lovely Holly, had said 'yes', as had Amy and the apparently new boyfriend. I was relieved that at least with this one I had the name written down in black and white: Finn, short for Findlay. All I had to do was to break the news to Marcus…

First thing the next morning, I summoned my manager, Alex 'Creepy' Crawley, to brief him on the case of Freda's nephew, Noah. I had decided that we better bring in the big guns on this one, as I could foresee that I would never get any peace at home from either Freda, or by proxy, Marcus, until we had investigated. By chance, the book of "Interview Techniques for Financial Witnesses" was still on my desk, and it occurred to me to practise my newly acquired skills on old Creepy. The first thing I recalled was the exhortation to maintain steady eye contact with the interviewee at all times. This was of course something of a problem: due to Creepy's unfortunate squint, which eye should I concentrate on? I decided that for the present, I would ignore that particular technique, and move swiftly on, as it were. The next idea was the so-called kinetic mirroring: *'When an interviewer adopts similar body positions and mirrors the interviewee's movements, a greater chance for rapport is realized.'*

I waited a moment for Creepy to settle himself in a low chair, and studied his posture through narrowed eyes. Here came the second problem: Creepy, who is quite a lanky individual, with long legs, had wrapped one leg round the other in a Gordian knot of flesh and bone. Quickly surmising that if I attempted a similar posture, I would most likely end up in A&E with a double hernia, I rapidly abandoned that technique as well.

Taking a surreptitious look at the book once again, I remembered that the next item on the agenda was to decide whether the interviewee was a listening person or a seeing one. The idea behind this is that people remember things in different ways, so that for instance, one person when recalling a memory or piece of information, will see it in their mind's eye, whereas other people may hear it in their mind's ear, as it were. These tendencies to recall often exhibit themselves in subtle ways. For example, a person whose predominant system is auditory will speak in hearing terms. 'I hear what you are saying', or 'that sounds about right', for instance.

Visual people, on the other hand, speak in terms of sight. 'Do you see what I mean?', or 'I get the picture' are probably much more likely to be used by visual people. Or so the theory goes. Also, according to the book, a clue to which type people are can be gained by studying in which direction they tend to look if asked a question. So if a person looks to the left, they are a 'seeing' type, or if to the right, they are more auditory. Or possibly it was the other way round? The idea once you have established this, is to ask questions in the way best suited to the individual.

Here again Creepy rather confounded this theory, since he consistently looked to both the left *and* the right at the same time. His response to my first question as to whether he could spare me a few minutes was, 'I can see my way clear to hearing what you say,' which further confused me. With a sigh, I gave up for the time being, and reverted to normal.

I briefly outlined the facts of the case of Noah Kirby and Kenny Mitchell, and passing him the files, bade him put other matters aside for the time being, and concentrate on this job.

After he had gone, I settled down to deal with the business of the day, but I had to admit, my mind kept wandering back to the telephone conversation I'd had with Marcus the previous evening. I had broken to him the news of the impending lunch party. He had adopted the clipped tone he uses when he is put out about something.

'That'll be fun,' he said, with an ironic edge to his voice, 'what are you going to cook?'

'Er, I'd rather hoped you would come to the rescue there,' I had replied.

There was a silence, and I could hear breathing over the phone. 'Please?' I had added.

'Hmm!' was the response. Then, 'Well, of course I will.' Another silence. 'The thing is,' Marcus had continued, in a slightly petulant tone, 'the thing is, Sam doesn't like me very much.'

'Oh no, that's not right! Of course he likes you!' I had rushed to reassure Marcus, though I have to admit that even to my own ears, I didn't sound very convincing.

'Well, resents me, then,' Marcus had said firmly.

'No, no, he doesn't. Honestly. I think you're being oversensitive. You both got on fine that weekend in London, didn't you?'

'I suppose so,' Marcus had reluctantly conceded, 'but I think that was largely because we were on *his* turf. I think it will be different at our house. Or rather, *your* house, which after all, was his home for a long time.'

It was my turn to be silent. I had to acknowledge there was a lot in what Marcus had said, however unpalatable it sounded to my ears. I had changed the subject at that point, and we had talked about this and that for a few minutes before ending the conversation. I was debating with myself whether I should do anything further or simply leave well alone and trust to luck, when Janet poked her head around the door and reminded me about rehearsals that evening.

'And we really must get around to practising for the Christmas Concert,' she had added with grimly pursed lips, making it sound more like a threat than an encouragement. I acquiesced in a vague sort of way, and after giving me one of her sharp looks, she withdrew. *Oh well,* I thought that evening as I hurried along the High Street to the church hall, *at least rehearsals will be a pleasant diversion from all this angst.* But as with so many things, here again I was proved wrong...

As I entered the hall, I saw that the cast and chorus were gathered around our director, Clive Pettit. I also realised, with a sinking feeling in my stomach, that he was giving one of his periodic 'pep' talks. These are designed, in his mind at any rate, to round out the characters in the libretto and put more flesh on their bones, so to speak. Unfortunately, they usually have the effect of causing confusion or downright annoyance in the minds of the actors he is supposed to be encouraging. And so it was, on this occasion. As I took my place in the circle around him, muttering an apology for my tardiness, he turned in my direction.

'Ah, Ben,' he started, 'how good of you to drop in.' I was about to make some excuse in response to this rather sarcastic greeting, but decided a dignified silence was probably a better course to take. I have to admit that I have been known to make similar *ironic* remarks to late arrivals at the office, so I have some experience in this field. Clive continued, 'As it happens, I was just coming to *your* part, my dear Ben. Now of course, previously you were to be Bill Bobstay — a decent, honest, hardworking sailor; a friend and support to Ralph. Willing to stand up to his superiors and to defend his principles. Very much the dominant one in the group. A strong physical presence, perhaps,' here he ran his eye up and down my frame, 'but possibly that is not essential.' I felt duly put in my place. 'Also, not the sharpest tool in the chest, shall we say. But things have moved on, and you have been promoted, in a manner of speaking, to Captain. As I see it, Corcoran *could* be played as a slightly stupid victim, or as a terrible snob who deserves all he gets. Either way, I'm sure you are well suited to the part, my dear Ben.' Clive beamed at me, as though he had bequeathed a great compliment, although I was not entirely sure it had come out that way. Clive continued, 'Of course, the Captain does need to have a strong stage presence and we have the difficulty that he does need to *appear* to be the same age as Ralph Rackstraw,' again Clive eyed me up and down, 'but I dare say we can get over that little hurdle.'

I was half expecting some ribald comment at this from some of the other cast members, particularly Randall Barrett, who was cast as the aforementioned Ralph Rackstraw, but was pleasantly relieved when this little speech was greeted with a polite silence.

'Oh, er, yes, well thanks for that, Clive,' I responded, 'most — er — *useful*.' Clive beamed at me, then putting his hands up in his characteristic manner, turned to Janet, who was standing alongside me.

'Now Janet, or should I say, Buttercup, I also like the idea — but it is by no means written in stone — that Buttercup is a bit of a pest, ahem, sexually speaking -sneaking glances at sailors' bottoms, copping a quick feel of bulging biceps, and that sort of thing.'

I could feel Janet stiffen in rage beside me, and could imagine the lips compressing into a thin line. Then, in a low voice, but clear for all to hear, Randall muttered, 'Should come quite naturally to her, then.'

Janet gave a low snarl of rage, rather like a caged tiger that has been prodded by an itinerant keeper, and for one second, I really did think she would pounce. Luckily Clive, who had obviously heard the remark as well, and I, both moved swiftly at the same time.

'Do you think we should make a start as we're short of time?' I gabbled, whilst simultaneously, Clive clapped his hands and said, 'Well, that's enough from me for now. Let's get cracking!'

We hurried into our positions, though I noticed Janet moving rather reluctantly, and casting viperish looks in Randall's direction. Fortunately, she soon seemed to lose herself in her performance, no doubt to the relief of the rest of the cast and Clive in particular. At one point whilst not required on stage, as it were, I found myself standing next to Randall. I turned to him and looked him in the eyes. 'Bit of an unkind thing to say about Janet, wasn't it?'

Randall looked down on me in a not entirely friendly fashion. He gave a shrug. 'Just a joke.'

'I'm not sure she saw it that way,' I responded coolly, 'I think perhaps an apology is called for.'

Another shrug. 'Don't think that's going to happen any time soon.'

'No?' I pondered for a moment, then went on, 'That's a shame, because it would be awful if Mrs Barrett were to find out about the goings-on at the Manor House Hotel, wouldn't it?'

Randall looked at me steadily. 'You know, Ben, I don't think it's quite ethical is it, to resort to blackmail? What would the Institute say?' I was about to protest, when he continued in a suave fashion, 'anyway, by Mrs Barrett, I take it you mean my soon-to-be *ex*-wife?' He gave a mirthless laugh. 'Sorry to disappoint you but that ship's already sailed, old pal.' He walked off, leaving me kicking myself for being outsmarted so ignominiously.

There was a short break in proceedings just then, and our director, Clive, beetled over. 'I saw you in conversation with Randall,' he started, 'and from the look on your face, it was not a pleasant one.'

It was my turn to shrug. 'You could say that,' I replied, then outlined the essence of our exchange.

Clive tut-tutted. 'I know he can be difficult sometimes, my dear Ben, but he *is* very talented, and for the sake of the Society, I would urge you not to upset him too much. I don't want to lose him as well as Derek.'

I pulled a face. 'Well, OK, I'll try. But he does have this habit of getting under everyone's skin and causing trouble.'

Clive sighed. 'I know, I know. The trouble with Randall is he's his own worst enemy!'

'Not whilst I'm around, he isn't!' I retorted curtly, and moved off.

It was quite late by the time the rehearsal finished, and I was exhausted. The role of Captain Corcoran is a large one, and it needed all my powers of concentration. Although often the role is described as being for a baritone, parts of it are more suitable for a lyric baritone or tenor. Clive had thoughtfully adjusted the music in places to make it more suitable for my voice, but it was still something of a strain. In particular, I was dreading the opening of the second act when I have to sing 'Fair moon, to thee I sing', which as I have mentioned before, is quite challenging. More challenging still is the fact that throughout the show, I am the object of the affections of Buttercup, better known as my fearsome office manager, Janet...

A few days passed, and arriving home late one evening I was surprised to see lights on all over the house. Before I could put my key in the door, it had been wrenched open and there stood Marcus. He wrapped me in a tight hug so that I could barely breathe, then releasing me said, 'Looks as though you could do with a drink.' He gave my hair a playful ruffle and I followed him through to the kitchen and sat down at the breakfast bar. 'One large chardonnay coming up!' he said, matching the action to the words. I raised my glass in acknowledgement.

'Notice anything?' Marcus asked after a moment.

'Erm…' I looked around. 'Any clues?'

Marcus tut-tutted in a good-natured way. 'Honestly, Ben, you are hopeless! The decorators, man! They've finished and gone!'

'Oh, yes, well I realised *that*,' I tried to sound nonchalant, 'I thought you meant something else.'

Marcus gave me one of those 'you-don't-really-expect-me-to-believe-that' looks and said, 'Well, what do you think? Come on, take a look with me.' He pulled me up and started walking around the house. I had to admit that it all looked very good.

'And luckily, all done before your birthday lunch tomorrow,' Marcus had added. My heart gave a lurch. Truth to tell, I had forgotten about *that* as well, and I wondered how my children would react…

Next morning, I was woken early by Marcus, who gave me a birthday card and present, but said he couldn't linger because he had the lunch to see to. He busied himself in the kitchen most of the morning, whilst I tried to assist by setting the table, selecting some wines and making helpful comments. Seeing two pans on the hob, I lifted the lid of one and sniffed. 'Mmm, smells interesting,' I said, then pointing to the other pan, I added, 'What's that? The antidote?' and received a wet tea-towel at full bore in the stomach. 'Ouch!' I cried, 'that hurt!'

The guests were due around midday, and a few minutes before, Marcus went up to shower and change, then came down to the kitchen where I was setting out some champagne glasses in readiness. He was wearing dark trousers that were a little on the snug side, shall we say, and an open-necked striped shirt that was revealing a little more chest hair than was entirely seemly. Particularly at lunchtime. Particularly with my children. I was about to say as much, but thought better of it, and confined myself to pretending to brush something off his front and casually doing up a further button. Marcus looked as though he was about to speak, but he too obviously thought better of it.

The door-bell rang and I went to answer it. Sam and Amy and their other halves crowded in and I exchanged kisses with the girls, a handshake with Finn, and a slightly awkward hug with Sam. Marcus, who had been hovering in the background now came forward and the process was repeated, except that he and Sam confined themselves to an overly formal shake of the hands. I opened the cards and gifts that they had brought and Marcus poured out the Moet. Sam had been looking around during this time, and suddenly said, 'Have you been decorating, Dad?' There was a slight edge to his voice which made me feel uneasy.

'Yes, yes, we've had the painters in this last week. Have a look around.' The party trooped out, led by Marcus who provided a detailed commentary on the colours used. Holly and Finn, of course, had not seen the place before, and were naturally interested to nose about. We returned to the kitchen, and I went around refilling glasses. As I paused in front of Sam, I said, 'Well, what do you think Sam?'

He scowled back at me. 'What do I *think*? I think, how could you, Dad, how could you?'

I was taken aback. 'What do you mean?'

'I mean, this place was created by mum, and you've just tried to erase her from the scene.'

I went cold. 'That's not fair, Sam. I'm not obliterating her memory. This place is my home, not a shrine. Your mother is still there in my heart, in my mind.' We were standing a little apart from the others, and speaking in low tones, so I don't think they actually heard what was said, but they could tell from our body language that all was not well.

'I think it all looks lovely, Dad,' said Amy coming over and giving me a kiss on the cheek, 'clean and fresh.' Sam scowled once more. Holly now came, and taking my arm, said, 'Will you show me the garden, Ben? Sam is always going on about how lovely it is.'

'Or have you altered that too?' Sam muttered, whilst Holly shot him a look.

'I'll come as well!' Amy cried, and took my other arm. The two girls pulled me along and through the French windows into the fresh air. Their bright chatter and infectious enthusiasm soon made me put Sam's outburst to the back of my mind.

When we returned, Sam was leaning against a worktop, drinking champagne, with a surly look on his face, whilst Marcus and Finn appeared to be having a fine old time, laughing and joking. I was slightly concerned to see that the recalcitrant button on Marcus's shirt had come undone again, and the shirt front gaped open. I also saw that Marcus had his arm around Finn's shoulders as he was telling some story, and noticed Amy's eyes narrow as she too clocked this. I wanted to say to her that this was just Marcus's way, particularly after he'd had a couple of glasses of wine, and that it did not mean that he had designs on her boyfriend, but I decided that it was probably better just to ignore it. Instead, I distracted Marcus by asking if it was time to sit down and begin serving. 'Yes, right, let's get going,' he agreed.

We sat down and Marcus served the starter. 'Do the wine,

Ben, will you?' he said, and as I stood to do this, I noticed Sam and Amy exchange glances. They didn't say anything, but the look was clear enough: Marcus had unwittingly echoed what Julia used to say to me, and the kids were clearly not comfortable with the idea that Marcus had apparently replaced her.

We began to eat. I had Sam and Amy on either side of me, whilst Marcus, sitting at the other end of the table, had Holly and Finn. My children seemed unusually reserved, and I found myself struggling to make conversation. In contrast, the other end of the table was lively and chatty, and appeared to be having a very jolly time. Sam seemed to pick at his food, and in the middle of the main course, suddenly turned to me and said, 'Was it your idea to do all these changes? Or was it his?' He tossed his head in the direction of Marcus.

I made a determined effort to stay calm. 'Oh, I think it was a bit of both,' I said in as light-hearted way as I could manage.

'And who chose the colours? I bet it was…'

'Drop it, Sam!' Holly's voice rang out like the crack of a whip.

Sam flushed and for a moment looked as though he was going to argue with her, but thought better of it and stared down at his lap. There was a sudden rush of conversation around the table as everyone else began talking at once. After a couple of minutes, Holly suggested to Sam that they clear away the plates. This was obviously an excuse for her to get him alone and speak to him, and I could see the two of them talking in low voices at the other end of the kitchen. Evidently, whatever Holly had said was effective because when they returned to the table, Sam made a determined effort to be sociable, and the rest of the meal passed in comparative harmony.

They left in the late afternoon, apparently all due at the same party in town that evening. I felt drained as I cleared away and washed up. 'Was it all OK?' Marcus asked anxiously, coming up behind me as I was at the sink.

'Yes, yes, it was great. Super food,' I replied, 'thanks.'

Marcus hovered by me. 'Did I do something wrong?'

I paused with my hands in the warm water, then turned to him. 'Why do you ask?'

Marcus shrugged, 'Oh, just that Sam and Amy didn't seem too happy.' He paused, then added, 'And the way *you* looked at me too.'

I could feel my heart beating. How could I say that it was the mere fact that he was there at all that was the problem? I dried my hands, then put them on his shoulders and said, 'No, Marcus. You didn't do anything wrong. Not at all.' Moving away, I added lightly, 'Although you might want to rethink the shirt thing...'

Later I went for a run, saying to Marcus who was sprawled on the sofa in front of the TV that I needed to work off the lunch. I ran for a long time, harder and faster than I normally do, wondering as I did so, what I was running away from...

Monday morning as I made my way along the High Street to the office, my feelings of despondency had still not lifted. Although on Sunday I had done my best to be bright and breezy, I'm not sure I entirely fooled Marcus, as I caught him once or twice casting pensive looks in my direction. However, I did not feel ready to discuss matters with him and assiduously changed the subject if it looked as though it were heading in the direction of family relationships. On one of these occasions, I had related to Marcus the events at the rehearsal on Friday evening, and the insulting remarks made by Randall *vis-à-vis* Janet. Even Marcus, who it has to be admitted, has a bit of a crush on young Dr Barrett, was appalled. 'What a b-----d! He needs taking down a peg or two!' I agreed, but admitted that my hitherto useful weapon of the threat of spilling the beans on Randall's amatory pursuits to his wife, was now rendered ineffective because of the forthcoming divorce. Marcus agreed that this was a nuisance but added, 'I'm sure we can do something though,' and had looked thoughtful.

I had barely sat down behind my desk when Janet waltzed into my room. 'Just thought I'd better tell you in person, in case you haven't checked your automated diary,' she began, 'that you have an appointment shortly with a Mr Noah Kirby.'

I decided to ignore the little dig about the diary and leaning back in my chair said, 'And Good Morning to you too, Janet. Who's Noah Kirby?'

Janet rolled her eyes heavenwards. 'That case that Tom Bremner passed to you the other week. The missing money from the old people's home. Remember?'

'Oh, that,' I replied quickly, 'yes of course. I had momentarily forgotten the gentleman's name.' Janet looked doubtful at this. 'Right, thanks. Oh, and could you ask Alex to step in, please. And ask him to bring the files on that case.'

'Dammit!' I thought, as I had totally forgotten about the case in view of other events that had happened over the weekend. I would have to quickly go through the facts, and hope that Alex 'Creepy' Crawley had managed to produce some sort of defence.

Alex duly appeared a few minutes later and lowered himself into a chair. In response to my request to give me a *resume* of the facts in the matter of Messrs Kirby and Mitchell and with his gaze apparently fixed on the filing cabinet behind me, Alex began.

'Well, Ben, as you will recall, these two gentlemen were employed by the Riverhill Residential Home, and amongst their duties, they took residents to the shops or on outings. Very often, they also had charge of the old folks' money, and obviously, they were supposed to look after this and account for all expenditure. After each trip, they had to fill in a sheet, showing how much they had been given, what had been spent, and the balance to be returned to the home and/or the residents themselves.'

I nodded, 'Yes, yes, I recall all that. And the accusation is that they stole some of this money?'

Alex assented. 'Plus, they were accused of spending excessive amounts on the trips themselves. When they were confronted with these accusations, Kenny admitted it.'

'But Noah didn't?'

'No, that's right,' Alex agreed, 'and then this DC Sparkes, who was investigating, made a schedule of the amounts taken by Kenny from the resident's funds, and compared it with cash deposits in Kenny's bank account. And unfortunately for Kenny, he found that the amounts were pretty much the same.'

'How much are we talking about?'

Alex referred to his file. 'Just under £16,000, over a period of two years.'

'So how does Noah fit into this? Apart from going on these trips with Kenny,' I asked.

'Well, Kenny was prima facie the one in charge of the money, and was responsible for accounting for it, that's true. But the problem was, there were bank transfers over this period from Kenny's account to Noah's, of around £9,500, which on the face of it were related to the money that Kenny has admitted he took.'

I put the tips of my fingers together and leant back in my chair. 'I see. So Noah is being charged with possession of criminal property, that is, the £9,500 that was transferred to him by Kenny?'

Alex nodded again. 'Yes, that's right. Furthermore, Kenny

apparently admitted this and was also charged with concealing criminal property — the amounts he transferred to Noah — as well as with stealing the money itself.'

'And Kenny pleaded guilty to all this?'

'Yes, that's right. Which makes our job more difficult.'

I considered this. 'Well, it doesn't help, that's certainly true. But just because Kenny pleaded guilty, a court is not entitled to assume that Noah is too. For instance, Kenny might have been advised to plead guilty to *all* the charges rather than risk further investigations. Plus, there could well be a reduction in his sentence by entering a guilty plea early on.'

Alex shrugged. 'I guess so.'

I leant forward in my chair. 'So, have we got anything to help Noah? Presumably, because Kenny pleaded guilty, the prosecution evidence has not been challenged.'

Alex stroked his chin whist continuing to address the filing cabinet. 'I suppose so. Well, we've not really got a lot so far. I've requested some further documents — for instance, the records of the Riverhill Residential Home, as we haven't seen those yet.'

'OK,' I said, 'but that won't necessarily help, because the point at issue, so it seems to me, is the monies transferred from Kenny's bank account to Noah's. The records of the home won't add anything to that.' I had taken the file from Alex and was skimming through the documents. 'Mm. Just a moment, judging from these bank statements of Kenny's, he seems to have other accounts. Have we got statements for all of those?'

'No, Ben, I don't think we have.'

I shut the file. 'It might be worth getting hold of those. Oh, and has Noah given any other plausible explanation for why these sums were transferred to him by Kenny?'

'Not that I've seen,' replied Alex, standing up.

'Right, well I'd better ask him when he comes in. OK, thanks for that Alex — I'll get back to you later.'

Alex left, and Janet rang through a few minutes later to say Noah had arrived, so I did not have much time for preparation. It does not always prove necessary to actually see these clients in person, but I generally like to, as it helps me with the background, and it is often surprising what you can learn in a little general conversation. A peremptory knock on the door heralded the arrival of Noah, and I rose from my seat to greet him.

There was a joke circulating some years ago at the expense of a well-known politician of the day. It went: 'Why do people take an instant dislike to *so-and-so*? Because it saves time!' That epigram ran through my mind on meeting friend Noah Kirby. From the tattoos on his forearms to the earring dangling from his left lobe and the look of smirking contempt on his rather fleshy lips, I can honestly say that I did not warm to Mr Noah Kirby. I looked for some resemblance to Freda-wot-does, but found none, and surmised, as it turned out correctly, that he was the son of Freda's husband's sister, and consequently, there was no blood relationship. 'If he were to be made honest by an act of parliament, I should not alter my faith of him', a line written by my illustrious playwright namesake, also occurred to me after a few minutes' discussion. However, being professional, I put these unwelcome thoughts firmly to one side, and tried to deal with the matter in hand in an objective fashion.

I had an idea that I would again try the methods outlined in my book 'Interview Techniques for Financial Witnesses' and started with the 'kinetic mirroring' as suggested. This involved my slumping in my chair with my right leg forward and the left ankle crossed onto my right knee, whilst my arms swung down by my sides, and making an attempt to chew imaginary gum on the left side of my mouth. Before I could start speaking, Noah paused in his own mastication, with real gum in his case, and in a broad Brummie accent said, 'Are you taking the piss or something?'

I hastily sat upright and adopted my more normal posture, whilst assuring him that, I most certainly was taking nothing from him, let alone *that*. I mentally consigned 'Interview Techniques for Financial Witnesses' to the waste-bin, and carried on.

I asked Noah if he understood what he was accused of, and the evidence against him. He shrugged and looked bored. 'Yeah, well I'm done for, aren't I? Kenny pleaded guilty, didn't he? and landed me right in it.'

I put the tips of my fingers together as I replied. 'Well, yes he did. But as you know, you are accused of possessing criminal property, in other words, the £9,500 that Kenny transferred to you, which on the face of it came originally from the old folks. Now,' here I parted my hands and pointed my forefinger at Noah, 'I am not a lawyer, but it seems to me that one could at least argue that either: a) the £9,500 was *not* paid from the money Kenny admitted he took, or b) it *was* from that money, but you didn't know or suspected that it was. Also, of course, it could simply be that he was repaying some money that you had previously lent to him.' Running my eye up and down Noah as he slouched in the chair opposite, it was hard to think that he would ever be in a position to lend anybody anything like those amounts, even over a period of two years. 'Was that what happened, Noah? Did you lend Kenny money?'

Noah, looked away from my gaze as he answered. 'Yeah, that was it. I lent Kenny money.'

'And I suppose it would be too much to hope for that you

kept some sort of written record of these loans?'

Noah shrugged once more. 'No. I don't go in for writing stuff down.'

This was not a surprise. 'How did you keep track of these loans? There must have been quite a lot of them?'

'Yeah well, you know, we just sort of knew how much and all that stuff. I trusted Kenny, he's a straight sort of guy.'

Not that straight, I thought, *he's admitted pinching sixteen grand from the old folks at the home!* Out loud I said, 'Possibly so, but we could do with a bit more than a character reference. After all,' I went on, recalling my words to Janet a few days before, 'blind trust is not an internal control!' Noah merely looked baffled at this comment, so I moved on quickly.

'I don't suppose you know if Kenny had another bank account, do you? And if so, why?'

Noah gave a grin. 'Yeah, Kenny went on and on about this new account he'd opened, which gave interest, even though it was a current account. He's pretty savvy about money, is Kenny. But he said it was a bit of a pain because he had to keep paying money into it each month to get the higher rate of interest.'

I made a note of this. Strange to think that someone who was prepared to steal thousands of pounds from vulnerable old people was so fastidious about their personal finances. We talked a bit further, though without any further useful information being revealed, and Noah left, with a promise that he would try to recall the dates and amounts of the money he had lent to Kenny. I did not however think it worth holding my breath over that one. I leant back in my chair and flicked through the bank statements again, then compared them with the schedule of money stolen, according to DC Sparkes. A little idea was forming in my mind, and I dashed off an e-mail to old 'Creepy' Crawley with some instructions on the matter.

I turned my attention to other work matters and the day passed by. It was late afternoon when my mobile buzzed and a message flashed up from Tom, suggesting a glass of wine in 'Et Alia' after work. I quickly replied with an affirmative, and passed the invitation on to Marcus. I finished what I was doing, then made my escape before Janet found some reason to delay me. Much as I admire Janet's abilities in the work-place and indeed in the operatic society, I can find her a little trying at times. I was also becoming vaguely aware that our on-stage amorous entanglement in the forthcoming production of *HMS Pinafore* might be sending out the wrong signals. Much as I admire Janet, I don't admire her in *that* way. I was also having second thoughts about our proposed duet 'I've got you babe' in the Operatic Society's Christmas concert, thinking that it too might be misconstrued.

I rattled along the High Street the few yards to the wine-bar, where I found Tom already ensconced with a couple of glasses on the table waiting. He rose on my arrival and greeted me with a welcoming pat on the back. 'I'm ready for this!' I exclaimed, raising my glass and holding it up in salutation.

'Bad day?' Asked Tom in a sympathetic tone.

I slurped a mouthful of wine. 'Oh, not really, I suppose. Just things, you know.' I had another mouthful, then said, 'Incidentally, I had a chat with Noah Kirby today. You know, the case you sent me about the thefts from the old folks' home.'

Tom nodded. 'Oh, yes? Any progress on that front?'

I grimaced. 'Not sure. I've got a couple of thoughts, but we'll have to see how it goes. Can't say I warmed to the guy, though.'

Tom shrugged. 'Well, you don't have to *like* the clients, you know. That's the thing about being professional — you do your job to the best of your ability, no matter what your personal feelings are.'

'Well, yes, quite, and I believe I do,' I replied slightly stiffly.

Tom interrupted, 'Yes, yes of course you do. I wasn't trying to imply anything else.' He gave my arm a reassuring squeeze.

I relented, and went on to voice my misgivings over Noah's veracity.

Tom grimaced. 'Tricky,' he said, 'but on the other hand, from what you say, he hasn't said anything which is demonstrably untrue, has he?'

'Well, no, not so far,' I admitted.

'So then, I think you have to give him the benefit of the doubt. And if I were to play devil's avocado for a moment, to borrow your Freda's phrase, you could argue that all you have to look for are holes in the prosecution's argument. After all, it's up to them to prove the case "beyond reasonable doubt", not for you to *prove* some alternative thesis.'

'I suppose so,' I replied, a little glumly, 'but I would rather I was convinced that the client was innocent!'

'The trouble with you, young Ben,' here Tom ruffled my hair in an avuncular fashion, 'the trouble with you is that you worry too much!'

'And that's not the only thing I've got to worry about,' I went on, draining my glass. Tom signalled for a barman to replenish our drinks before saying, 'I thought there was something up. What is it? Marcus?'

I shook my head. 'No, no. Well, yes *and* no. I mean, indirectly it is, I suppose.'

Tom looked at me with a raised eyebrow. 'Perhaps you'd like to elaborate,' he said dryly.

I paused for a second as our drinks arrived, then went on to describe the scene at my lunch party two days earlier. 'And the thing is, Tom,' I finished up, 'the thing is, Marcus asked me if he'd done something wrong. He knows that Sam is a bit wary of him, even though I try to dismiss the idea. Even Amy didn't seem quite as accepting as usual the other day. But Marcus hasn't done anything *wrong*, it's just the fact that he is there at all that is the problem. And, I have to be honest, it makes it worse that he's a man. I mean, in Sam and Amy's eyes, I suppose it looks as though I'm trying to replace their mother with him. But how can I say all that to him? And what can I do about it? I don't want to have this rift between the kids and me. Or me and Marcus. It's tearing me apart.'

I must have been more emotional than I thought, as I suddenly felt my eyes going moist, and Tom looked at me in alarm before digging in his pocket and proffering a tissue.

'Well, I'm not sure I know what the answer is, old chap,' he said gently, patting me on the shoulder as he spoke, 'but I'm sure things can be resolved. You're all lovely people — you, and Sam and Amy, and Marcus too — I'm sure you can sort it all out.' He produced another tissue and blew his nose, and I looked at him in surprise: it seemed his eyes were damp too. At that moment, he suddenly pointed, and said, 'Ah, look who's here!'

I looked around and saw Marcus had just entered. Tom stood up and rushed over to him, then steered him towards the bar. I was about to join them when I was accosted by a client, and got waylaid into a conversation. By the time the client had left, Marcus and Tom were on the way back to our table with more drinks. 'What were you two in such earnest conversation about?' I asked as they sat down.

'Oh, just this and that, you know,' said Tom airily and

quickly started talking about some complicated case he was involved with at work.

'So what were you and Tom *really* talking about?' I asked Marcus later as we were sitting at the breakfast bar in the kitchen. He gave me one of his 'shifty' looks, by which I mean he looked me straight in the face without flinching.

'Oh, nothing, really,' he replied in an overly nonchalant way, 'as Tom said, just this and that...'

A couple of days passed and although my mood had not grown any lighter, I tried to disguise this behind a façade of good humour. I strode into the office one day and meeting a couple of members of my staff, greeted them by saying, 'My gallant crew, good morning, I hope you're all quite well!' They mumbled something in response and drifted off.

'I don't think they quite got that those are your first lines as Captain Corcoran in "Pinafore",' a voice rasped behind me. It was Janet, of course. Whirling round, I greeted her too. She gave me a curt nod and stalked off. Janet plays 'Buttercup' and amongst the first things I do in the show is to comment about her, 'A plump and pleasing person!' In reality, I have to say that Janet is certainly *not* plump, and in general, not particularly pleasing either. Still, willing suspension of disbelief and all that...

I had barely sat down behind my desk when Alex 'Creepy' Crawley appeared.

'Got a minute, Ben?' he asked lugubriously, addressing the waste-bin in the corner of the office.

'Certainly, certainly,' I replied, 'have a pew!' I indicated the chair on the opposite side of the desk, and Alex sank down. He opened a file on his knee, and began addressing the filing cabinet.

'It's about this case of Noah Kirby,' he began, 'I've done some work on the stuff we've got, along the lines you suggested,

Ben.'

'Good,' I replied, 'does it help Noah's defence, at all?'

'Well, it's interesting,' Alex said, 'here, look at these.' He produced some notes from the file, and passed them across the desk to me. I picked them up and began to read.

'You see from those, Ben, that although DC Sparkes concluded that the total of the money allegedly stolen by Kenny is roughly similar to the unaccounted-for bank deposits in his account, within three or four hundred pounds, the timing and pattern of the supposed thefts and deposits doesn't tie up.'

'Mmm,' I mused, 'and this graph you've done here, showing the cumulative totals of each on a day-by-day basis, demonstrates that.'

'Yes,' said Alex, 'you can see the mismatch between them. It shows that at least *some* of the deposits occurred *before* the cash thefts Kenny admitted to, which means that those deposits can't have related to the thefts.'

'Well, that's good from our point of view,' I said, 'though it's odd that Kenny's team didn't apparently point this out in his defence. What about this other bank account of Kenny's? Have you managed to get statements for that?'

'Yes, Kenny's lawyers were actually quite helpful on that. You can see from those that, until two years ago, Kenny's salary was paid into the original account. He then transferred most of it to this "new" account as soon as he was paid. Then there is often a series of smaller transfers back to the "old" account, presumably as and when Kenny needed spending money.'

'Yes, that would tie up with what Noah said. Kenny needed to make regular payments into this new account to qualify for the higher interest rate.'

Alex nodded. 'Then from about two years ago, the salary

was paid into this new account. There are still transfers out from that account to the original one, as before.'

'OK,' I said, 'that's fine as far as it goes. Does it help Noah?'

Alex nodded again. 'Well, yes. And if we look further at the transfers from Kenny to Noah, they seem to be more closely related to either Kenny's salary receipts, or transfers into his account from the "new" bank account, rather than any alleged "thefts". In fact, only about £300 looks unaccounted for in this way.'

'The final bit of the jigsaw is to show that Noah really did "lend" Kenny money from time to time as he claims, and Kenny paid it back. Any joy with that?' I asked.

'Yes certainly,' Alex confirmed passing me a sheet of paper, 'if you look at this schedule here, you can see the amounts going each way. Again, the totals are roughly the same, within a few pounds this time.'

'So this all supports Noah's assertion that the amounts he received from Kenny were merely repayments of earlier informal loans to Kenny. Presumably he made these in cash, which Kenny paid into the bank. Perhaps it was to ensure he had enough going in each month, to get his higher rate of interest. Well, that's good, well done, Alex.'

'Yes, it does support Noah's story,' Alex agreed. He went on, 'There are other amounts deposited in the "new" bank account, for which we don't have any explanation, though.'

I shrugged. 'Well, they don't really need to concern us, I don't think. It's the movements *between* Noah and Kenny that we need to concentrate on, as that is the evidence on which the prosecution are relying.'

Alex said brightly, 'And of course if all this was a bit dodgy, why do it through bank accounts which can be traced? Why not just stick to passing cash between them, which can't be?'

'Well, it's a good point, and one which occurred to me as well,' I said, 'on the face of it, you would think that implies the transfers are above board, I suppose.' I stood up. 'Good, thanks Alex. If you could just tidy all that up for me, I'll complete the report and get it back to Tom Bremner.'

Alex unravelled his limbs from the chair in which he had been ensconced, and sidled out of the room. I had a vague feeling I'd just said something which was important, but I couldn't quite remember what it was…

A few more days passed. There was a further rehearsal for "Pinafore" one evening which proved somewhat chaotic. For once, our director, Clive Pettit was rather late. The cast and chorus milled around for a while, and started chatting away to each other, so that the noise level grew. Suddenly, there was a loud clapping of hands, we all looked, and there was Randall standing in the centre of the room, hands raised. 'Ladies and gentlemen, *please,'* he began, in a fair impression of Clive's clipped and prissy tones, 'if you are going to behave like the kindergarten, I will have to treat you as such. When I say "Shhhh!" you all have to turn to the person next to you and go "Shhhh!" at them.'

There was some muted laughter at this, and I had to admit to myself that Randall had caught Clive's manner very accurately. Unfortunately for all concerned, Clive himself had entered the room before Randall had finished speaking, and now stood just behind him. His usual slightly green complexion was now suffused with a tinge of red, rather as if one of the French Impressionists were attempting to paint a set of traffic lights. 'Thank you *so* much, Randall,' Clive intoned, with a heavy dose of irony. Randall did not reply, but merely gave a careless shrug, and stood aside. Whilst Clive was going through some instructions to the chorus, I found myself standing next to Janet, who had a somewhat grim expression on her face.

'Bit much of Randall to do that,' I commented.

The lips went thin. 'That's putting it mildly!' she replied.

In an attempt to lighten the mood, I said, 'Well, you know the end of the first act with Ralph Rackstraw?'

Janet looked quizzical. 'Ralph Rackstraw? The part Randall is playing?'

'That's right,' I confirmed, then went on, 'and that bit where old Rackstraw says he is going to kill himself, but the ensemble persuades him not to?'

Janet nodded.

'Well how about this time we don't bother trying to persuade him!'

I trudged back home after the rehearsal, for once not feeling inclined to look in at 'Et Alia'. I was aware that my daughter Amy had not been in touch since the lunch party, apart from a rather stiff e-mail of thanks. This was disturbing: unlike her brother, Amy is usually on the phone or messaging frequently. I steeled myself to put a call through to her when I got in, pouring myself a large glass of wine as I did so. Fortunately, Marcus was out at the squash club, so I didn't have to worry about being overheard.

'Hi, love, it's Dad,' I said, probably unnecessarily, as Amy picked up.

'Yes, hi, how are you?' I tried to decide if the tone was a little less fulsome than always.

'Oh, fine, fine. Thanks. You?' We chatted about this and that for a few minutes, though I had the impression that Amy, like me, was choosing her words rather carefully. Finally, I decided to take the bull by the horns. 'Listen, Amy, my love, I just wondered if everything was all right.'

'All right? Why shouldn't it be all right?' Amy's tone was sharp, unlike her normal manner.

'Oh, well, I don't know,' I started, then said, 'well, it's just that I thought you seemed a bit er... well, *reserved* shall we say the other day at lunch.'

There was a silence for a few seconds. 'Oh, well, I wasn't going to say anything...'

'Was it Marcus?' I asked abruptly.

Amy gave an intake of breath. 'No... well, I don't know...well, actually,' Amy cleared her throat loudly, 'well, it was just when we came in, and there he was with his arms all over Finn...'

I tried to give a breezy laugh. 'Oh, that's just Marcus's way. He's like that with lots of men...' oh, no I thought, that makes him sound as though he's promiscuous, 'I mean people. And Finn is a good-looking bloke. I could understand...' I trailed off, vaguely aware that if I was not careful, Amy might start to think I had designs on the hapless Finn myself. 'It's just his way,' I finished lamely.

'Oh, yes?' Amy did not sound convinced.

'What about Sam?' I tried changing tack

'What about him?'

'What does he think about it. About Marcus, I mean?'

Amy clicked her tongue. 'I can't speak for Sam, Dad. You'll have to ask him yourself.'

I could feel myself getting exasperated. 'Well, what do you want me to do, Amy?'

'Do?' Amy sounded cool, 'You must do what you think best, Dad. As always.'

We had a few more minutes of desultory conversation before the call ended. I sat at the breakfast bar, clutching my glass of wine, in a black mood. So engrossed was I in my thoughts that I failed to hear the door open and Marcus enter the room, with the result that I jumped violently when he wrapped his arms round me from behind, spilling my drink.

'Hey, your nerves must be in a bad way! Not like you to waste good wine!' he cried playfully, 'what's up?'

I gave a grimace and shook my head, 'Oh, nothing, nothing, just some case at work I was mulling over.' I stood up. 'Drink?' I asked, and tried to give a reassuring smile, but I had the feeling that Marcus was not convinced.

I passed a sleepless night, finally falling into a troubled slumber as a grey, sickly dawn permeated the room.

Nor was my mood improved the next day. Mulling on Amy's retort that if I wanted to know what Sam thought, I should ask him myself, I put a call through to my son the following morning. On reflection, that was probably a bad idea, as Sam was at work, and clearly not in a mood for chit-chat. However, at the time, I felt I had to speak to him as soon as I could.

I started in emollient tone. 'Look, Sam, I'm very sorry if I upset you by doing things in the house. I didn't realise it would bother you so much.'

Sam gave a sort of snort, which I found hard to interpret. I pressed on, pouring what I thought was oil on troubled waters, though the effect was more akin to pouring oil on an already out of control conflagration.

'Look, Dad,' Sam eventually said, in a cold tone, when my expressions of regret finally faded away, 'you know the issue is not so much the changes, but the fact that *he* was behind them all.'

I tried hard to keep my voice level. 'By *he,* I take it you mean Marcus?' I asked. Although I could not see Sam, I sensed he gave a 'well, of course' sort of shrug. I continued, 'What is your problem with Marcus? What is it you want me to do?'

'Well, that's a matter only *you* can decide, Dad,' responded Sam, with a tone of chilling finality.

It was a struggle to concentrate on work matters after that, but the business of the day had to be dealt with. I did my best to put on an insouciant air when Janet appeared in my room towards the middle of the day.

'Billings for you,' she said shortly, dropping a pile of paper onto my desk with a bang. I leaned back in my chair and put my hands behind my head.

'You know Janet, sometimes, I think of myself as a Captain Corcoran in real life. This firm is my ship and I am the captain. I have my worthy crew to help. I have to plot a course, and steer us through the turbulent waters of the commercial world, lashed to the wheel whilst the storms of economic uncertainty try their utmost to push us off course, until we reach the calm waters of success and the safe haven of profitability.' I felt quite pleased with my nautical analogy.

'Unfortunately, if you don't get on with this invoicing, the ship in question will turn out to be the Titanic, and it will go down with all hands! Now, should I get you a cup of tea, or perhaps you'd prefer to splice the mainbrace?' Janet retorted in a crisp tone.

She disappeared and I was left with the thought that the (probably apocryphal) practice of making mutinous crew-members walk the plank was perhaps not such a bad idea...

Settling down to work, I dealt with the invoicing, then at the bottom of the pile of papers, I came across the report that Alex

'Creepy' Crawley had prepared on the case of Noah Kirby. I read through it, then picked up my phone and put a call through to Tom Bremner.

His stentorian tones boomed out, 'Bremner speaks!'

'Ah, Tom,' I began, 'we've finished our look at the case of Noah Kirby. You know, the chap involved in the old people's home.'

'Yes, yes, I remember,' Tom affirmed, 'you'd better send it across to me, but perhaps you could just summarise the outcome.'

'Sure,' I replied, and quickly rattled off the conclusions we had come to, that the timings of the payments from Kenny to Noah were not directly linked to the thefts from the home which Kenny had admitted to, and that they could be repayments of loans from Noah to Kenny.'

'Of course,' I concluded, 'we can't absolutely prove that these were all repayments of loans — not surprisingly, neither Noah nor Kenny kept any written records of all that.'

'No, quite. But I think from what you say that there is sufficient doubt about it all that the prosecution wouldn't be able to proceed. After all, it's up to them to prove their case beyond reasonable doubt, not for you to prove an alternative.' As this exactly echoed the proposition I had put to old 'Creepy' Crawley, I could not fail to agree. 'Anyway, I'll have a word with the powers that be, and see if we can get the CPS to decide not to proceed.'

'Great, thanks Tom. That will be a great relief to Freda at least.' I hesitated for a moment, debating whether to unburden myself to Tom. Before I could decide, he spoke.

'And what else is troubling you, Ben?' For all his bluff and genial air, Tom has a remarkably sensitive and perspicacious side.

'Ah, yes, well, it's like this, Tom.' I recounted my conversations with Sam and Amy.

'And I think they would rather that Marcus wasn't around any longer,' I finished, 'so I find myself torn between them all.'

'Have you said all this to Marcus?' Tom as always went to the crux of the matter.

'No, how can I?' I replied, 'it would only make things worse between him and the kids. And the worst of it is that he is being perfectly OK with them. It's Sam and Amy who are being difficult.'

'Possibly, possibly,' Tom mused, 'but you are dealing with raw emotion here. It's all very well to say they should be happy for you, but you can't necessarily alter the way they feel.'

'So what's my best course of action, Tom?'

'Well, probably what you do best, Ben,' Tom gave a mirthless laugh.

'Namely?'

'As you frequently put it yourself: masterly inactivity!'

I took Tom's advice to heart, and ostrich-like, buried my head in the sand, as it were. The next few days passed uneventfully, although I caught Marcus looking at me thoughtfully from time to time. In an effort to avoid talking to him about what was troubling me, I regaled him with all the minor gossip and chit-chat from both the office and the 'Pinafore' rehearsals. I had just finished recounting the incident with Randall impersonating Clive Pettit, our operatic society director, when Marcus's mobile rang. Glancing at the screen, he answered it, but immediately walked out of the room. I could hear the odd word, but could not make out who was at the other end. The conversation ended with Marcus saying, 'Right, I'll see you there,' and he came back into the kitchen, where I was sitting on a bar stool, pretending to read the paper.

'What was all that?' I asked casually.

'Oh, just a work thing,' Marcus replied, equally casually. I glanced up, and he gave me one of his 'shifty' looks, which as I have mentioned before, consists of him looking straight into my eyes without blinking. I debated with myself whether to challenge this, but decided against it, and just nodded. Marcus went on quickly, 'Now, what were you saying? Oh, yes, Randall. He's becoming a bit of a nuisance. We'll have to think of something to do about him. I wonder what…'

The following morning, Marcus announced that he had a meeting in town, and wouldn't be back until late that evening. I thought it odd that he hadn't mentioned this before, and it crossed my mind that it was something to do with the phone call from the previous night. However, before I could quiz him on this, he said he was in a hurry and dashed out of the door. I was just in the process of locking up and leaving for the office myself, when I heard the scrunch of tyres on the gravel drive, and turned to see an old Nissan pull up. It was of course our housekeeper, Freda-wot-does. I gave a muted curse, as I usually try to avoid direct contact with her, but putting on a purposeful expression, I called, 'Morning Freda, how are you? Sorry, I must rush off to work.'

'Oh, Mr J, morning to you too. But hold on a minute will you, I've got something I must say to you.' Thinking this was probably a request for a new vacuum cleaner or something, I said, 'Can it wait, Freda? Perhaps Marcus can deal with whatever it is tomorrow? I really must dash.'

'Oh, no, I must say it now, Mr J. You've got to grasp the nettle whilst the sun shines!'

'How very true,' I replied in a dry tone, 'now how can I help you?'

'Oh, you've already done that Mr J,' said Freda, crossing the drive towards me. I pushed open the door, and bowing to the inevitable, we went into the kitchen. 'Yes, Mr J,' Freda continued, taking off her coat and scarf as she spoke, 'I must say, it's another feather in your bow.'

I looked at her blankly.

'Our Noah!' Freda cried, 'he rang us last night to say that the solicitors had been in touch with him, and the case against him has been dropped. According to that nice friend of yours, Mr Burner…'

'Bremner,' I interrupted, absent-mindedly, 'you mean, Mr Bremner.'

Freda, who had been waiting with mouth open ready to carry on speaking continued, '…Mr Bremner said it was all down to you and your report.'

'Oh, good,' I said, 'of course, I'm pleased about that. For your sake, as well as young Noah's. I hadn't actually heard that from Tom Bremner, so it must have only just happened.' As I spoke, I had a recollection that there was a missed call on my mobile from Tom, which I had omitted to return. Probably he was calling to tell me the good news. 'Right, well, thanks for telling me, Freda, and I'm glad I could have been of help. Now, I really must go.' I beat a hasty retreat, before Freda could regale me with more of her mixed and mangled metaphors.

In truth, I had forgotten all about Noah and his friend Kenny since concluding our report and sending it to Tom Bremner: I had been too preoccupied with my own affairs. But the conversation with Freda reminded me of something which had occurred to me following my discussion with old Creepy Crawley, and on reaching my desk, I buzzed through to Janet. She appeared before me in a matter of seconds. 'Ah Janet, there you are. What kept you?' I said in an ironic tone. Janet, who despite her many virtues, has no sense of humour whatsoever, was about to protest, but I held my hand up and stopped her. 'Never mind that now, Janet. Could you just find a number for this person, please, and get them on the line for me as soon as you can? Thanks.' I pushed a piece of paper over to her, and she picked it up and read it. She looked as though she was about to question me, but I said quickly, 'I'll explain later, Janet.' She shrugged, and disappeared.

I next put a call through to Tom. 'Oh, hi, Tom,' I began when he answered, 'sorry I didn't get back to you yesterday. Were you going to tell me about the Noah Kirby case?'

'Ah, yes, Ben, that's right. I was going to say…'

'…that the CPS have decided they're not going to prosecute. Yes, Freda told me this morning. She said you'd been in touch with Noah, and then he told her.'

'Ah, right, I see,' said Tom, 'yes, well, it was all down to you. Once they'd seen your report, they realised there was really no case to answer. Well done!'

I was silent.

'You don't seem to be very pleased about it, Ben,' said Tom sharply, 'I would have thought you would have been gratified that you presented such a successful defence.'

'Well, yes of course, I am, that's true,' I started, 'it's just that…'

Tom snorted. 'Look, Ben, as I've said before, goodness knows how many times, it's not your job to go ferreting around finding out things. It's up to the prosecution to prove their case beyond reasonable doubt, not for you to provide an alternative theory, and if the prosecution can't prove their case, because of your investigation, then so be it. End of.'

'Yes, I know, but…'

'The trouble with you, Ben, if I might say so, is that you think too much.'

'OK, OK,' I protested, 'let's leave it, should we?'

'Fine with me,' said Tom, 'anyway, whilst you're on, I was going to say, how about a session at "Et Alia" after work? Marcus is away isn't he, so you've no need to rush home.'

'Yes, OK, that would be great,' I said, 'see you there about six thirty.'

As I put my mobile down, a thought crossed my mind about something Tom had just said, but before I could pursue it, my desk phone trilled. It was Janet. 'That call you asked for,' she said, 'I'll put you through…'

Just before six thirty that evening, I was gathering my things together and tidying my desk, ready to set off for the wine-bar, when Janet entered. 'You've had a lot of mysterious phone calls this afternoon,' she said, 'are you going to tell me what you've been up to?'

I gave the side of my nose a tap. 'That's for me to know and you to find out,' I said with a knowing wink. The arms folded: a dangerous sign, as I have mentioned before. I hastily added, 'But if you'd care to join me at "Et Alia" for a refreshing glass of sauvignon blanc, then I will reveal all to you. And Tom, come to that.'

Obviously, curiosity overcame Janet's normal moral scruples, and she readily agreed.

We locked the office and set out the few yards along the high street to the wine-bar. Pushing through the door, we headed for our normal spot, where I could see Tom was already ensconced. There were two figures at the table adjacent with their backs toward us, but as I got nearer, I realised with a jolt that it was none other than Randall Barrett, sitting with the girl who had taken the part of Josephine in our latest production. I could feel Janet stiffen beside me, but undaunted, I gave Randall a half-wave of acknowledgement, which he studiously ignored. We greeted Tom and sat down by him, whilst he waved a hand so that within a micro-second, one of the barmen had come over to take our orders.

'I do wish I knew how you did that,' I said in a slightly peevish tone.

Tom gave a wry smile, then turning to Janet said, 'It's not so often we see you in here, Janet. Special occasion?'

Janet pursed her lips. 'Certainly not. But Ben here talked me into it.'

This was slightly stretching the truth, I thought, but decided not to say anything. Tom gave me a thoughtful look. 'It's funny,' he said, 'because something rather odd has just happened, which I wanted to talk to young Ben about. I wonder if the two things are connected?'

I tried to look inscrutable. 'Well, hard to say until I know what you're on about.'

'I was just going to tell you,' said Tom, 'you see, the thing is, I've just had a call from Noah Kirby again...'

'Saying how thrilled he was with the work I did, and he wants to pay double my fee, no doubt?'

'Well, not exactly, Ben,' said Tom, looking at his most magisterial, 'as I suspect you very well know. He was calling to say that he has just been arrested again!'

'Really? That was quick work!' Both Janet and Tom looked as though they were about to pounce on this remark, when Tom, who was facing the entrance of the wine-bar, instead gave me a hefty nudge and said, 'Well, I'll be...! Look who's just come in!'

I twisted round in my seat, expecting to see some business crony of Tom's, and gave an involuntary cry of surprise. Making their way through the crowded bar were Sam and Amy...

'Mind if we join you?' Sam asked, with a sheepish look.

By this time, I had stood up in surprise. 'Of course! But what are you doing here?'

'Hello, Dad,' Amy gave me a hug and kissed my cheek, 'bit of a long story. Aren't you going to offer us a drink and a seat?'

'Yes, sorry, here, I'll get some chairs. Oh, you know Tom of course, and do you remember Janet?'

'Yes, yes, we certainly do,' Sam and Amy confirmed.

Tom beckoned the barman, who as usual, arrived in a microsecond to take the order. Tom turned to Janet and said, 'Perhaps we'd better leave the family to their reunion?'

'Oh, no, please, it's fine, isn't it Sam?' Amy interjected, giving her brother a hard look, 'don't move on our account.'

'No, don't, please,' Sam affirmed, though with perhaps less sincerity than his sibling.

As they were speaking, I pulled up two more stools, and they sat down.

'This is a lovely surprise,' I began as I took my seat once again, 'so what is the long story. Oh, and before you begin, do you need to stay over? It might be getting a bit late to get a train back to town.'

'Yes, we're going to stay the night,' Amy replied, 'in fact, that's why Marcus has gone home, to check the beds are made up.'

'Marcus?' I asked, puzzled, 'Marcus is with you? I thought he was in town at a meeting?'

Tom got up at this point and said, 'Perhaps I'll go to the bar and see about some more drinks. Give me a hand, Janet, will you?'

I shot Tom a look. 'Do you know something about all this, Tom?'

'Be back in a tick,' Tom said hurriedly, moving off and dragging Janet, somewhat reluctantly after him.

I turned back to Amy. 'I think perhaps you'd better tell me what's going on.'

It was Sam who spoke. 'Let me do this, Amy,' he started, putting a hand on his sister's arm. 'You see, the thing is, Dad, that I think we, well, particularly me, owe you an apology. I wasn't very nice to you at your lunch party the other week.'

I was about to protest, but Sam held up his hand. 'No, no, I was wrong. I shouldn't have said what I said, and I'm sorry.'

'And I'm sorry too, Dad,' Amy chipped in, 'I was being silly about Marcus and Finn.'

'Well, it doesn't matter now,' I replied, 'though I appreciate the gesture. But what's brought all this on? And what has Marcus got to do with it?'

Sam cleared his throat, and giving a sideways look at Amy went on, 'Marcus messaged both Amy and me the other day, and said he was coming up to town, and could we meet for coffee or a drink or something.'

'Right, well he didn't say anything to me about that,' I interrupted, 'but what did he want?'

'He didn't say in advance. He was just insistent we all met. He said it was very important.'

I gave a nod. 'And?'

'So we agreed we'd have a coffee around midday. And then Marcus told us that you were so upset about how we'd both been, and that he, Marcus that is, felt responsible. He said that he loved you very much, but that if that meant causing a rift between us and you, Dad, then he would go away. He said he knew you always put us first, and that was quite right, but he realised that you were being torn in two, and he couldn't bear to see you like that.'

I felt a myself giving an involuntary sob, and did my best to disguise it by clearing my throat loudly.

'He said that? So what did you say?'

Amy took over. 'We were both a bit shocked, I think. We hadn't really thought about how you and Marcus felt, I suppose. But we talked for a bit, and Sam and I came to realise some important stuff.'

'Stuff?'

'Yes,' Amy carried on, 'we know that you loved mum, like we all did. But she's gone from us now. Sam and I have got our own lives to lead. But so have you, Dad. We can't expect you to just carry on like a latter-day Queen Victoria and be in permanent mourning for the rest of your life. We want you to be happy, and if that is with Marcus, then that's great. It doesn't mean that you've forgotten mum, or are trying to erase her memory. You've just got to live a different sort of life now.'

Sam chipped in, 'Yes, what Amy says is right. And Marcus is a really nice guy. The best.'

I could feel the tears well up in my eyes. 'Thank you. Thank you both. You don't know what that means to me. Are you sure? You know, you can't help the way that you feel...'

'...but you can help the way you behave,' Amy cut in, 'I know, mum used to say that. But we do both feel the same. Honestly. Be happy, Dad, please, for all our sakes.'

The tears were streaming down my cheeks now. I wiped at them, and cleared my throat and tried to pull myself together. 'Thank you, Sam, thank you Amy,' I coughed, then added, 'though I'm not entirely sure I want to be likened to an old queen…'

Tom and Janet arrived at that moment, bearing a bottle of bubbly and some fresh glasses.

'All well?' Tom asked anxiously. He looked relieved when he received nods of affirmation. 'I thought we could have this as a bit of a celebration,' he went on, pouring out the fizz and handing it around, 'oh, and look who's here! Just in the nick of time!'

I turned, and there was Marcus making his way across the room towards us. I half stood, waiting to fling my arms around him. He gave me a cheery wink, but then suddenly spotted Randall and his lady friend. Quickly altering direction, he went up to their table.

'Randy!' he exclaimed, and before the hapless Randall could move, Marcus had enveloped him in a bear-hug, and given him a resounding, noisy kiss full on the lips. 'Thank you for the other night. You were great! No wonder they call you Randy!' he exclaimed, giving the startled Josephine a lascivious leer. 'We must do it again soon, if I can get rid of…' here he gave a nod in my direction, '…and you can get rid of your older sister here.' He gave another leer at Josephine, playfully ruffled Randall's hair, and sauntered over towards me.

'That'll serve old Randall right for being so horrible to Janet and everyone else,' he said to our group in an undertone as he sat down beside me.

Meanwhile, Josephine had stood up, and said through gritted teeth, 'You bastard!' to Randall, then stalked off towards the door. Randall went after her calling, 'No wait, I don't know what he was on about. Wait!'

All started to laugh bar Janet, who confined herself to a thin, grim smile of satisfaction. 'You shouldn't have done that you know,' I admonished him, 'though it was quite funny.'

'Well, perhaps not,' said Marcus, 'though he had it coming. It just sort of occurred to me when I saw him sitting there. Anyway, what's this? Bubbly? Are we celebrating?'

I picked up a glass and gave it to him. 'Yes, I think we are. Here's to all of us, eh?' We all clinked glasses. 'Anyway,' I went on, 'I think you've got some explaining to do, haven't you?'

'No time for all that,' cried Marcus, 'I've just come from home, and Freda is on the warpath. Something to with some nephew called Noah. "There's a whole new can of worms coming home to roost" apparently, and "he's got more skeletons in his dirty washing than I've had hot dinners". I'm not sure what all that's about.'

'Ah, I think I can help you there,' I said, 'according to Tom here, young Noah has just been arrested. Again!'

'Again?'

I nodded, and quickly ran through the story of Noah and his friend Kenny.

Sam asked, 'Why has he been arrested then? I thought you'd got him off the charge of receiving stolen money.'

'Yes, come on Ben, I think you have a bit of explaining to do too, don't you?' Tom gave me a piercing look.

I gave a shrug. 'Yes, the report we prepared put a stop to the original charge. But I did have the feeling that all was not right.'

'In what way?' Janet asked.

'Well, a couple of things, I suppose. For a start, this money that was going backwards and forwards. Where would Noah get the money from in the first place, to be lending it to Kenny. Noah doesn't earn a lot, and he runs quite a fancy car, plus paying rent and so on. It didn't add up.'

'And what else?' Marcus chipped in.

'Well, the main thing really was why didn't Kenny and his team put up some sort of defence, and say that some of the money comprised loans from old Noah. He just pleaded guilty to the thefts, straightaway. It was a conversation with Alex "Creepy" Crawley that made me ponder on that point.'

'And what conclusion did you come to?' It was Amy this time.

'That the reason he pleaded guilty so quickly was that he didn't want any further investigation into his affairs. And the reason for that, presumably, was that he was doing something else which was worse than nicking cash from the old folks' home.'

'And that would be?'

'Drugs,' I replied promptly, 'Not that I have any proof, of course, but it did seem to me a likely explanation.'

'So what did you do?' asked Sam, curiously.

Janet intervened. 'Oh, I know the answer to that one. That's why you had me chasing around all afternoon. You had a talk with the original investigating officer, didn't you? DC Sparkes, wasn't it?'

I bowed my head in acknowledgement. 'Yes. I suggested to him certain lines of enquiry, which he seems to have pursued with enthusiasm.' I took a sip of champagne. 'You see, I wondered if there had been any problem with missing drugs from the old people's home. I think that might have been how it started. Then subsequently, Kenny, and through him, Noah started dealing more generally. The so called "county line" thing. But it's just a theory.'

Tom said, 'You are a funny one, Ben. You can't leave well alone, can you?'

I shrugged. 'Perhaps. But I didn't feel comfortable about it all. I *knew* there was something funny going on. It all stems from a lack of internal control, I suppose.'

Five faces looked at me blankly. 'Yes,' I carried on in a thoughtful tone, 'a lack of control at the old people's home meant that it was easy for Kenny to steal the money, and possibly drugs, in the first place. And look where all that led.'

Afterwards, we retired to my house, and Marcus rustled up an impromptu supper, at which we all drank rather more wine than was entirely sensible, Janet included. She and Tom staggered off around eleven, then Sam and Amy went to bed, conscious that they had an early start to get back to town the following morning for work. Marcus and I cleared up, then throwing caution aside, I sat him down by me on the sofa, and poured us both a glass of wine.

'So tell me, were you really prepared to walk out if Sam and Amy hadn't have relented?'

Marcus grinned sheepishly. 'Well, yes. But it was a pre-emptive strike. I'd rather left of my own accord than have you throw me out.'

'I wouldn't have done that!' I cried.

'Wouldn't you?' Marcus turned my face to his and looked at me. 'No, don't answer that. But you were thinking about it, I could tell. So I took a calculated risk. Actually, it was Tom who suggested I talk to Sam and Amy.'

'Tom? Ah, so that was what you were talking about that evening in the wine-bar?'

Marcus shrugged. 'I suppose. And then he called me after you'd had those telephone conversations with Sam and Amy. Anyway, I took his advice, and the rest is history.' He took a swig of wine. 'But I knew in my heart of hearts it would be OK.'

'You did?'

'Yes. Because I know the kids love you and want you to be happy. Deep down.'

I gave a muted snort. 'Yes, well, perhaps so, though they have a funny way of showing it at times.' A thought struck me. 'And you of course told Tom that you were going up to town today to see Sam and Amy. That's how he knew you would be late back. And I suppose it was Sam or Amy on the phone to you last night, saying where to meet?' Marcus gave a rueful nod. 'Still,' I took a slurp from my own glass, 'all's well et cetera, et cetera. We're together, the kids seem happy, I've salved my conscience over the Noah affair. And you,' I gave Marcus a poke in the ribs, 'you gave Randall something to think about!'

Marcus grinned. 'Yes, I did, didn't I? Just sort of came to me when I saw him there. Actually, I did quite enjoy that bit — giving him a hug. Surprisingly muscular, isn't he?'

I gave him a harder poke. 'That's enough of that! Anyway, you've sorted him out — for the time being at least...'

Ben Jonson and a Problem of Presentation

'No, no, no, my dears, this really won't do at *all*,' Clive Pettit's hands went up in his characteristic fashion, 'can we do it again, *please*. And this time, Ben, could you *try* to be a bit more, er, *ladylike*? I know willing suspension of disbelief and all that, but there *are* limits, you know!'

We were rehearsing for the operatic society's annual Christmas concert. In a moment of weakness, I had given way to my bombastic office manager's choice of song for the duet we were to perform. For the umpteenth time, I was regretting my capitulation in this matter: I had suggested we perform 'Baby, it's cold outside', but this had been rejected by Janet, reinforced by her feminist group cronies, on the grounds that the song in question had undertones of female subjugation by predatory males. Instead, we had compromised on the old Sonny and Cher classic, 'I've got you, babe.' In a rash moment, I had suggested that we swapped roles, so that I sang the Cher part, and Janet the male one. Although Clive had expressed some doubts about the wisdom of this at the time — the phrase 'drag-queen fest' seemed to echo in my mind— we had persevered. Too late, I was beginning to come around to Clive's point of view...

I was relating all this to my old pal Tom Bremner in our usual corner in 'Et Alia' an hour or so later. 'Perhaps I should have insisted on something else after all,' I said, gazing mournfully into a large glass of oaky chardonnay, 'my voice really isn't suited to this one. Besides which...' I trailed off.

'Besides what?' asked Tom, 'come on Ben, spit it out!'

'Well, it's just that Janet keeps looking at me with large eyes. She's been like that to some extent since I took over the part of Captain Corcoran in "Pinafore". You know, she was "Buttercup" and she and Corcoran end up as an item.'

Tom put down his glass and regarded me with a look of suppressed amusement. 'You mean, you think she's got - or is getting — a "pash" on you?'

'Well,' I bridled slightly at his tone of disbelief, 'is it so surprising?'

'Bearing in mind the circumstances, yes, it is,' said Tom. 'Honestly, Ben, love you as I do — er, in a platonic sort of way of course,' he added hurriedly, 'sometimes you *do* have an exaggerated sense of your sex appeal!'

'Really?'

'Yes, probably Janet was just throwing herself into the part, if you see what I mean.'

'If you say so.'

Tom cleared his throat then carried on, 'Anyway, moving on, so to speak, I had a couple of things I wanted to speak to you about. I did ring your mobile earlier, but you didn't answer.'

I relented from my attitude of hurt sensitivity. 'Oh, sorry, I was probably rehearsing. I haven't looked at my phone since I left the office. What did you want to say?'

'Firstly, there's a personal injury case I want you to look at.'

I nodded, 'Fine, fine. What's it all about?'

Tom spread his hands, 'Well, probably not worth a great deal. A woman was thrown to the floor of a bus when it braked suddenly. She broke an arm and her jaw in the fall, plus other more minor injuries, and has been unable to work for some while.'

I nodded. 'What line of business?'

'Self-employed physiotherapist. So you can see why it's been difficult for her to work.'

'Yes, of course. OK, well, send the file over to me and we'll have a look. Now, what was the other thing?'

Tom coloured slightly. 'Well, I know it's a bit of an imposition — and you probably won't want to do it — and I could understand why, I wouldn't be that keen myself, to be honest. But it would go down well.'

'Yes, but what is it?' I asked impatiently.

Tom looked surprised. 'Didn't I say? It's this over sixties club that the church runs. They have their meetings and so on in the church hall where you rehearse.'

'And?' I said, thinking Tom seemed to be taking a long time to get to the point.

'They want a speaker for their next meeting. They wrote to me, but I can't manage the date they suggested, so I volunteered you!'

'Oh, gosh, great, thanks a bunch!' I said sarcastically, 'and when do they want this talk? And on what subject?'

'Didn't I say that either?' Tom looked at me guilelessly, 'well, as to what — I thought you could talk about some of your cases — the more interesting ones, anyway.'

I flattened my lips into a thin line, of which even Janet would have been envious. 'And when is this fascinating presentation due to take place? You haven't mentioned that as yet.'

Tom shifted uncomfortably in his seat. 'Ah yes, well, in point of fact it's — er — Thursday.'

'Thursday? You mean the day after tomorrow?'

Tom nodded.

'Christ, Tom, you might have given me a bit more notice!'

Tom hung his head. 'Yes, sorry and all that. I forgot all about it to be honest. But if you really don't want to, I'll try to find someone else, or just come clean and tell them we can't do it.'

I looked at him in exasperation. 'Oh, all right, I'll do it. But I don't know what I'm going to say, or when I'm going to prepare it.'

'Oh, thanks Ben, you're a pal!' Tom looked as though he was going to hug me, but thought better of it and gave me a pat on the shoulder instead. 'I can at least get us another drink in. Same again?'

'Oh, I'm not sure I've got time now,' I retorted, 'but if you twist my arm, OK then!'

'Anyway,' Tom continued a minute or so later as the barman miraculously appeared with refills, 'why don't you get Marcus to help? He's used to doing all these power-point things isn't he?'

'Yes, he is,' I took a mouthful of chardonnay, 'actually, he would probably do the whole thing much better, but he's going to be away Thursday. I'll rope him in though, don't worry!'

The house was still in darkness when I opened the front door some half an hour later, which meant Marcus was still at the squash club. *Pity*, I thought, *I could do with running this talk thing by him now.* Luckily, I didn't have to wait long before I heard the sound of someone trying to insert the key into the lock of the door. I pre-empted Marcus by opening it for him.

'Couldn't seem to get the key in,' he beamed affably at me.

'No, always difficult to hit a moving target,' I agreed, 'how much did you have to drink tonight?'

'I only had a quick pint,' he replied in a huffy tone.

'Of what? Gin?'

'Ha, ha, very funny!'

'Anyway, come here and sit down,' I continued, pulling him

into the kitchen and pushing him onto one of the stools by the breakfast bar, 'I want to pick your brains.'

'I better have some wine, then,' Marcus replied, 'I always think better on a glass of wine.'

Stifling the response. 'Don't you think you've had enough?' I poured out two glasses of chardonnay.

'Cheers!' We clinked glasses.

'What it is,' I began, 'Tom has landed me with doing a talk to some old fogeys' group at the church hall on Thursday, so I could do with a bit of a hand.'

'Ah,' Marcus gave me a wink, 'well, of course! Delighted to assist. First off, remember the old five "p" adage.'

'Five p? What's that?'

'Proper preparation prevents poor performance,' Marcus replied promptly, 'though in your case, I might make it the more complete nine "p" version.'

'Which is?'

'Prior proper preparation prevents poor performance by the person putting on the presentation,' he intoned, with a grin.

'Most helpful,' I said primly.

'No, but seriously, what are you going to talk about?'

'Well,' I started, 'Tom did suggest just talking about my work and so on.'

Marcus looked less than impressed. 'Not sure about that,' he mused, 'you don't want to get too technical and bore them all with those whatsit tables and section 42 offers.'

'Ogden tables,' I said absent-mindedly, 'and Part 36 offers. Part 36 of the Civil Procedure Rules.'

Marcus waved a hand dismissively, 'Yeah, yeah, whatever. The point is, you don't want to be tedious and go on about all that stuff.'

'Well, I wasn't intending to, as a matter of fact. What Tom suggested was that I talk about some of the more interesting cases in my experience of forensic accounting.'

Marcus gave me a look expressing incredulity that *any* aspect of accountancy could be regarded as interesting. 'Well, I'm sure I can find something, even without your help,' I went on in a testy tone.

Marcus put his hands up in a gesture of submission. 'OK, OK, keep your hair on! Let me think,' he paused and took a slurp of wine, 'Yeah, I know, I suppose for instance you could talk about how you found out about that hotel scam. And then there was the guy falling off the wall. That was quite a clever bit of detective work, actually.'

'Right, good, that's more like it. If I put a few thoughts together, could you knock up a power-point thing for me tomorrow?'

'Knock up a power-point thing?' Marcus mimicked, in a deprecating tone, 'is that what you think I do all day?'

'Isn't it?' I asked innocently, and winced as Marcus cuffed me around the neck.

'Anyway,' he went on slyly, 'if it all goes a bit quiet, bring on Janet and go into your Sonny and Cher routine.'

'You mean, give them a bit of a laugh?'

'No, more that it'll make the accountancy thing seem quite good in comparison!'

It was Marcus's turn to wince as I returned the cuff.

'No, I'm only kidding. Of course, I'll do it. Better get on with it first thing — we don't have much time.'

'Yes, I know,' I went, 'I'd better not make too much of the detective thing though — these cases are mostly a question of analysis of data and hard slog. I bet I don't have any "detecting" to do for months.'

But here again, as so often, I was proved wrong…

I was in the office early the next morning, deciding that I would draft out my talk first, before getting embroiled too much in the business of the day. I set my mind to it and slaved away for an hour or so, then e-mailed the draft to Marcus so he could 'knock up his power-point' thing as I had put it the previous night. I had just pressed 'send' when Janet waltzed into my room, bearing a parcel.

'Tom Bremner,' she announced curtly.

I was feeling in a light-hearted mood now that I had put the dreaded talk to bed, so to speak, so I answered in a playful tone, 'Oh, surely some mistake, Mrs Mathieson! Looks more like a file to me!'

I was rewarded with a look that to describe as 'withering' would be inadequate. She banged down the package on my desk and snapped, 'No, I mean this parcel is from Tom Bremner, of course!'

'Really?' I replied in a tone of heavy irony, which as usual, was completely wasted on Janet.

'Yes, really! Anyway,' she went on in a more conciliatory tone, 'I wanted to talk to you about something else.'

'Oh, yes? Is it to do with work, because if not, can we leave it until later? I've got a lot to get through today.' Janet's lips thinned in their usual way when she was displeased about something, but ignoring that sign, I ploughed on, and added, 'Yes, that reminds me, can you clear my diary tomorrow morning, please. I'm going across to the church hall at eleven to give a talk to the old fogeys.'

Janet's hands went to the hips: another dangerous sign. 'If

by "old fogeys" you mean the over sixties club, I might remind you that *you* will be an old fogey yourself one day!' She turned and stalked out of the office murmuring something that sounded remarkably like 'if I don't throttle you first, that is!'

A quotation came to mind: 'Men have their mothers forced upon them, but their wives, or in this case, *office managers*, are their own choice.' I turned my attention to the package on my desk, but at the back of my mind it struck me that Janet had presumably wanted to talk about something apart from work, and I wondered idly what that could be.

I started reading the notes on the case Tom had presented to me. The claimant in this case was an Amanda Hunt. La Belle Amanda had been a passenger on a number 22 bus and she was making her way down the aisle, just prior to alighting, when the bus driver had suddenly stopped, causing her to be thrown forward violently. She had fallen awkwardly, catching the side of her face on a metal hand rail, and breaking her jaw, then also breaking her arm when she hit the floor of the bus. She had not been paying attention to the road at the time, being concerned only that she did not miss her stop, and was unable to explain why the driver had braked. As Tom had disclosed, Amanda was a self-employed physiotherapist, and consequently, her injuries rendered her unable to work, and would do so for some time to come. Fortunately, the prognosis was good, and the expectation by the medics was that she would make a full recovery with no long-term problems. The file contained some details of Amanda's earnings and expenses, sufficient on the face of it for us to calculate fairly readily the loss of earnings. Luckily, from her point of view, she did not own premises or employ staff of her own, but rented space and services from a more senior physiotherapist, who had established a sports injuries and physio practice not far from the surgery of my old rival, Dr Randall Barrett, in King Street. So far, this all seemed straightforward, but it crossed my mind that there was no explanation given for the bus driver's sudden stop, which had precipitated the injuries Amanda had suffered. I rifled through various papers, then found a statement from the driver in question, to the effect that he had stopped sharply in order to avoid a collision with a car which had pulled out in front of him.

I made a few notes then looked up as there was a tap on my door. It was Alison from Business Services, better known by her *soubriquet* of 'Alice in Ledgerland'.

'Alex asked me to give these to you, Ben.' She placed a stack of files on my desk.

'Oh, right, thanks Alice — er — I mean Alison,' I replied, 'though I don't know why he had to summon you to act as his runner.'

'Oh, he didn't, Ben. I just happened to be in his room and I offered to bring them. We were talking about a job I'm doing for him,' she added, a touch defensively. A slight blush crept across her cheeks, and I thought again that I detected a burgeoning romance between them, at least on Alison's side....

'Of course,' I said smoothly, 'oh, and could you perhaps do me a favour and hand this file to Alex? Thanks.'

Alison picked up the Amanda Hunt file and almost skipped out of the room, no doubt pleased to have another opportunity for a rendezvous with her *inamorata,* so to speak. I pondered for a few moments on the subject of office romances. I have to say that I don't really think they are a good idea: 'Don't dip your pen in the office ink' was a saying that sprang to mind. If the romance is going well, then the couple involved are often too busy staring into each other's eyes to actually get on with any work. But worse still if the romance is *not* going well. In this case, there are tears and arguments and sullen silences, and the rest of the staff get dragged in to taking one side or the other. Then that in turn causes dissent between members of the workforce, which often continues long after the lovebirds themselves have kissed and made up. However, there was remarkably little that I, or indeed anyone else, could realistically do about it. As Gilbert and Sullivan put it in *The Gondoliers,*

'Try we life-long, we can never,
Straighten out Life's tangled skein.'

I pressed on with the business of the day. Around lunchtime an e-mail appeared from Marcus with an attachment incorporating the talk and presentation for the following day. I gave instructions to Janet that I was not to be disturbed, and set about rehearsing. I have to hand it to Marcus that he had managed to spice up my rough draft with some amusing and pertinent graphics, so the effect to my eyes at least, was quite reasonable. Fortunately, the talk only had to last twenty to thirty minutes, so it was not too taxing a job.

The next morning, I arrived at the Church Hall, familiar of course because it was the venue for rehearsals of CAOS, and sought out the organiser of the Over 60s group, Hannah Phelps. A stoutish woman with wild grey hair that erupted from her scalp like cooling lava was pointed out to me, and I sped over to introduce myself.

'Ah, Mr Johnstone, good morning,' she began.

'Er, actually, it's Jonson,' I responded, 'Ben Jonson. You know, like the sixteenth-century dramatist.'

'Yes, of course,' she said vaguely, 'I must make a note. For my introduction.' She smiled, then scrabbled in a voluminous hand-bag for some paper and a pen. 'Yes, now let me see,' she shuffled pieces of paper, 'and you're a lawyer?'

'Er, no, I'm a forensic accountant. Tom Bremner's the solicitor.'

'Is he speaking as well?' Hannah looked puzzled, 'I thought we were just having the one talk today.'

I could see this was going to be a trying morning. 'No, Tom Bremner, the solicitor, the one you originally asked to come, is not able to be here, so he asked me to come in his place.'

'Ah, I see,' Hannah looked as though light had finally dawned, 'and you're going to talk about the law?'

I took a deep breath. 'No, I'm a forensic accountant, you see, so I thought I would be better advised to talk about that.'

'Forensic?' Hannah looked perturbed, 'You're not going to show pictures of dead bodies and things, are you? It could be a bit upsetting for some of our regulars.'

'No, I think you're confusing me with a forensic pathologist,' I said with as much patience as I could muster, 'I'm an accountant. There won't be any dead bodies, I assure you,' I added, though looking around at the members of the group who were making their way into the hall, I wondered if I was making a bit of a rash promise…

I had roped in Alice-in-Ledgerland to help me and to stand by in case of technical issues with the presentation, so we quickly set up, ready for the talk.

At precisely eleven o'clock, Hannah rose to her feet and giving a somewhat ineffectual rap on the table to attract attention, began to speak.

'Welcome Ladies and Gentlemen to the Over 60s group. Today, we are going to have a talk from the distinguished — er — accountant,' here Hannah referred to her notes, 'distinguished accountant, Mr William Shakespeare!'

I rose to my feet to somewhat muted applause. 'Thank you, Mrs Phelps, though I had better say that my name is actually that of another sixteenth-century playwright, Ben Jonson.'

Hannah gave me a sharp look. 'Jonson? I thought he was that man who kept a diary.'

'Ah, I think you must be getting confused with *Doctor* Johnson,' I smiled, 'Samuel, that is.'

'Dear me, I'm so sorry,' Hannah said, 'Ladies and Gentlemen, please welcome Dr Ben Samuel.'

I decided to leave it at that point, and instead plunged into my talk. Fortunately, all went well, and I was gratified by the apparently enthusiastic applause when I had finished. The rapture was somewhat modified when I overheard two elderly men later confessing that they had turned their hearing devices off for the duration and were applauding because it was time for the tea and biscuits…

Although I was personally quite keen to make a quick escape after my little presentation, Hannah Phelps was insistent I stay for some refreshment, and pressed a cup of tea into my hands. 'Can I tempt you to a fig-roll?' she asked, passing a plate of rather moribund looking biscuits. I gave a deprecating smile and replied that I was trying to avoid all temptations at present.

As I sipped my tea, Hannah started to speak. 'Actually, Mr er, er…'

'Jonson,' I added helpfully.

'Yes, Mr Jonson, I did want a little word with you, now that I understand what you do in your work.'

'Oh, yes? You have a problem?'

Hannah looked round to ensure we were not going to be overheard. 'It's like this,' she began. 'You know it's always difficult to get volunteers to be officers of a little voluntary organisation like this?'

I nodded. 'Yes, it's a problem, I'm sure. So many people don't want to be bothered with such things, particularly as they are er, getting on in years, shall we say.'

'And especially posts like Secretary and Treasurer,' Hannah agreed, 'so when our previous treasurer died quite suddenly, oh, about a year and a half ago, we were a bit desperate. Then this new man joined, and immediately volunteered. Dennis, his name is, Dennis Saunders.'

'Right. Don't think I know the chap, but go on.'

Hannah sighed. 'Well, Dennis seemed an answer to our prayers. He had retired from one of the big banks, in quite a senior position, so he knew about money. But then there were marital problems, and his wife left him.' Hannah took a gulp of tea, then continued, 'well, I'd heard about this, so I said did he want to carry on. But Dennis said yes, he would, because it gave him something to do and took his mind off things.'

'Well, I can understand that,' I said as Hannah paused for another sip, 'but then what?'

'Well, over the summer, we began to hear grumblings in the town that some of the association bills were not being paid. You know, we hold events, so there's expenditure on food and drink, room hire and so on. We, that is, my husband Harry and I, tackled Dennis about it. He sort of brushed it aside, and said that because of some confusion at the bank about transferring money between the two accounts we have, some cheques had bounced.'

I thought, but did not say, that in this day and age of online banking and 24/7 access to the bank accounts, this sounded a little thin.

Hannah brushed a recalcitrant strand of hair from across her eyes and continued. 'So anyway, Dennis assured us he was

177

sorting it out, so that was that. For a few weeks, at least. Then I got a letter from the bank about a credit card that had been applied for on the club's account. Well, I didn't know anything about it, and so Harry and I had another go at Dennis, who finally admitted he had asked for one. But he had never asked the management committee for approval.'

'And you were suspicious as to why he wanted one?' I asked as Hannah paused.

'Well, I don't know a lot about these things, but Harry used to help Reg Smith, the previous treasurer, and said there was really no need for Dennis to have one. So in the end, we confronted Dennis and insisted that he hand over all the books and so on.'

'And he did?'

Hannah nodded. 'Oh yes, to be fair, he did so straightaway. But unfortunately, it consisted of a Sainsbury's bag full of a pile of bills, bank statements and so on. It was a total mess. We were wondering what to do next, but then listening to your talk today, I thought that perhaps…?'

I sighed inwardly. 'You'd like me, or my firm rather, to have a look?'

'Oh, would you? We'd be ever so grateful.'

A thought struck me. 'But surely you have a firm of accountants who do annual accounts and so on? I think you ought to mention this to them first.'

Hannah pulled a face. 'Well, we do usually use a firm. Huxleys.'

'Ah!' I saw the problem. Huxleys was of course the firm whose founder and senior partner had been helping himself to clients' funds, and had been exposed by me. I went on, 'But they have been taken over and I'm sure everything is fine now.'

'I think we, that is the management committee and I, would be happier if *you* had a look into it,' Hannah said firmly.

I hesitated for a moment. Although I never like to turn work down, the problem with a small charity such as the Over 60s is that the time costs my firm were likely to incur in this sort of work were probably going to be pretty high in relation to the income of the organisation. Often, in these cases, I end up having to do a lot of work myself, and not charging the time, or else having to take a big hit on my firm's recovery rates. Which was all very well, and at times, I am happy to do it. But nevertheless, I do still have to pay my staff and all the other overheads, so there is a limit to my charity...

'Please?' Hannah had noticed my hesitation.

'Yes, of course,' I conceded, thinking, *Oh, well, perhaps I'll get my reward in heaven...*

Half an hour later, clutching a plastic bag full of jumbled receipts, bank statements, cheque-books and invoices, I was back at my desk. Alice-in-Ledgerland, at my behest, accompanied me, and I explained the background to her. 'So could you start by going through this lot and make some schedules of receipts and payments, please, Alice, er, I mean Alison,' I said, 'and could you get on to Huxleys, and see if we can get any information for earlier years. Oh, and I'll ask Alex if he could supervise, so if you have problems, which I think you may well, you can consult with him in the first instance.' I noticed that she looked rather pleased at that prospect and wondered if I might be inadvertently encouraging the nascent romance...

However, I needn't have worried as it turned out. Alex 'Creepy' Crawley had declared that he was snowed under with work, and could I find someone else to supervise? Although he was probably correct about being very busy, it did just cross my mind that he was making an excuse not to be in too frequent contact with the fair Alison. I said as much to Janet later that day, who merely pursed her lips even more tightly than usual and muttered something about 'good job too!' Janet and Alison, it has to be said, have never seen eye-to-eye, particularly after the unfortunate incident with the stationery cupboard door. However, not wishing to leave Alison entirely unsupported, so to speak, I had a thought and e-mailed Gary Lincoln, asking him to act as mentor. Gary, our efficient but neologistic tax manager, had instantly replied:

'Wilco. Can you BMUTS me on this ASAP as I'm not ITL.'

I was still trying to decode this message that evening, trying my utmost to resist the urge to plead ignorance to Gary and ask him direct what on earth he was talking about. As Marcus was away overnight, I had messaged Tom to arrange to meet at 'Et Alia' for a glass or two of *vin* very *ordinaire* after work. When I arrived, I found him in our usual corner, with a bottle and two glasses already set up.

'Good man, Tom!' I cried 'I'm ready for this!' I sensed that Tom did not have quite his usual air of raffish bonhomie, but we chatted away affably enough for some minutes. I repeated Gary's incomprehensible message, but Tom declared himself as baffled as I was.

'Oh, how did your talk go today?' he asked after a while, 'sorry, I forgot to ask. Sorry too that I landed you with it.'

'It went OK, I think,' I replied, 'apart from Hannah Phelps confusing me with an eighteenth-century lexicographer!' Tom looked bemused by this, but did not make any comment. 'Tom,' I said, 'is everything all right? If you don't mind me saying so, you don't seem quite your normal self this evening.'

Tom pulled a face. 'Yes, sorry, Ben, you're right. In fact, I'd better tell you now. You know that case I passed over to you the other day? The girl who fell on the bus?'

'You mean Amanda Hunt? Yes, I know. What about it?'

Tom took a hefty gulp of wine. 'I've just heard today from the bus company's insurers.'

'And?'

'And they are denying liability.'

'What?' I cried, 'how come?'

Tom spread his hands in a gesture of exasperation. 'They are saying that it was not the bus driver's fault, because he had to stop rapidly to avoid a collision with a car. And they've provided a statement from another passenger which confirms this.'

'Dammit! And of course, Amanda can't say what happened because she wasn't looking at the road ahead!'

'No, quite,' Tom replied, 'so I'm not sure it's worth pursuing, to be honest. And in the meantime, you'd better stop work on the loss of earnings and so on because it doesn't look as though we'll get any costs back from anyone.'

I sucked air between my teeth. 'Well, I don't suppose our time costs are very great as yet. Still, it's annoying — well, particularly for Amanda Hunt, but also for you and me. More time written off!' I took a mouthful of wine, 'and whilst we're on the subject of such things, I've got another job on now which is probably going to cost me a packet!'

Tom raised an eyebrow in enquiry, and I explained to him what Hannah Phelps had told me about the treasurer of the Over 60s and her request for us to investigate.

'And it occurred to me,' I added, 'you said you were a trustee of this charity, aren't you?' Tom nodded and I continued, 'shouldn't you have been aware of all this? Surely you have a duty to look at the finances at the management committee meetings?'

Tom stood up suddenly, red in the face. 'Honestly, Ben, you can be a pompous little prick at times!' and stalked off, leaving me staring after him in astonishment.

'Am I pompous?' I asked Marcus later when he skyped me at home.

'Yes,' was the uncompromising and uncomfortably swift response.

'No, no, take your time to consider your answer,' I said, somewhat nettled at this.

'I did,' Marcus retorted.

'Any other complaints then whilst I'm about it?'

'Well, you are a bit grumpy, especially in the mornings. And you do have an exaggerated view of your acting and singing abilities. And you do seem to think that everyone fancies you. Even Janet, apparently.'

I stared at him on the screen. 'How did you know that?'

Marcus shrugged. 'Oh, I think Tom mentioned it the other day.'

'You often have little chats about me then, do you?' I was starting to feel irritated.

'Yes, I suppose we do.'

'And why is that?' I could feel my lips thinning in a fair impression of those of my esteemed office manager.

'Because we both…care about you!'

'Even with all my faults?'

'Surprisingly, yes!' Marcus almost shouted. In softer tone, he went on, 'Look, I know you're fishing for compliments, so here we are: I think you are funny and witty and intelligent and straightforward and honest, and I don't want to be with anyone else. Satisfied?'

'Well…'

'Oh, yes, and you're not bad looking either. In fact, quite hunky — in a sort of way, of course. If the light is dim, that is!'

'I see, "May very well pass for forty-three in the dusk with the light behind me" type of thing?'

Marcus moved his hands apart in a gesture of assent. 'That sort of thing.'

I mellowed. 'OK, well, thanks for all that. But what am I going to do about Tom? I really didn't mean to upset him. He's not usually so sensitive.'

Marcus considered for a moment, then said, 'Probably he's a bit concerned. If he's a trustee, then, as you said, he does have a responsibility to ensure good governance. And I suppose the group, charity whatever it is, could sue him?'

It was my turn to consider. 'I suppose so, although it might be a bit unlikely. And all he needs to do is show he acted reasonably. But it wouldn't reflect too well on him, or more importantly, his firm.'

'Anyway, you'd better do something about patching up things with him PDQ!' Marcus waved a finger at me sternly.

'Yes, you're right. I'll try to get him ASAP.' I was about to end the conversation, but Marcus had reminded of something. 'Oh, and by the way, or should I say BTW, what on earth do the acronyms "BMUTS" and "ITL" mean?' Marcus looked puzzled, so I explained about Gary's cryptic message of earlier that night.

'Search me!' Marcus seemed bemused, 'look, must go, I'm still with the crowd. Ciao!' The screen went blank, but not before I had a glimpse of a group of Marcus's colleagues seated around a table at what looked like a very swanky restaurant. It was funny, I mused to myself, how much of what Marcus calls *work* seems to involve eating and drinking in exotic locations…

Taking Marcus's advice, I tried calling Tom's mobile, but there was no reply. I left a brief message on his voice-mail, asking him to call me back, and was just pouring myself a restorative glass of chardonnay when there was a ring on the doorbell.

'Who the hell is this?' I wondered as I padded down the hall. A familiar figure was silhouetted on the glass of the door, and as I pulled it open, Tom burst in and enveloped me in a bear hug so tight that I had trouble breathing for a moment. 'Good God, Tom, put me down, you're going to suffocate me!' I gasped, then added, 'though naturally I'm delighted to see you too!'

Tom released me from his vice-like grip and hung his head. 'Ben, look, I'm really sorry. I shouldn't have said what I said. Can you forgive me?'

I scoffed and said, 'Well, I've just spoken to Marcus and he confirmed that I *am* a pompous prick at times, so it is I who should be apologising to you!' Tom grinned and I added, 'Anyway, come through to the kitchen. You're just in time — I was just pouring myself a glass of wine. Come and join me.'

Tom nodded acceptance and followed me to the breakfast bar, where I quickly found another glass and filled it up.

'Cheers!' We clinked glasses and settled ourselves on the bar stools.

'Look, Ben,' Tom started after a couple of mouthfuls of chardonnay, 'you were quite right. I *should* have known what was going on at the charity. And I feel a bit guilty about all this, so if you have a problem with fees and so on with the work you're going to do, I'll see that you get paid.'

'What? From your own pocket? Well, that's very decent of you, Tom, but I'm not sure I could accept that.'

Tom waved a finger at me, 'Well, let's see should we. We'll talk it over at the appropriate time. But the important thing is that you do a thorough job — which I'm sure you will,' he put in hastily, 'I don't want there to be any issues here.'

I shrugged. 'Well, OK, sure thing.' We clinked glasses again. 'Actually, Tom, on another matter, I've just been thinking.'

'Always dangerous, I've noticed,' Tom pulled a wry face.

I gave him a playful punch on the arm. 'Yeah, thanks pal. But it's about this bus case. You know, Amanda Hunt.'

'Yes? What have you been thinking then, old chap?'

'It occurred to me that these days there's probably CCTV on the buses.'

Tom considered. 'Yes, possibly.'

'And,' I went on, 'it's possible isn't it that it might have picked up the registration number of the car that caused the bus driver to do the emergency stop.'

Tom nodded.

'Therefore,' I continued eagerly, 'we could trace the driver, or rather, the driver's insurers, and make a claim against them. I mean, Amanda could.'

Tom considered for a moment. 'Well,' he said eventually, 'yes, in theory, I suppose we could. But it might be a bit of a long shot, though.'

'But worth a try, surely?' I urged.

Tom gave a rueful laugh. 'You never give up, do you, Ben? That's what I admire about you. Well, one of the things, anyway.' He slurped another mouthful of wine. 'OK, I'll get on to it first thing in the morning, eh?' How about that?'

'Great! Now, how about another glass? Oh, and it's getting late. Why don't you stay over? I can lend you some of Marcus's things if you like.'

Tom was just saying yes to this suggestion when my laptop pinged. It was a message from Marcus. 'Got the answer to

"BMUTS" and "ITL" for you,' he announced, 'you'd never have guessed it!'

I had to admit to having a slight headache the next morning. Tom and I had stayed up too late and had more glasses of wine than was entirely sensible, and it had taken some effort on both our parts to arise and make ourselves presentable for the working day. I was glad though that Tom had come around the previous evening, and we had made up our little spat. 'Life's too short,' he had said, slurring his words a little, as we had made our 'goodnights' at the top of the stairs, and somewhat to my surprise, he had again enveloped me in a tight hug, before patting my shoulder with a great, hairy fist.

I picked up the photograph of Julia which stood on one side of the low sideboard in my office. A matching frame at the other end held one of Julia with our children, Sam and Amy, taken when they were aged ten and eight. I gazed at her image for a while, then turning it over, read the quotation from my sixteenth century playwright namesake, pasted on the back:

She is Venus when she smiles,
But she's Juno when she walks,
And Minerva when she talks.

I felt my eyes moisten. A peremptory knock on the office door, heralding the entry of Janet, made me hastily replace the photo and dab at my eyes with a finger before swinging around to face her. 'Got something in my eye,' I said quickly, in response to her expression of enquiry. She shot a glance at the frame I had so rapidly put down, and her normally severe expression softened for an instant.

'Would you like me to get it out for you?' she asked, the thin lips relaxing ever so slightly.

'Thank you, but no, that won't be necessary,' I replied, then added quickly, 'Did you want me for something?'

The expression tightened and regained a more familiar aspect. 'Just this morning's post,' she said in a clipped manner, 'oh, and there was one other thing.'

My heart sank at this. 'Yes? And what was that?' It was an effort to keep my tone neutral.

Janet pierced me with one of her looks, but I returned the gaze unflinchingly. 'Yes,' she went on, 'it's about this piece we're doing for the Christmas Concert. I don't think it's working, is it? Or more specifically, I don't think *your* bit is working.'

My initial instinct, as always with Janet, was to argue. But on this occasion, I had secretly to admit that I thought the same, and in fact our director, Clive Pettit, had said as much earlier in the week. I didn't reply for a moment, but finally said, 'So what do you suggest.'

Janet took a deep breath, obviously steeling herself to say something difficult. For a moment, I thought she was going to refuse to perform with me at all, but she suddenly blurted out, 'I think we might be better to go with your suggestion after all. You know, the "Baby it's cold outside" thing, only with the roles reversed, and you being the chap saying that he really can't stay.'

If I hadn't already been sitting, I think I would have *had* to sit out of sheer shock.

'Do you mean that?' I started, 'won't your feminist action group have something to say about it?'

'Not at all,' replied Janet stoutly, 'in fact they're fully in favour. I ran the idea past them yesterday. They consider it is a refreshing and ironic synthesis of female empowerment.'

I wasn't at all clear that I understood the sentiment, but I nodded sagely. 'Well, good, let's do it then. Thank you, Janet.'

'Well see if you can get this one right,' she returned, marching out of the room.

'Yes, miss!' I mimicked, sticking my tongue out at her retreating back, and thinking that the resemblance to Miss Norbury, my primary school teacher, grew ever more marked. I had hastily to compose my features into a more normal aspect as she suddenly reappeared and said, 'Don't forget, full dress rehearsal this evening!'

'Dammit!' I thought. Of course, I hadn't actually *forgotten* but I had put it to one side, in a manner of speaking. The operetta on this occasion was 'HMS Pinafore' with me in the actually pretty major role of 'Captain Corcoran' and Janet as 'Buttercup'. The rehearsal tonight was to be followed by performances on Friday and Saturday evenings, and a final afternoon one on Sunday. I could have done with a totally clear head, and kicked myself for not having had an early night the previous day as I had originally intended.

The rehearsal did not go well. There were multiple missed cues, the curtain stuck on two occasions and Josephine, my stage daughter and female romantic lead, seemed to be suffering from an acute attack of amnesia. I too found it a great strain: my slight headache had persisted all day, and was if anything rather worse than it had been in the morning. I also felt a stinging at the back of my throat, but tried to dismiss it all as a mild attack of nerves. Matters were not helped of course by the personal relations between myself, 'Josephine' and Randall Barrett, who played the male romantic lead. Randall and I have never exactly hit it off, but matters deteriorated when Marcus had marched up to Randall one evening in the wine-bar, kissed him full on the lips, and implied that they had had a night of passion together. As Randall had been romantically involved offstage with 'Josephine' and had in fact been sitting with her at the time, this had led to the cessation of relations between the two, despite my intervention and pleadings that this had all been a practical joke, albeit a rather clumsy one. Randall naturally blamed me as much as Marcus, and refused to accept my assertions that I had no hand in it and did not know in advance what Marcus was going to do.

Poor Clive, our director, was feeling the strain. He was constantly mopping his brow with a handkerchief, and his complexion, which as I may have mentioned before, has a hint of green at the best of times, turned through chartreuse and sage, to end up as something Marcus rather caustically described as "Shiny Shamrock". Marcus had turned up towards the end of proceedings and was eyeing me somewhat anxiously.

'Are you OK, Ben?' he asked, 'you look a bit pale.'

'Oh, I'm all right,' I replied, a little brusquely, 'just a bit of a headache. Not surprising after that horlicks of a rehearsal.'

'Oh, I don't think it was too bad,' Marcus said reassuringly, 'after all, don't they say that if a dress rehearsal is terrible, the first night will be great?'

'They may *say* that,' I replied, 'but on the whole I think that is wishful thinking, hope and a touch of denial!'

Marcus shrugged. 'Well, anyway, I thought you were really...' his voice tailed away a little, as he seemed to search for the right word, '...really quite creditable!'

'Thank you for that ringing endorsement!' I was feeling irritable by now.

'Right, time you went home,' said Marcus and pulled me firmly across to the dressing rooms, 'you need a hot toddy and an early night!'

I did as I was bid, but if I had hoped that by the next morning

I would feel one hundred per cent again, I was sadly disappointed. I managed to struggle through the day, but with a throbbing head, and to my alarm, a voice that was getting decidedly croaky. Around half past three, Janet flung open my office door and stood before my desk.

'Someone to see you!' she exclaimed.

'Really? I wasn't expecting anyone. There's nothing in my diary.'

Janet gave me a look as if to say 'well that doesn't mean anything.' She has always been rather sniffy about my automated diary. 'No, I've arranged this for you. Come in!' she called as there was tentative rap on the door.

I looked up, and to my utter surprise, in walked Randall Barrett.

'Good Lord!' I exclaimed, 'what in the world are you doing here?'

Randall pulled a wry face but before he could speak, Janet interrupted.

'I asked Randall to come. I managed to track him down, and I told him you are obviously not well, and he very kindly offered to come and see if he can patch you up.'

'Patch me up?' I bristled, 'I'm not some old banger you're trying to get through its MOT!'

Two pairs of eyes regarded me steadily as if their owners didn't actually agree with that remark, but did not *quite* like to say so. Finally, Randall spoke.

'Perhaps you could leave us, Janet, and I'll take a look at Ben. Close the door behind you, if you would.'

'Do you want me to undress?' I said, still in a state of surprise.

Randall looked at me coolly. 'Only if you really want to, but personally, I wouldn't have thought it necessary if I'm only going to look at your head and throat, which I understand is where the problems lie.'

I felt somewhat foolish, but I responded to Randall's questions, and he looked down my throat and ears, and also into my eyes, which I found rather disconcerting. There is something uncomfortable about being in such close proximity to another human being who is not your spouse or a member of your family. Or your lover, of course...

Randall finally said, 'Well, I don't think it's anything too serious, Ben, but you've got a bit of an infection. I'll give you these,' he produced some tablets from his bag, 'take one straightaway. Then some painkillers, and also this,' he rooted in his bag again, and produced a spray bottle. 'Use this just before you go on stage, and then at every opportunity during the show. It should help you keep your voice going.'

'OK, well, thanks very much Randall. I appreciate it. You didn't have to do this.'

Randall snapped his case shut. 'Well, I'm a professional. Like you, Ben. And sometimes you have to do things because you *are* a professional. In any case, it's for the good of the whole show — we don't have any understudies, do we, so if *you* can't perform, we're all a bit buggered!'

'Well, anyway, I appreciate it. And I wanted to apologise again. You know, that thing with Marcus in the wine-bar. I really had no idea what he was going to do.'

Randall grimaced. 'Well, perhaps. I was pretty pissed off at the time though. And it didn't help, you lot all laughing like hyenas.'

'Well, no, I can see that.'

'And "Josephine" went off me in big way, not surprisingly.'

191

Randall pursed his lips. 'Although there wasn't any future in that actually. I was trying to dump her anyway, so it saved me a job, I suppose. Does make the performances a bit trying though.'

'Yes, I suppose so.'

Randall hesitated for a moment, then said, 'And as for Marcus, well, I suppose I ought to apologise to him as well.'

I was surprised. 'Apologise to Marcus? Whatever for?'

'Oh, that time in the wine-bar. You weren't there, but Marcus came up to me — I think he'd had a few by the way- and said "I think we're made for each other. Where have you been all my life?" Or something.'

'Christ! And what did you say?'

'I said, "I wasn't born for the first half, and anyway, I don't go in for balding old queens".'

'Ah! Well, yes, he wouldn't like that. He is a bit sensitive about the hairline, apart from anything else. No wonder he wanted to retaliate.'

Randall moved towards the door. 'Right, well, I'd better be getting on. See you later, Ben.'

'Sure. And thanks again, Randall.' The door closed and I swallowed one of the pills Randall had left. As I did so, I suddenly had a horrible thought: suppose Randall had given me an emetic or something...

I got over my little outbreak of paranoia, and by the time I got to the Little Theatre, was actually feeling better. I took Randall's advice, and sprayed my throat liberally at every opportunity, and managed to get through the evening without mishap. The old adage about a disastrous dress rehearsal meaning a brilliant first night was proved to be at least partially true: if not exactly *brilliant*, the performance was certainly OK, with no major hiccups, at least onstage. In the dressing-rooms after the show, whilst the post-mortem of the evening was taking place, Marcus joined the company in a celebratory drink. I managed to catch Randall's eye and beckoned him over. 'I think you two wanted a word with each other,' I said.

The two men eyed each other warily for a moment. It was Randall who broke the silence. 'Yes, actually, Marcus, I just wanted to say sorry for some things I said to you a while back in the wine-bar. It was wrong of me, and I shouldn't have done it.'

Marcus gave a rueful grin. 'And I'm sorry for the incident the other week. Funny, that was in the wine-bar as well. Perhaps it's something to do with the atmosphere. Shake?'

The two shook hands. 'Well, that's good,' I remarked, 'we can all move on now, can't we?'

Whilst pleased that peace had broken out, so to speak, I was a little concerned to note that Marcus, who has always had a bit of 'thing' about Randall, had reverted to running his finger around the inside of his shirt collar, something he tends to do when in the company of an attractive man. 'And talking about moving on,' I added, 'perhaps *we'd* better move on. I probably should get to bed and try and shake off whatever it is I've caught.' I grabbed Marcus' arm and we made our farewells.

I was rather late in to my office on Monday morning. The remaining two performances of *Pinafore* had gone well, and fortunately, my voice, helped no doubt by Randall's ministrations, had held up. By Sunday evening though I was pretty exhausted, and for once had not stayed long at the cast party following the last show. Marcus had left me to sleep in, and in fact it was only when Freda, our redoubtable housekeeper, had started clattering about, that I had fully come to. I had showered and dressed quickly, then crept downstairs, hoping that I might be able to avoid being drawn into a dialogue, as Freda's conversation tends to be larded with so many mixed and mangled metaphors that it is often hard to follow her drift. Unfortunately, I remembered that I had left my keys on the breakfast bar in the kitchen, so had to run the gauntlet of *la belle* Freda.

'Oh, morning Mr J,' she went as I entered, 'you're up then? Mr Marcus said you were still sleeping like a baby in the bathwater.'

It occurred to me that Marcus had probably said no such thing, but I let that pass.

'Yes, Freda, bit of a late night.'

'Oh, you've been burning the midnight candle after the horse has bolted, that's your trouble. You need to take care, you know. You're just like my hubby, Mr Bell.'

Having met Freda's husband on a couple of occasions, this was not a comparison that I felt was entirely flattering.

'Really? And how is Mr Bell?' I realised as I spoke this was a dangerous thing to say, as Freda's hubby seemed to be permanently on his sick-bed.

Freda gave a deep intake of breath. 'Ooh, terrible. Terrible sore throat. Can't speak. I says to him, "Well, as you can't speak, you'll just have testiculate!"'

I was tempted to reply along the lines of "let's hope he doesn't make a balls-up of it then", but decided it was better to refrain. I confined myself to a sympathetic 'oh dear, dear' and made my escape.

Around midday, my mobile went. It was Tom Bremner.

'Morning, Ben,' he started, 'oh, by the way, loved the show. Thought you were great,'

'Oh, good, thanks Tom. Yes, I think it went quite well. And luckily my voice didn't pack up. I was a bit worried on Friday that I would be completely hoarse. Anyway, what can I do for you?'

'It's about that bus damages case. You know, the physio who broke her arm.'

'Amanda Hunt?'

'That's the one! Anyway, I followed up your suggestion, and got the CCTV footage of the incident from the bus. It confirms what the bus driver said.'

'Really? And can you get the registration of the car involved?'

'Not sure. But we've also got the statement from another passenger, who managed to get part of the number of the car. If you like, I'll whizz the CCTV thing over to you.'

'Yes please, Tom, that would be great, thanks. So what next? Can you track the driver or owner of the car down from the DVLA?'

Tom snorted. 'I'm going to have to start calling you DCI Jonson of the Flying Squad! Yes, don't worry, we're on to it.'

'Good! Oh, and Tom, keep me ITL, won't you?'

'ITL? What the hell does that mean?'

I grinned. 'It's one of Gary's little acronyms. It means "In the loop" of course. *Everyone* knows that!'

There was a 'Hmmph!' from the other end, and the line went dead.

I thought it was just as well I had not brought up "BMUTS" as well, which I had gathered from Marcus stood for "Bring me up to speed". One can overdo these things…

Thinking about Gary Lincoln reminded me of the Over 60s club, and I gave him a buzz. 'Any progress, Gary? Or should I speak to Alice-in, er, I mean Alison?'

'No, I'm your man. I'll shoot through.'

'If you would, Gary, ASAP, so that you can BMUTS!' I

couldn't resist chipping in.

'Sure!'

'TTFN!' I added ruthlessly.

Gary came to my room and we went through the findings so far. Alison had been through the records, such as they were, and drawn up schedules of receipts and payments over the period for which Dennis had been Treasurer. She had also compared the bank statements to the accounts that Dennis had presented to the management meetings in connection with the main fund-raising events. As we had surmised, the charity's finances were in a deplorable state. Surpluses from the fund-raising events had not been paid into the bank, and on numerous occasions, cash had been drawn from the bank, even in months when there were no activities. In fact, the only time that cash wasn't being taken out of the bank was when there was no cash to be had there. In addition, there were a couple of receipts for items which were clearly Dennis' personal expenses, but which had been paid for with the charity's cheques.

Gary concluded that there seemed on these provisional findings to be a deficit of around £8,000.

'But, Ben, if I may lay my silver on the table, I don't think we can just say this guy has misappropriated the money. It's likely that there is stuff which has been paid for in cash — quite a lot of stuff, I would imagine. The main problem is that there's no cash book.'

I thought for a moment. 'Yes, so you're saying that if there is substantial cash expenditure — which there seems to be — and this is not recorded properly, or indeed at all, then the fact that surpluses from the fund-raising events are not banked doesn't necessarily mean that they've been pinched?'

Gary nodded. 'For sure. And, of course, in the absence of the cash-book, it's not clear what happened to the cash that Dennis withdrew from the bank. But if you look at these annual accounts this character has provided for the AGM, then it would look as though he would have had to have drawn some cash from the bank in order to pay those expenses which were not paid by cheque, or electronic payment, or the retained surpluses on those events.'

I was looking at some more schedules. 'So if you look at the expenditure based on the bank statements, and compare it with this schedule here,' I held up a sheet of paper, 'which is a list of those payments for which we have actual physical invoices and receipts, then there are several payments from the bank which don't show up on this sheet. Presumably because there is no invoice.'

'Plus, you can't discount the supposition that there are further *bona fide* expenditures which have been paid in cash and for which there are no receipts, for whatever reason.'

I leant back in my chair and put the fingers of both hands together. 'So apart from the fact that we can say with certainty that the records are a total dogs bollocks, we *can't* say with certainty that any money has been misappropriated. It could be that overall, Dennis owes the charity some money, or the charity may in fact owe Dennis some money.'

'That's about the size of it,' Gary confirmed.

'OK, good, thanks Gary. And thank Alice, er, I mean Alison for me, would you? She's done well.' I had to confess to feeling slightly guilty about my last staff appraisal for Alison, as I had in a fit of temper written, 'Works well only when under pressure and cornered in a trap', which was possibly less than fair.

I thought about the Over 60s case for a few minutes. I did not want to give the 'all clear' to Hannah Phelps just yet; I felt we needed a little more investigation first, which would involve interviewing the unfortunate Dennis Saunders. *Another case for DCI Jonson,* I thought.

Glancing through my e-mails, I saw that there was one from Tom. Opening it, I found there was an attachment. *Presumably the CCTV from the bus,* I decided, and clicked on it to view the footage. Nothing happened, and after a few minutes of impatient clicking, and railing at the exigencies of modern technology, I gave up and forwarded it to Janet, with an exhortation to deal with it. As an afterthought, I also asked her to track down the erstwhile Treasurer of the Over 60s and arrange a time for him to come to the office.

Other matters came to the fore, and it was after lunch when Janet put her head around my door and said, 'Have you got a minute?'

'For you, my dear Janet, all the time in the world!' I said in an ironic tone, though instantly regretted it, in case Janet should misconstrue my sentiments. I could not entirely discount the impression that Janet was coming to regard me as something more than just her employer...

'Three things,' she said firmly, standing before my desk and fixing me with one of her looks. 'Number one: that attachment from Tom Bremner. All fine, and I can't understand why you had any difficulty. Look, I'll open it for you,' and before I could say anything, she grabbed my laptop, and with hands flying around the keyboard, produced an image of the inside of the number 22 bus which had been the setting for Amanda Hunt's accident. 'I'll leave you to look at that at your leisure,' she added, lips compressing into a straight line.

'Good, thank you. Number two?' I prompted.

'Number two: Mr Saunders is coming in tomorrow to see

you,' Janet went on, 'No doubt you'll have noticed the appointment on your automated diary.' This was a dig at me, as Janet knows full well that I rarely remember to look at the thing.

'Yes, of course,' I said urbanely, noting Janet's slightly sardonic curl of the otherwise arrow straight lips, 'what time?'

'It's in the diary,' Janet said shortly

'Just remind me.'

Janet sniffed. 'Eleven thirty.'

'Thank you. Number three?'

Janet pulled up a chair and sat down opposite me. 'The Christmas Concert,' she began, 'now that we've got *HMS Pinafore* out of the way, we need to crack on with it. We haven't got that much time, you know, and the practices we've had so far are not much help if we're going change the song.'

'Yes, true. Look, this is what I think we should do. First, we do a couple of verses in the normal way, then we do the next two, where I put on a French accent, and finally we do the first two or three again, with me putting on a very British accent, but doing the woman's part. As a sort of stereotypical repressed Englishman.'

'Can you do accents?' Janet looked at me doubtfully.

I shrugged. 'Well, the English one should be fine. And I think I can manage a bit of a French twang. I'll get Marcus to help me there — his French is pretty good, what with all these trips to Brussels.'

'I suppose it might work,' Janet rose, 'but you need to put a lot of work into it! I'll arrange extra rehearsal time with Clive, but don't forget we've got to do all the group choir pieces as well.' She passed out of the room imperiously, leaving me thinking that if she did have a 'thing' for me, she was not showing much evidence of it today...

I turned to my computer and started to play the CCTV footage which Janet had set up for me. It showed the bus going down a designated bus lane, and to the right, a line of cars in heavy traffic. Suddenly, and without indicating, one of these had pulled into the bus lane, then disappeared into a side road. The bus had braked sharply to avoid hitting the car, which was of course not unreasonable in the circumstances. I played and replayed the clip several times, and although the make and colour of the car were easily identifiable — it was a metallic silver VW — the registration number was not legible, and nor was the driver identifiable. Tom had mentioned that one of the other passengers had managed to get part of the number, so I hoped for Amanda Hunt's sake that this would be sufficient to trace the owner and/or driver involved. Reluctantly, I turned my attention to other matters, though I had the vague sense that I was missing something.

Next morning, promptly at half-past eleven, Dennis Saunders was wheeled into my room by the implacable Janet. I bade him take a seat at the meeting-room end of my office, whilst Janet placed two cups of coffee on the table, and then opened up the files on the Over 60s case. He was a big, rather untidy looking man in his sixties, and I could detect the lines of strain around his face.

Before I could begin, he launched off. 'I haven't done anything wrong, Mr Jonson, I really haven't. Oh, I know the records are a bit of a mess, but I haven't taken anything that wasn't mine.'

I started to say that no one was suggesting at this juncture that he *had* taken anything, but that we were merely trying to sort the books out. 'I think that one of the big problems we have,' I said, 'is that there isn't a cash book to record everything.'

Dennis nodded. 'No. The previous chap didn't either. The records were a bit of a mess when I took over, and what with one thing and another, I've sort of trickled along without getting it all sorted out.'

'I see.'

'The thing is,' Dennis continued, taking a slurp of coffee, 'my wife left me last summer, and I just don't seem to be able to settle to things.'

'Yes, I think Mrs Phelps told me that. She also suggested that perhaps it was too much for you to deal with, and she would find someone else, didn't she?'

Dennis nodded. 'Yes, she did. But I thought it would give me something to think about, to take my mind off, well, you know, other things. But some days I can't deal with it, and then things pile up, you know?'

I made a non-committal response to that, then asked, 'Can you tell me why the surpluses on fund-raising events are not apparently banked?'

'Oh well, you see there's a lot of cash expenditure which crops up unexpectedly, so I found it easier to keep the spare cash in a cash box, as I was told to do. I do bank the surplus from time to time though,' Dennis added defensively.

I made a note, then said, 'And there are a few cheques for stuff that is obviously your personal expenditure. For instance,' I rummaged through the file, 'ah yes, there's one here from June which is payable to the DVLA for the tax on what I presume to be your own car.'

Dennis' face took on a defiant look. 'Well, the thing is, I've found on quite a few occasions I've had to put my hand in my own pocket to pay bills for the association, and so I thought on that occasion, as I didn't have my own cheque book to hand, they could repay me a bit.'

We talked for an hour or so, and as he was leaving, he suddenly asked, 'Do they think I've pinched the money? Are they going to the police?'

I made some bland response to this, and he disappeared down the corridor, with head bowed. I was left thinking over what he had said. Something had rung alarm bells in my head, but I couldn't now just put my finger on what it was...

A week passed by. True to her word, Janet had me practising frequently, which together with the more general practices for the ensemble pieces, meant that I seemed to be fully occupied. However, one day Marcus insisted I have an evening off. 'Let's go out for a bite,' he said, 'I've got some promotional vouchers for one of those new gastro pubs — why don't we give that a try?'

'OK,' I said, 'which one is it?'

'The Blue Boar,' Marcus replied.

'The Blue Boar?' I was trying to place it, 'oh, just a minute, I know. Isn't that the place down one of the back streets where they were always having brawls?'

'That's the one,' he confirmed, 'you're right, there often used to be trouble there. Actually, the locals used to call it "The Black and Blue Boar"!'

'Sounds charming.'

'Last time I went in there the barman said to me, "You're not a regular, are you?" and I said, no, how did you know, so he says. "Because you put your drink down"!'

I pulled a face, 'Well, I assume that was an apocryphal story, but I get the drift.'

'Anyway, not to worry, it's all been done up now. People say it's very good. Oh, and as it's a bit of a way, I'll call a cab.'

'Let's roll!'

We had quite a pleasant meal at the newly refurbished 'Blue Boar', though as Marcus rather sharply pointed out, 'If the white wine had been as cold as the plates, and the vegetables as warm as the water, we would have been a lot better off!'

Relaxing afterwards with a glass of wine, Marcus said, 'Not long now until we go to NY.'

'Yes, indeed,' I replied.

'You might sound a bit more enthusiastic!' Marcus complained, 'it's supposed to be a treat.'

'Yes, it is. Yes of course I'm looking forward to it. Just seem to have a lot to deal with before then.'

'Such as?'

'Well, there's this blasted concert for a start. I wish I'd never agreed to it, I mean, we've only just done *Pinafore* for heaven's sake! And there's a couple of cases I'd quite like to get out of the way before then as well.' I went on to tell Marcus about the problems at the Over 60s, and also Amanda Hunt's accident in the bus. We had by this time paid the bill and were walking from the 'Blue Boar' to the taxi rank. As we turned on to the main road, I slowed and gave Marcus a nudge saying, 'Actually, it was about here that the incident happened. I hadn't noticed before. The bus was in the bus lane, and there was heavy traffic alongside, when the VW pulled across in front of the bus and disappeared into Serpentine Road over there.'

'Yes?' Marcus, striding on ahead, didn't sound particularly interested, 'come on, it's freezing out here, let's get moving.' I hurried on to catch up with him, when a car emerged from Serpentine Road and turned onto the main road, travelling in the direction we were walking. Although it was dark, the bright street lights revealed its make and colour quite clearly: it was a silver

VW...

I was on my mobile to Tom Bremner first thing the next morning. I had messaged him the previous night, to say that I had spotted what might be the car involved in the incident with the bus, although annoyingly, I had not been quick enough to get its registration. I had been eager to phone him as well the previous night, but Marcus had persuaded me to refrain, pointing out quite sensibly that it was getting late and perhaps Tom would not be overly thrilled to start talking about work at that time of night, no matter how excited I might be. 'After all,' Marcus had said, being irritatingly reasonable, 'it might not be the same car.'

'Morning, Tom,' I began, 'you got my message, didn't you? About the car in the Amanda Hunt accident case?' Tom assured me that he had.

'Yes, Ben. So possibly, it could be a local person. Anyway, leave it with me, and we'll carry on with the info from the DVLA.' He paused for a second, then added, 'Oh, and I don't want to dampen your enthusiasm, but this is not conclusive proof that the car you saw last night, and the one on the CCTV footage are one and the same. And of course, we don't know who the driver was, even if the car is the same.'

'Perhaps we could get some "teccy" to enhance the video so we could read the number more clearly?' I suggested.

'All right, all right, Inspector Jonson of the Yard!' Tom replied, 'let's just take it one step at a time, hey? See how we get on.'

And with that, I had to be content for the time being.

As Marcus had pointed out the previous evening, our New York trip was fast approaching, and of course Christmas itself. Rather against Marcus' wishes, I had insisted that we be back for Christmas. I had of course asked Sam and Amy and their respective other halves for the holiday, though getting definitive responses out of them was proving to be more difficult. 'It is a bit tricky, what with Holly and Finn also having family they want to be with,' I had defended them stoutly, whilst Marcus had looked a bit dubious. In the end, all four were due to come from Christmas Eve to Boxing Day, before dispersing to other venues. In addition, much to his surprise, Marcus' recently divorced sister, Diana, had also accepted an invitation for Christmas Day and Boxing Day, though we were still in the dark as to whether she was bringing her two sons, Marcus' nephews. I was now beginning to panic about how we were going to accommodate and feed everyone, but Marcus waved these concerns aside with a maddening insouciance and simply declared that 'it will be all right on the night.'

These thoughts were just running through my mind when Janet arrived in my room, carrying a large plastic storage box, filled with files. 'What's all that?' I asked, in some surprise.

'The Over 60's files from Huxleys that you asked for,' Janet sniffed, dropping the box with a bang, 'and there's three more of these out in reception. They must have been jolly glad to get rid of all this junk.'

'I don't want them all in here cluttering up my room, thank you very much!' I cried, 'put them in Business Services out of my way.'

With an exaggerated sigh, Janet bent to pick up the box once more, but I interrupted her. 'No, wait, now I come to think of it, leave it. I'd better have a quick flick through this one.' Janet muttered something which sounded a bit like 'Well, make up your mind for heaven's sake,' and let the box fall. I added, 'But you can give the other boxes to Alice in Ledgerland, I mean Alison.'

I dragged the box round to the side of my desk, so that I could reach in from my chair without having to get up. I spent the next hour sifting through files and bank statements, then put them down and leant back in my seat, thinking. After a few moments, I opened my laptop and dashed off a message to Gary and Alison, with some instructions on what to look for.

Looking at my watch, I realised that I needed to leave and get over to the church hall for a further rehearsal for the CAOS Christmas concert, so I hurriedly tidied my desk and set off. Janet's desk was empty so I took it that she had already left. It was raining hard, and as I had no coat or mac, I kept my head down as I hurried along the pavement. As a result, I only got a glimpse at the last minute of the car speeding up the high street heading for a giant puddle just at the entrance to the hall. A torrent of water hit me, drenching me from head to toe in a tsunami of muddy brown liquid, and leaving me gasping for breath. 'Ruddy vandal,' I cursed and pushed open the door, then stood dripping in the lobby, debating whether to try and muddle through or dash back home to change.

'There you are at last,' barked a familiar voice, 'come on, no time to lose. Our turn next.' It was Janet, coming out of the ladies' cloakroom, seemingly oblivious to my plight. She pushed open the door to the main hall, and beckoned me to follow her. Shrugging, I squelched my way after her, and we went to the far end where we mounted the makeshift stage. Barely giving me time to draw breath, she signalled to Betty, our accompanist, to start our song. We had just got to the part where I am pretending to be a Frenchman, when Clive, our director, clapped his hands and bade Betty to stop playing.

'Sorry, Ben, am I missing something here? Why are you doing a Welsh accent?'

I bristled. 'It's a French accent, actually, Clive.'

'Oh?' There was pause. 'And whilst we're on it, is the bedraggled look meant to be significant?'

'No, Clive,' I replied as patiently as I could, 'purely coincidental. Now can we get on with it, please?'

Clive shrugged, mopped his brow with a handkerchief, and resumed his seat. I signalled to Betty to start again. This time, we made it all the way through, much to my relief. 'I think we need to tighten that up in a couple of places,' Janet glowered at me, 'well, at least *you* do.' I was about to slink off, but Janet went on, 'No, don't go yet. We're going to do the ensemble pieces, and you're needed. We're a bit short on men tonight.'

Looking around, I noticed she was correct. 'Yes, I suppose we are,' I went, 'where's Randall for a start? I thought he'd be here.'

Janet tut-tutted. 'Well, he *was* briefly. Then he got a phone call from one of his colleagues asking him to cover the out-of-hours, so he shot off.'

'Probably him that caused this!' I pointed to my wet and muddy attire, but before I could explain, Clive called us all to order and we were off again.

After an hour or so, we had a break for a few minutes, and I ambled off to the kitchen to get a drink. To my surprise, just emerging from the store cupboard was my erstwhile compere, Hannah Phelps, grey hair tumbling about her shoulders. We exchanged pleasantries, in which she referred to me as Dr Samuel, though I decided I didn't have the energy to correct her, but just as she was wishing me a good evening, I suddenly remembered something.

'Oh, Mrs Phelps, about the Over 60s accounts,' I began.

'Yes? Have you got anywhere with that?' she asked.

'Yes and no,' I went, 'but I'll have to come back to you shortly on that particular matter. No, it was something I noticed on some earlier accounts, actually. Do you have some equipment or something bought on finance?'

She looked puzzled. 'Finance?'

'Yes, I mean a loan to buy, oh I don't know, a photocopier, or computer or something.'

'Well, we do have a computer, but I think it was donated by Mr Bremner's firm. Why do you ask?'

'It's just that I noticed some payments going out quite regularly, marked...' I stopped suddenly as I had a flash of realisation. 'Oh, no, don't worry, I see I've made a mistake.' I hurried away, before she could say anything further. I needed time to think...

I trudged back home thinking hard. The house was in darkness as Marcus was away overnight, so I rooted in the freezer for something to eat, then stuck it in the microwave whilst I divested myself of my damp and muddied clothing, and took a shower. I threw on a dressing-gown and went back to the kitchen, retrieved the meal from the microwave, and whilst starting to eat, took out my mobile and called Tom.

'Ben, where the hell are you?' Tom's voice boomed around the kitchen as I had put my mobile on speaker whilst I ate, 'I thought you might have come across for a quick one after rehearsals.'

'I was going to, Tom, but I had to come back to change,' I quickly explained the mishap with the puddle. 'But,' I went on, 'I wanted to speak to you about a little matter. The Over 60s in fact. There's something I think you should know...'

Next morning, I was in early at the office, and was already at my desk by the time Janet arrived. 'Couldn't sleep?' she enquired, with an imperious look over the top of her glasses.

'And Good Morning to you too, Miss Norbury, er, I mean Janet,' I replied curtly. Really, the resemblance to my teacher was most unnerving. 'No, just a busy day ahead. And in fact,' I went on, 'as you're here now, there's a couple of things I need you to do urgently for me, please.' I scribbled a note on a sheet of paper and handed it to her. She scanned it, then raised her eyebrows in query. I shook my head and said, 'No time to explain now. I'll tell you later.'

Janet, for all her faults, is very industrious and efficient, and she was soon back in my room. 'All arranged as you asked for. Eleven o'clock. Do you need the Board Room?'

I shook my head. 'No, we'll be fine in here, I think. Oh, and that other matter — did you find out?'

Janet looked at me quizzically. 'Yes, you were quite right about that. But why did you want to know?'

I tapped my nose and tried to look mysterious. 'That's for me to know, and you to find out,' I replied. If I was hoping to make her intrigued, I was disappointed.

'Oh, I expect I will before too long,' Janet said airily, 'you aren't much good at keeping things to yourself, are you?' With that, she left the room.

I didn't have time to dwell on Janet's cutting remark, as I summoned Gary and Alison and gave them too some instructions. 'The meeting's at eleven, which I know doesn't give you a lot of time, but just cover the essentials and give me the bare bones, will you?'

'Sure thing, Ben,' went Gary, 'we'll pop it on the top shelf and turn up the heat, then just hum a few bars for you.'

This was a mixture of office metaphors on an almost Freda-wot-does scale, and I was tempted to make some riposte along the lines of 'now we're cooking on gas', but thought better of it and just asked them to get cracking. I turned back to my laptop, and once again opened the CCTV footage from the bus on which Amanda Hunt had suffered her injuries. I played and replayed the clip, trying to zoom in on the offending VW that had caused the bus driver to brake so violently. Yes, there it was. If I went in close enough, I could just make something out on the top of the windscreen. Not conclusive perhaps, but a pretty fair indication I would have thought...

Just on the dot of eleven o'clock, Janet appeared, and with a vestigial knock on the door announced, 'Your visitors are here.' She stood back and in walked Hannah Phelps, closely followed by Tom Bremner.

'Good morning, good morning,' I started, 'come in. Let's go and have a seat over there.' I nodded in the direction of the low sofas at the far end of my room. 'Oh, and Janet, could you rustle up some tea, please?' I turned away as I said this, but out of the corner of my eye I could have sworn that Janet pulled a face and made a mocking little curtsey, presumably in protest at my request to act as tea-lady. Luckily, my two guests were oblivious as they were already heading across the office.

Hannah was first to speak. 'What is all this about, Dr Jonson,' she began, pulling at strand of wild grey hair which had escaped from the multi-coloured Alice-band she had wedged on her head, 'Have you found anything out about Dennis Saunders?'

'Well,' I started, 'oh, and by the way, please call me Ben...'

'Oh, I'm so sorry,' Hannah interrupted, 'please go on, Dr Ben.'

I ignored Tom's stifled laugh and continued. 'Well, it is of course to do with the Over 60, Mrs Phelps, which is why I've asked Tom — er — Mr Bremner, I mean — to join us, as Chairman of the Trustees. I've complied an interim report here,' I picked up a file which Gary had deposited with me a quarter of an hour earlier, 'and in brief, our investigations would suggest that although there is no doubt that Mr Saunders' record-keeping was pretty abysmal, to say the least, I don't think one could say that he had actually misappropriated any funds from the society. It is true to say that surpluses from fund-raising events have not been banked, but there were obviously also considerable cash expenditures, and so just because the surpluses weren't banked doesn't necessarily mean that they were stolen. Overall, I cannot say with any certainty that Dennis Saunders owes the society money, or if in fact it is the other way round, and the society owes *him* some money. In other words, I do not believe there is any evidence that a crime has been committed in this instance.'

We were interrupted by the arrival of Janet with a tray which she banged down with quite unnecessary force on the table, and walked off.

'Don't worry, Janet, I'll pour,' I called after her. She simply replied 'Thanks,' and carried on out of the room. As I have commented before, irony is wasted on her.

Tom leaned forward and said, 'So your recommendation is that we take no further action, is it Ben?'

'Well, I think you could do with finding another treasurer perhaps,' I replied drily, 'but I don't think there is anything to be gained by going to the police, for instance. They wouldn't be interested, not with the lack of evidence.'

Hannah Phelps looked relieved. 'So that's it? Thank goodness for that.'

'Ah well, not exactly,' I went on, 'you see, I said that there is no evidence that a crime has been committed in *this* instance.

However, we have obtained the records of the society for earlier years, and we think that there may well be some defalcations, to coin a phrase, previously.'

'Why do you think that?' asked Hannah.

'Well, the records are in fact almost non-existent for these earlier years. There are some rudimentary schedules drafted by someone — possibly the previous treasurer, Reg Smith — or possibly by someone at Huxleys, the accountants. Nothing seems to correlate with anything else, and the bank account seems to be totally up the Swanee, to use a technical term. But there are a considerably number of cash payments, which end up in "purchases of food and drink" in the accounts, but aren't called that on these schedules. They are labelled, which is why I asked you last night if you had a loan for purchasing equipment. I thought you see that they may be payments under a hire-purchase agreement.'

Hannah looked at me with wide eyes. 'I'm not sure I understand you.'

I continued, 'You see, these payments were labelled "HP" which at first I thought stood for "hire purchase", but then I realised that they were in fact initials. HP.'

Hannah took a sharp intake of breath. 'And you're saying that I took money from the society? That those initials are mine?'

I shook my head, 'No, I'm suggesting that the initials HP don't stand for Hannah Phelps. They stand for *Harry* Phelps, your husband...'

By five thirty that afternoon, I was exhausted. I messaged Marcus and suggested we retire to Et Alia fairly soon, then sent the same to Tom Bremner, adding 'Was I right?' This was a reference to a little conversation between us earlier that day, when I had made a suggestion in the Amanda Hunt case. There was a rapid response, merely saying 'Yes & yes!' I gave a little chuckle at this, just as Janet swept into my room with a sheaf of paper.

'No, Janet, whatever it is, it will have to wait until tomorrow!' I began.

To my surprise, Janet shrugged and replied, 'OK, that's fine. No hurry.'

Taken off guard, I said, 'Good! I'm off to the wine-bar — why don't you join us? I can fill you in on the events of the day, if you want.'

Janet gave me a slightly superior smile. 'I told you that you were no good at keeping things to yourself.' I was about to make some protest at this, but she carried on, 'But yes, why not?'

'Fine!' I went, 'oh, and just see if Gary and Alison are around, will you? They may like to join us so I can fill them in as well.'

Janet motored off, and I quickly tidied my desk, and headed out of the door.

We all squeezed into our favourite corner of Et Alia. I vainly signalled for the barman to take our order, but I must have, without realising, donned my cloak of invisibility. 'Oh, for heavens sakes!' Janet exclaimed and with a peremptory wave of a hand, a barman appeared.

'Why can't I do that?' I started to say, just as Marcus appeared.

'Must be your after-shave!' he grinned, ruffling my hair before sitting down. I made a mental note to mention to him to kindly refrain from doing that to me in front of the staff. I have a feeling it is not good for my authority.

At that moment, Tom ambled in and remarked, 'Quite a gathering! What's going on?'

'Ah, Tom,' I rejoined, 'I was just about to tell the troops here about this afternoon's events. I think they deserve to know — after all, it was Gary and Alison here who did the basic report.'

'And you sprinkled your fairy-dust on it,' Gary cut in. There was a bit of a silence at this, whilst Tom muttered, 'That could have been better put!' I think Gary was blissfully unaware of what he had said because he continued to look around expectantly.

I carried on, 'Yes, well, I'm not sure I would put it quite in those terms, but never mind.' I turned to Marcus, 'We're talking about the Over 60s club thing here, Marcus. I told you that the records were in a mess, didn't I? Well, after some good work done by Gary and Alison, we decided that there was no real evidence that any money had been taken by the current Treasurer. But, when we looked at earlier years, under the previous Treasurer...'

'That the one who died?' asked Marcus.

'Yes, that's right, Reg Smith was his name. Well, we found some funny goings-on there, and in particular, these payments apparently marked as "HP". Now originally, I wondered if there was in fact some equipment or something that the association had bought under a hire-purchase agreement. It would have been a bit odd, but it was a possibility. But Mrs Phelps soon put me right, and said there was no such thing. Then it came to me that "HP" was in fact someone's initials. And of course it so happens that Mrs Phelps first name is Hannah, so at first glance, she would look like the culprit, if you like to put it in those terms.'

'But it wasn't?' Gary and Alison both spoke at the same time.

'No, because by chance, Hannah's husband is named Harry, so he too has the initials "HP".'

'So how did you decide it was him?'

I spread my hands out. 'Well, for a start, I didn't think Hannah Phelps looked the sort to take money from the club. But, that aside, she made some comment about Harry helping out, which gave me the first inkling. Then in one of the boxes of files we got with the old accounts in, there was a receipt from Huxleys saying they had returned the records to *Harry Phelps,* not Reg Smith, which is what you would have expected. And finally, Dennis Saunders made some comment about not banking cash but keeping it in a box, "as I was told to do". Told, in fact, as it turns out, by Harry Phelps. Possibly because he had ideas about pinching some more, but he didn't in fact get the opportunity.'

'But don't the accounts need to be audited or something?' Janet intervened, 'surely Huxleys would have noticed something was wrong in that case?'

'Ah, well,' I responded, 'actually, because this is a very small, unincorporated charity, it doesn't need any sort of audit or independent examination in fact.'

'So what did Huxleys do then?' Janet snapped back crisply.

I gave a mirthless laugh. 'You may well ask! No, to be fair, the charity still has to file reports to the appropriate authorities, and in fact, in this case, the trust deed setting up the charity stipulated annual accounts had to be prepared, although it doesn't mention an audit. So Huxleys prepared rudimentary accounts from the information supplied, which in this case was sketchy, to say the least.'

'So you don't think they were in any way involved?' asked Tom, peering over the top of his glasses, 'I mean bearing in mind what old Keith was up to.'

'No, I don't think there is any evidence of that.'

Marcus butted in, 'But why did this Harry Phelps do it? And what about the treasurer, this Reg Smith? Was he on the take as well?'

'Well,' I replied, 'when we spoke to Hannah Phelps, she not surprisingly, didn't know anything about it. So at her suggestion, she rang Harry and asked him to come to the office on some pretext or other. This he duly did, and when Hannah confronted him, he completely crumbled, and told us all.'

'Which was?' Janet cut in.

'Well, that this Reg Smith was getting a bit past it, and said something about needing a hand to Harry one day. Harry started helping him, unbeknownst to Hannah, and then realised he could cream off money, with very little chance of anyone noticing.'

'How much did he take? And why in particular?' Tom asked.

'Well, we're not talking big bucks here, but I suppose it amounted to a few thousand over a period of time. Not a great sum in itself, but of course significant in terms of the size of the organisation. As to why, well, gambling was the problem. Harry became hooked on all types, again unbeknownst to Hannah, and took just to feed his habit. Then of course, it all came unstuck when Reg died suddenly. Harry wanted to take over from him, but Hannah said she didn't think that would be appropriate, and so Harry had to watch whilst Dennis Saunders took over. Of course, he was scared at first that Dennis would rumble something, but fortunately for Harry, Dennis was so disorganised that he didn't. Then Dennis was accused of taking money...'

'Yes, that's what I think is the worst thing of all, that Harry didn't come clean there and then and save poor old Dennis all that angst!' Tom interrupted.

'Yes, that was bad,' I agreed, 'and of course it puts Hannah Phelps in a difficult position. She has resigned, not surprisingly, which is a shame because she actually did a good job.'

'Despite thinking you were either William Shakespeare or

Dr Samuel Johnson, rather than plain Mr Ben Jonson!' Marcus laughed.

I grinned. 'Oh, it was quite funny really. But I feel sorry for her. I don't know what will happen with Harry — it'll be up to the trustees, won't it Tom?'

'Yes, we'll have to consider the position,' said Tom, thinning his lips almost as much as Janet does, 'although Hannah has straightaway said she will personally make good any losses. But anyway, that's for another day.' He took a large slurp of wine. 'Now moving on, Ben, there is that other matter, isn't there?'

'You mean the Amanda Hunt case?'

Tom nodded, but Marcus asked, 'Amanda Hunt? Is that the bus accident case?'

I confirmed that was correct.

'So, you need to find the driver and/or the owner of this VW, did you?' Marcus asked.

'Oh, we've done that now, thanks to Ben,' Tom grinned, 'he gave me some information before, and I was able to confirm that he had the correct car and driver. And we've been in contact with him, and now his insurance company, so I think Amanda Hunt will get her claim paid after all.'

'OK, OK, so put us out of our misery,' Marcus complained, 'you are both grinning inanely, so it must be someone we know. Who?'

'Ah, well, you mustn't let on that it was me who found out,' I said, raising a finger to my lips, 'Mum is definitely the word here.'

'OK, but tell us for Pete's sake!' Marcus almost shouted.

'Randall Barrett!' I replied, and was gratified by the stunned silence that greeted this revelation.

'Randall?' asked Janet, 'So that's why you asked me what

kind of car he had. But how did you know it was him? I thought you couldn't read the registration number on the CCTV footage.'

'Ah, no more we could!' I exclaimed, 'at least, not all of it. But it was that other evening at the rehearsal. You remember that I arrived soaked to the skin and covered in mud because a car had driven through a big puddle just as I was hurrying down the road?' Janet nodded. 'Well,' I went on, 'although I didn't really get a good look at the car, because I had my head down against the rain, I did at the last-minute glance up and saw a sticker on the top passenger side of the windscreen. And I did notice the car was a VW. Then Janet here said Randall had just left the rehearsal room because he was on call. And that jogged a memory with me: the sticker on the windscreen was one of those "Doctor on Call" stickers that they use in case they have to park on yellow lines or something.'

'And?' Marcus prompted.

'Well, I also had an inkling that I had spotted something similar on the car in the CCTV film. So I looked again, and there it was. And then I got someone to check on the registration number of Randall's car, and Bingo! The registration matched with the bit we already had. So, I then passed that little snippet on to Tom, and Robert, as they say, is your uncle!'

'Another triumph for Inspector Jonson of the yard!' Tom clapped me on the shoulder, almost making me spill my drink. I tried to look modest, but I'm not altogether sure I was successful...

'A good day's work then,' said Marcus as we wended our way home a little later, 'but you seem a bit quiet. What's the problem?'

'Baby, it's cold outside,' I replied.

'Well, it's a little chilly certainly, but it's not that bad. And since when have you started calling me "baby"?'

'No, you oaf!' I cried, 'I'm talking about the operatic society concert! I'm doing "Baby, it's cold outside" with Janet, and the concert is tomorrow!'

Ben Jonson and the Big Apple

I slumped in my seat and closed my eyes. Whatever happened to the mystique and glamour of air travel? Not so much the jet set and café society, rather the EasyJet set and the Nescafe society. The drive to the airport had been bad enough, with heavy rain and traffic tailing back for miles: at least it had been in a chauffeur driven car, courtesy of Marcus' company.

But it is the whole airport process that I find so appalling. The undignified scramble through security, feverishly trying to undo watches and belts, extracting phones and wallets from their hiding places, whilst balancing on one leg to remove shoes. Next, the departure lounge, where the passengers are corralled like recalcitrant sheep, and shooed along corridors to be penned up behind railings. And the interminable shuffle to the boarding gate, trying to look cool with the boarding pass on the mobile, only to find that it has turned itself off, and you hold up the entire queue as you try to coax it back into life. And the surreptitious look at the fellow passengers, trying to decide who you *don't* want to be seated next to - the overweight and the screaming kids, generally.

Then once aboard, the airlines do their best to alarm the nervous amongst us by droning on about what to do if you stop breathing, and how you must *not* inflate your life-jacket…

And those budget airlines, whose pilots are so grimly determined not to lose an iota of time that they taxi around the airport trying to emulate a Grand Prix driver. And it's worse later, when they fling the aircraft down on the runway like a sack of potatoes. As Marcus rather cuttingly said last time we flew to Europe, 'Did we just land, or were we shot down?'

I often think that instead of the rather bland announcements on landing, the cabin staff *really* want to say, 'Ladies and gentlemen, please remain in your seats until Captain "Bomber" Harris and his crew have brought what's left of the airplane to a screeching halt at the gate. Then once the smoke has cleared and the alarms silenced, we'll open the doors so that you can pick your way through the wreckage to the terminal building.'

I was aroused from my musings by a tap on the shoulder. I opened my eyes to find a young steward before me, proffering a glass of something that purported to be champagne. 'With the compliments of the gentleman in Business,' he announced.

'Which gentleman would that be?'

'Big guy, designer stubble, plunging neckline…'

'That would be Marcus!'

I must do something about those shirt buttons…

I sipped the frothing liquid and sighed. Well, at least I hadn't been totally forgotten by Marcus and his chums, who looked as though they were all set to party for the next four days.

In truth, I was actually quite pleased to have a bit of peace and quiet on my own — if you can call sitting cheek by jowl with two hundred or so other bodies in the economy section of a passenger jet, being alone. The last couple of days had taken their toll. Apart from work matters to clear up before I departed, there was also the Christmas festivities to prepare for, since we were due to be back on the day before Christmas Eve. Then of course, there had been the Operatic Society's annual Christmas concert…

I had felt surprisingly nervous in the hours before the event.

I was by now quite used to performing but somehow, when made-up and dressed in a period costume to perform in one of G&S operettas, it is easy to hide behind the persona of the character you are playing. This performance, naked and exposed, so to speak, was to coin an expression I gleaned from my housekeeper, Freda, 'a kettle of fish of a different colour'. As it was, waiting in the wings to go on with my singing partner, the formidable Janet, I began to wish that we had after all stuck with our original 'I've got you Babe', with yours truly bewigged and begowned in the Cher role. At least I could have sought refuge in the disguise…

A voice behind muttered, 'Break a leg!' and as I turned, I saw it belonged to Randall, who had just come offstage. I didn't make a reply because although ostensibly a theatrical exhortation of good luck, I had a sneaking suspicion in Randall's case that he meant it more literally. A nod from Janet and we were on…

'Darling, you were sensational!' Tom put on a faux- camp voice as we celebrated in 'Et Alia' a couple of hours later. I tried to look modest, but fear I didn't succeed.

'Yes, thank you, it *was* all rather gratifying,' I said.

'Certainly was! Don't you think so, Janet?' Marcus turned to my office manager, and quickly added, 'and of course, I mean *both* of you. A tremendous performance.'

Even the normally po-faced Janet unbent sufficiently to give a small smile. 'Yes, it wasn't too bad. At least Ben here didn't stumble over his lines like he normally does!'

I was about to protest at this uncalled-for slur, but Marcus gave me a surreptitious nudge in the ribs and cut in, 'Well, I've never heard anything like it. There was a standing ovation when you finished.'

'Really? I thought it was just everyone rushing to get to the bar for the interval drinks,' Janet replied in a cool tone, but I could see that in reality, she was as pleased as I had been at the audience reaction. There had indeed been a standing ovation, accompanied by whistles and shouts of 'encore', which after a hasty conferral with the orchestra and our director, Clive Pettit, we had managed to perform. I had a sneaking suspicion that the ovation had been orchestrated at least in part by Tom and Marcus, together with some of their cronies, but nevertheless, I had to admit to enjoying that brief moment of adulation.

As I downed my second glass of chardonnay, and basked in a warm glow which was not totally due to the alcohol, I felt myself relaxing and prepared to have a short snooze before the pre-packaged meal was served. It was not to be, however. My companion in the adjacent seat suddenly snorted at some article he was reading in his newspaper.

'Bloody government!' he exclaimed, 'political pygmies, the lot them. And the opposition are no bloody use either! Oh, for the old days, when even if you didn't agree with them, you knew where you were going. What we need is some actual leadership!' He fulminated in this manner for a few minutes, before eventually running out of steam.

'Sorry about that,' he apologised, turning to look at me, 'just had to get that off my chest.'

I replied that it was quite all right and to think nothing of it. I was preparing to resume my doze, but before I could close my eyes again, he added, 'Justin.' He stuck out a hand. 'Justin Fields.'

I was about to respond, 'Better than just *out* of fields,' but managed to stop myself in time, and rather awkwardly grasping his hand in return, replied, 'Ben. Ben Jonson.'

'Ah!' Justin looked at me narrowly, 'like the runner?'

I was used to this. 'No,' I said, 'no "h". Jonson, like the seventeenth century playwright.'

'Oh, yes?' He mulled this over for a second. 'And are you a playwright?'

I gave a somewhat mirthless laugh. 'Well, hardly. I'm actually an accountant. A forensic accountant.'

Justin nodded. 'Right, interesting.'

I wasn't sure whether this was a statement or a question, and opting for the former, made no response. Justin went on, 'Different field myself. Logistics.'

Again, I was not certain of how to respond to this, so I changed tack and asked, 'Business or pleasure?'

Justin looked puzzled.

'I mean, this trip,' I went on, 'are you going to New York for work or for fun.'

His face cleared. 'Oh, I see, sorry. No, I live in New Jersey, so I'm going back home.'

'Right, I see,' I said, 'but your trip to the UK was business, was it?'

'Not exactly, no,' Justin's brow furrowed, 'on the other hand, it wasn't exactly fun, either.'

I didn't say anything, but took another sip of wine, as I had a feeling there was more to come. So much for my little nap, I thought.

Justin continued after a moment. 'No, it wasn't exactly a pleasure trip,' he repeated, 'quite the reverse. I went to see an old friend who was seriously ill in hospital.'

'Dear, dear. But you said *was* ill. Has he recovered?'

Justin grimaced. 'Well, no, he died. He lasted just long enough to make a new will, and appoint me as executor before he went into a coma, and that was it.'

'Gosh, I'm so sorry,' I went, 'how sad. But at least you got to see him before he — er —passed away.'

Justin shrugged. 'I guess so. Anyway, enough of that. What are you doing in the Big Apple?'

I hesitated a moment. Somehow, I didn't really want to go in to all the complications of why I was on this plane, and who with, so I equivocated and replied, 'Oh, just a quick visit to some friends.'

'But you've obviously got friends on this flight as well, haven't you?' I must have looked puzzled, because Justin quickly added, 'I mean, that champagne you got from the cabin crew whilst we were still on the tarmac. That came from Business so the steward said.'

I'd forgotten about the unexpected drink, courtesy of Marcus, but before I could reply, the curtain to our little section of the cabin was wrenched open, and there stood Marcus himself. Grabbing me by the wrist he exclaimed, 'I've come to rescue you from your dreary little existence here in steerage. Come with me!' He yanked my arm and hauled me up.

'Just a sec, what's going on?' I spluttered.

Marcus gave a broad grin and a lascivious wink. 'Got you upgraded, didn't I? There was a spare seat up front, so I asked the cabin manager if you could have it. He was a bit reluctant at first, but then my pal Tony weighed in. Turns out he knew the cabin guy — well, he does this run so often — and he put in a word, and Robert, as they say, is your uncle. Job done!'

'Looks like your lucky day!' Justin chipped in, giving me what my mother would have called an old-fashioned glance.

'So it appears,' I replied lightly, rummaging in the overhead locker for my hand-baggage. I handed the bag over to Marcus' outstretched hand and turned to Justin. 'Well, looks like I'm going to have to love you and leave you,' I began, wincing to myself as I realised what I had just said, 'but it's been a pleasure to talk to you.'

Justin gave a small smile, and reaching for his wallet, produced a card. 'Same here. My number and so on — perhaps we'll meet again.'

'Er, yes, perhaps,' I replied, fumbling in my jacket. I found a small stack of business cards in an inside pocket and handed one over to Justin. 'Here's mine, by the way. Hope you enjoy the rest of the flight.'

I followed Marcus forward in the plane to business class, and he ushered me to my seat. 'Seemed a nice bloke.' There was a slight edge to his tone which made me look up at him. Surely Marcus wasn't jealous? I wondered whether to make anything of this, but decided against it, and merely shrugged and said, 'Yes, he was pleasant enough, I suppose.' Marcus looked as though he was about to say something further, but I pre-empted him by adding, 'Anyway, now I'm in the pound seats, where's my wine? And the menu - I need to choose what I'm going to eat.'

Marcus grinned, and with a mock salute said, 'Certainly sir. And should I get one of the eunuchs to fan you, or perhaps peel you a grape?'

'That would be kind,' I replied coolly. Two can play at being sarcastic, I thought.

The flight passed uneventfully, albeit in a slight haze of alcohol, and it seemed no time before we touched down at JFK. As advised by the frequent fliers to New York, we sprinted off the plane to ensure we got to immigration ahead of the other passengers. In spite of the dire warnings I had heard about US immigration, we were through remarkably swiftly, and the immigration staff were scrupulously civil.

Not surprisingly, a bevy of stretched limos had been sent to collect our party, and we were whisked rapidly away from the airport towards Manhattan Island. 'Where's the hotel?' I asked, 'on Central Park?'

Marcus pulled a face expressing disdain. 'Good God, no!' he cried, 'that's so twentieth century! No, we're headed for Soho.'

'Ah!' I nodded sagely, though without any very clear idea where that was. However, knowing Marcus and his company, it would doubtless be very swish. And expensive. 'At least I'm not paying for the room…' I murmured to myself.

'What was that?' Marcus turned from peering out of the limo windows towards me.

'Oh, nothing,' I reassured him, 'Oh look, isn't that the Chrysler Building?' I managed to distract his attention by pointing. After a few minutes, we were decanted from the limo into the foyer of our hotel, which as I had surmised, was very smart, if not particularly large.

Noticing my look, Marcus commented, 'It's what they call a boutique hotel.'

I nodded sagely. 'Ah yes, a boutique, which is of course French for a place where you get half of what you expected for twice the price!'

The formalities of checking-in having been accomplished, we found ourselves in our room, which although by this time it was dark, appeared to offer spectacular views of the New York cityscape. I tried playing with the myriad of light switches by my side of the bed. 'Bloody typical!' I remarked after a few minutes' investigation, 'all these switches, but I still have to get up to turn the table lamp off!'

Marcus pulled a face. 'Oh yeah? Well, never mind all that now. Quick shower and change, and then we're off!'

'Where to?'

'We're meeting the others downstairs, then we're going for something to eat. Oh, and by the way, you'd better have this.' Marcus produced a sheet of paper and thrust it in front of me. Headed 'Accompanying Person's Program' it detailed the activities which had been planned for those of us not actually on the payroll of Marcus' firm. A quick scan confirmed my worst fears.

'Well, OK, but actually I don't fancy spending two days in Macys and Bloomingdales, thank you very much! I don't go into a shop at home if I can avoid it, so I don't propose doing so now.'

This fact Marcus could not dispute. I had my childhood scarred by my mother hauling me around shops in the school holidays. I vividly remember her on one occasion looking for a pair of shoes. In the first shop we entered, she found some she liked, but insisting on seeking out possible alternatives. Some three hours and several shops later, we returned to the original outlet and purchased the first pair she had tried. When I protested about this, to my mind, monumental waste of time and effort, I was treated to a sharp retort, followed by a sulky silence for the rest of the day. Even Julia had been unable to persuade me to change my ways, and had on several occasions been reduced to buying a pile of clothes for me to try on at home, and return the items I had discarded the following day.

'OK, OK,' replied Marcus, putting his hands up, 'keep your hair on! But don't forget I'm tied up most of tomorrow in a meeting. What will you do?'

'Oh, don't worry about me,' I said airily, 'I've got a few plans…'

The time difference of course worked in our favour, so after a reasonable night's sleep, we were up and about at quite an early hour in the morning. Marcus set off with his colleagues for their meeting, after leaving me with instructions how to get to the office. 'Should be through by mid-afternoon,' Marcus said as they were leaving, 'so call for me at say, three thirty?'

'OK, have a good day y'all,' I responded ironically.

'And don't forget that it's the party later!' he added.

I had my schedule all worked out, and as soon as Marcus had gone, I set off for the waterfront. I decided to run the gauntlet of the subway, and half an hour later found myself at the terminal for the Staten Island Ferry. As well as being free, I had been advised that on the return trip it provided an iconic view of Manhattan and the Statue of Liberty. And so it proved. Although a bracing voyage — it was late December after all, and there was a biting wind, with just the occasional hint of a snowflake — I had to admit that the views were spectacular. Next on the agenda was a trip to the Statue itself, and a climb up inside to the viewing places in the crown. After that, Ellis Island, with its museum and former immigration station, then back to Manhattan. I had heard that the 'Top of the Rock' — that is the observation platform at the top of the Rockefeller Center — was a must-see, so I headed back to the subway. The advice had been good — again the views were spectacular, and although bitingly cold, the sun was shining and the air was clear. The Empire State Building was not far away, although I had to admit to a slight feeling of disappointment at its curiously flat sides: the Chrysler Building was much more eye-catching to my mind, if rather less iconic.

Feeling by now in need of a little culture, not to mention somewhere warm and out of the cold air, my next stop was the Met, pausing only to acquire a sandwich on the way. Although it tasted very good (chicken, bacon and avocado on rye, easy on the mayo), it proved a challenge to manage, requiring jaws the size of a great white shark to stand any chance of getting through all the layers, not to mention the trail of bits of filling that I left behind me as I made my way up 5th Avenue.

Before I knew it, time had marched on, and a look at my watch revealed I had only a few minutes to make my way to the rendezvous with Marcus, so I scurried out of the building and headed downtown once more.

I made it to the office block and whizzed up to the fifteenth floor, as instructed, with a minute to spare. Pushing open the door to reception, I approached the desk, behind which sat a dark-haired woman in her forties, who was studying a screen with intense interest. I stood in front of her for some moments, but so intent was she on the task before her, she did not seem to notice my presence. I gave a slight cough, and dragging her eyes reluctantly from her terminal, she looked up at me in enquiry.

'I'm meeting someone here. Marcus. Marcus Wright,' I began.

'And you are?'

'My name's Jonson. Ben Jonson. You know, like the playwright?' I was met with an expression of polite incomprehension. Inspiration struck. 'Or the athlete,' I added, 'only without the "h".' No, too complicated. A fog seemed to descend on the receptionist. 'Could you just tell him Ben's here?' I pleaded.

'Oh, sure,' she drawled, 'why don't you sit down while I call him?'

I sank down into a low leather chair. Just then a guy of around forty, wearing a shiny suit that was at least two sizes too small for his frame, which if I was in a charitable mood I would describe as 'burly', twinkled up to me and asked, 'Can I help you, sir?'

'Oh, it's OK, thanks,' I started, 'I'm waiting for Mr Wright.' Too late I realised what I had said.

There was an infinitesimal pause, then with the suggestion of a wink, the man replied, 'Aren't we all, eh?' and twinkled away again.

I felt myself colouring, and hastily picking up a paper, pretended I was engrossed in it. So successfully did I manage this, that I gave quite a jump when a hand fell on my shoulder and a familiar voice said, 'Come on, time to get going!'

I struggled up from my chair. 'Hi Marcus, yes let's hit the road.' I was anxious not to linger any longer than was necessary.

'Gloria been looking after you?' Marcus nodded in the direction of the dark-haired receptionist. 'Hi Gloria, how are you, hun?' Marcus affected a fake American accent as he said this, 'see you at the party later, eh?' He gave a double click of the tongue as he finished.

'Sure thing, honey,' Gloria replied.

'Oh yes, Gloria has been most — er — helpful,' I went, 'come on, Marcus, let's go!'

'All right, all right, I'm coming,' Marcus went, 'what's the hurry?'

I didn't feel like explaining that one, so I added, 'I could do with a drink.'

'Fine,' said Marcus, 'I know this great bar on top of a hotel near Central Park…'

'Actually, I was thinking more of a nice cup of tea,' I interrupted, 'how about going back to our hotel. I think we can get one there. Anyway, we could do with pacing ourselves before the party tonight.'

'OK, well perhaps you're right,' said Marcus.

'Anyway, I'm whacked with sightseeing, so I could do with

a breather,' I went on as we descended to the ground floor. Giving a resigned shrug, Marcus followed me out of the lift and exiting the building into a bitingly cold east wind, hailed a taxi. 'I'm not walking far in these temperatures,' he exclaimed as we clambered in, 'cold enough to freeze the proverbial!'

Back at the hotel we made ourselves comfortable, and I ordered tea from room service. It arrived with commendable despatch, but as I feared, with hot water in a jug and separate tea-bags. By the time the water had hit the tea, it was probably 15 degrees below boiling, with the result that the tea was less than satisfactory. 'Why is it that you can never get a decent cuppa outside the UK?' I complained, 'it's really not difficult! But in Europe, they give you a glass jug of hot water, which has probably just been put in the microwave for a moment or two — no such thing as a proper kettle there!'

Marcus, coming out of the shower, threw a wet towel in my direction. 'Oh, stop whinging,' he laughed, 'I told you it would be a better idea to have a cocktail on the top of that hotel.'

'Yes, well, no doubt there will be plenty to drink later,' I pointed out, 'and I'd quite like to retain *some* liver function tomorrow!' I put my cup down. 'Right, well I'd better have a shower myself and get ready. Is it far to this place?'

Marcus shook his head. 'No, only a couple of blocks. That's partly why we chose this hotel. We can walk there and...'

'...and crawl back on our hands and knees?'

Marcus pulled a face. 'Ha, ha very funny! No, I was going to say that we can always get a cab back if we want.'

Our breath hung in the frosty air as we made our way up Broadway, and in spite of the light pollution, stars coruscated in an inky sky, diamonds on a black velvet cloth. It was not long before we arrived at our destination, an impressive stone building with Doric columns, reminiscent of a Roman temple. In response to my murmur of admiration, Marcus chipped in, 'I think it was originally a bank when it was built in the early 1920s.'

'I feel as if we should be wearing togas and sandals going in here,' I remarked.

'Well, funny you should say that, apparently we did have a "do" here a year or so back, where the idea was to come in togas. Unfortunately, a couple of the guys had neglected to equip themselves with suitable undergarments.'

'And?'

'Well, let's just say there was an incident in which the revolving doors played a major part...'

'Ah! That must have been embarrassing.'

'Yes, they could hardly conceal their dismay...amongst other things,' Marcus grinned, then went on, 'so since then, it was felt it was safer to stick to ordinary clothes.'

'Good decision!'

We entered through the revolving doors, luckily without problem, and mounted the stairs, at the top of which we were relieved of our outer garments, then were ushered in to the main reception room.

'Stone me, this is quite something!' I muttered in Marcus's ear. He shrugged and said airily, 'Oh it's not much, but we like to call it home!'

The room was enormous ellipse, with at one end a row of tall Doric columns, in front of a raised dais, once again emphasising the temple-like nature of the building. Overhead, a vast, glazed dome covered the centre of the floor, whilst on the walls were projected artificial vistas, so that it seemed one direction looked over New York harbour and the statue of Liberty, not unreasonably, whilst opposite was a point of view film of what looked like the Cresta run. Dining tables, each seating around a dozen people, were arranged around the perimeter of the oval, and in the centre was a large, six-sided bar, surrounding a tree covered in thousands of tiny white lights.

'Let's go over to the mixologist first,' Marcus suggested, propelling me gently across the floor by means of a hand on my elbow.

'Mixologist? What the heck's that?' I asked, puzzled.

'A drink, you twerp!' Marcus replied inelegantly as we arrived at the bar, 'now what would you like? How about a "Widow's Kiss"?'

'Very kind, but I'm spoken for, thanks,' I retorted, 'I think I'll just stick to some champagne, if that's on offer.'

'Of course,' Marcus spoke to the barman, and ordered for himself something called a 'Corpse Reviver'. After taking a long pull on it, Marcus offered me a taste. I gave it a dubious sniff.

'God, that smells lethal — the sort of thing you'll regret tomorrow!' I handed it back to Marcus, who merely grinned cheerfully and took another gulp.

'Well, I must go and mingle a bit,' he said, 'should I introduce you to people as we go?'

'No, it's all right, you go and mingle,' I said, heaving myself onto a bar-stool, 'I'll be fine here.'

He disappeared into a throng of party-goers, showering kisses, hugs and pats on the back as he went.

'Great guy, isn't he?' A low voice made me spin around on my stool, to find a tall, thin, angular woman, with long, straight black hair, had taken the adjoining seat. There was more than a faint resemblance to Cruella de Ville...

'Er, well, yes, I think so,' I muttered in reply, not quite sure what to say.

The woman held out a thin hand. 'Veronica, but everyone calls me Very.'

I paused for a second wondering whether to reply, 'Very pleased to meet you, Very,' or perhaps, 'Very, very pleased to meet you,' but thinking that the latter could be misinterpreted as too effusive, settled rather lamely for, 'Oh, hi, I'm Ben.'

'Ben?'

'Jonson. Ben Jonson. Like the 17th century playwright.' Blank look. 'Or the athlete. But without the "h".'

'OK, Ben Jonson without the "h" what are you doing here? You're not one of us, are you?'

'By "us" I take it you mean an employee of the firm, and you're quite correct,' I said, sounding even to my own ears rather pompous, 'but I'm here with Marcus, actually.'

'Oh, you're *that* Ben! Of course, I've heard a lot about you from Marcus.'

'All good, I hope?' I gave a nervous laugh.

Very looked at me through narrowed eyes. 'Mostly.'

This was hardly encouraging, and I was toying with the idea of moving away and going in search of Marcus when Very suddenly spoke once more. 'Aren't you the guy who sniffs out frauds and stuff?'

'I'm not sure I'd put it in quite those terms,' I replied, 'I am a forensic accountant by profession, and part of the job description does include investigating fraud from time to time, I suppose.'

'Marcus seems to think you're some sort of super sleuth.'

I made a self-deprecating little snort and spread my hands out, 'Oh, hardly that.'

Very raised a pencil-thin eyebrow. 'You see,' she said, 'I could do with a bit of advice…'

'Where on earth did you get to? I've been searching high and low for you this last half hour!' Marcus sounded quite cross as he put an arm around my shoulder some half an hour later.

'Were you getting worried about me?'

'Well, no, not worried exactly. I just wanted to make sure that you were enjoying yourself, that's all.'

'Ah, bless!' I poked Marcus playfully in the midriff, 'Actually, I've been having a little tete-a-tete with this woman called Veronica, sorry, *Very*. Or should I say, Very sorry?'

'Veronica? Bloody hell, what were you talking about with her?' Marcus looked stunned.

'Oh, I'm not sure I can tell you at the moment,' I said in a slightly arch fashion, 'who is she anyway?'

'Veronica is world-wide head of marketing, so in fact she is effectively my boss!' Marcus replied, 'I hope you haven't said anything that'll cause trouble.'

'Of course, I haven't, bonehead, what do you think I am?' I retorted, before adding, 'well that is to say, it shouldn't cause *you* any trouble...'

Veronica had suggested we move to a quiet room to the right of the dais for our chat, and thoughtfully commandeering a bottle of Bolly as she got down from her stool, led me across the floor. In the distance I could see Marcus in the middle of a group, talking loudly, with one arm round Gloria the receptionist, and another round a rather good-looking guy in his thirties with short, blonde hair. 'Looks like Marcus is enjoying the party,' I commented, but Very merely nodded and ushered me through the door, and gestured me to take a seat.

'OK, Very, what can I do for you?' I asked, as she poured us each a fresh slug of champagne.

'It's like this, Ben,' she began, taking a sip from her glass, 'I took on this new employee a few months ago, who seems great. In fact, that's the problem — too good to be true. And I get a funny feeling that there's something not quite right.'

'Well, you need to give me a bit more information, I think,' I started, 'and without pre-judging anything, I have to say that I have found that people who really know their business often have a good instinct about such matters. We accountants and auditors can trawl through the detailed figures to our hearts' content, but we don't necessarily have the feel that those running the show do. Anyway, carry on.'

Veronica started to talk. She refused to name the person involved — 'no point, Ben Jonson without the "h" because you wouldn't know them' — but they were involved with sales, and crucially, part of the remuneration was based on sales figures. Veronica explained how this was calculated, and that her suspicions were aroused when she happened to notice that their overall pay seemed to be a fair degree higher that the predecessor's had been, although there had not been any material alteration in pay scales.

'So the question is, Mr Jonson without the "h", can you tell me what I should be looking for or at?'

'In other words, how would I fiddle the books?' I asked ironically. A sudden horrible thought struck me. 'This hasn't got anything to do with Marcus, has it? I really don't think he would do anything like that.'

Very assured me that the person concerned was not Marcus, so I relaxed and started to think. 'In broad terms, if someone is trying to boost the profit, either of their company, or just their section of it, then you are looking at overstating revenue, and/ or *understating* expenses. So the first thing to look at is this guy's invoicing.'

'Sure, but how could that be manipulated?'

'Well, the easiest way is for them to produce totally fake invoices. But that of course would probably be picked up fairly quickly because someone would notice that these aren't being paid — unless they're managing to divert funds from other customers, in a process we call "teeming and lading". But from what you've said, I don't think they could do that.'

Very nodded, 'OK, go on.'

I took a slurp of bubbly and continued, 'So I would guess that what he might do is overbill in one period, then issue credit notes in the next for instance. Of course, there is a limit on how long he could continue to do that, but if he's not been with you long, then he might get away with it. In addition, if you include work-in-progress in your revenue line,' here Very nodded confirmation, 'then the work-in-progress figure could be inflated, thereby increasing the apparent revenue, and consequently his pay, if it is based on that figure.'

Very had produced a pad and pen from her handbag, and was busily scribbling notes, so taking another mouthful of champagne, I set off again. 'Also, I think you mentioned that the revenue line includes expenses which are rechargeable to the client?' Very nodded. 'That being so, then I would look carefully at those to see if they are being manipulated.'

We talked through these items for a while longer, and I made some suggestions as to what Very should be looking at.

'Well, thank you Ben,' she said finally, 'I must let you get back to the party and Marcus, of course. In the meantime, I'll just go over to the office for a while. Catch up with you later.' She put her pad and pen in her bag and snapped it firmly shut, then added, 'There is one other thing I wanted to ask you...'

'Mm, well I wonder who Very was talking about,' Marcus mused after I had given him a brief synopsis of my discussion.

'Well, I don't know — she was very (ha, ha, no pun intended!) careful *not* to mention names. And it would probably be just as well not to speculate — you don't want to start casting aspersions on some poor innocent.'

'Fair enough!' Marcus agreed, 'anyway, come on let's go and sit down — we're ready to eat!'

He led me across the floor to a table where it seemed his 'team' had taken up residence, and I was ushered into a chair. Food and drink suddenly appeared and I found that I was ravenous. Tucking in to a large piece of steak, I noticed that my neighbour's plate, belonging to a rather large girl of around thirty, was completely devoid of meat. Pointing my knife, I commented to her, 'I take it you're vegetarian?'

She nodded. 'Isn't everyone now?'

Glancing in front of me where there seemed to be the better part of a well-endowed ox, I thought this was possibly a comment a little wide of the mark, but buoyed probably by a bit too much, Bolly replied, 'Now tell me — are you vegetarian because you love animals? Or is that you hate plants?'

Obviously, my attempts at humour were not appreciated in the Big Apple, so to speak, and the woman merely gazed at me for a second, then turned to speak to the neighbour on her other side.

A voice in my ear made me turn my head. It was the young, blonde chap that I had seen earlier with Marcus. 'Just thought I'd come and say "hi",' he went, 'I've been hearing all about you, from Marcus.'

Instinctively I gave my usual response to this opening

gambit. 'All good, I hope?'

He shrugged. 'Mostly.' It was an unnerving repetition of what Very had said earlier. 'No, I'm kidding,' went on the young man, with a disarming smile, 'it's nothing but undiluted praise. I'm Zachary, by the way, Zachary Horn.'

There was a name to conjure with, I thought. I toyed with the idea of making some comment along the lines of 'you usually blow your own trumpet, then' but decided against it, and stuck out a hand. 'Pleased to meet you, Zachary.'

'Call me Zak.'

'Zak, then. And I'm Ben, but please call me — er — Ben,' I finished feebly, thinking that I must watch how much champagne I imbibed.

'And I see you've met Dalia,' here Zak nodded in the direction of my vegetarian neighbour.

'Oh yes, we're old friends,' I returned, 'we share a mutual interest in animal welfare.' Zak looked a bit at sea, so I quickly continued, 'so, tell me Zak, how do you fit in to the organisation, and how do you know Marcus?'

Zak pulled up a chair and slumped down beside me. 'I'm on the sales side,' he began, 'though I haven't been with the organisation for that long. I did my induction process in Brussels, though, which is where I met Marcus.'

'Really?'

'Yes,' Zak continued, 'Marcus and I had many an evening in the bars and restaurants of Brussels.' Possibly seeing my expression alter somewhat, he added swiftly, 'Along with the rest of the team, of course.'

'Of course,' I confirmed, though thinking it strange that Marcus had never mentioned the young man's name…

After a few minutes' conversation, Zak moved off, to be

replaced almost at once by Marcus. 'Just thought I'd move around the table and talk to everyone,' he murmured, then nodding in the direction of Zak, 'I see you've met the star of our sales team. What do you think?'

'Very pleasant. We had a nice chat — particularly about the night-life in Brussels.' I fixed Marcus with one of my best Janet-like gimlet looks, but he returned my gaze with equanimity.

'Oh, yes? Anyway, he's a good bloke — Very did well to hire him.'

'Very did very well!' I scoffed as Marcus rolled his eyes upwards, 'but I thought she was boss of marketing, not sales?'

'Yes, that's right, although sales does come partly under her remit. But the European head of sales was away ill for part of last year, and Very took a more hands-on role for a time.'

I nodded, but a thought struck me. 'You said he was the star performer?'

'Yes indeed,' Marcus affirmed, 'apparently his figures are really good — much better than his predecessor.'

'And no doubt he earns commission or bonus on those figures?' Marcus confirmed that this was indeed the case, and I began to get an uncomfortable feeling as my earlier conversation with Very replayed in my mind. 'Funny, you never mentioned him when you were apparently in Brussels together and painting the town red?'

Marcus gave me one of his shifty looks, that is, he looked straight into my eyes without blinking. 'Oh, yes? Must have slipped my mind.'

I let it go, though it came back to me the way Marcus had his arm around young Zak earlier that evening...

We finished eating and Marcus grabbed me and took me around, introducing me to his colleagues, who it must be said, all seemed intent on having a good time. I was in a group trying to explain the activities of the Operatic Society, and in particular, the fascination I had with the Savoy Operas of Messrs Gilbert and Sullivan, which seemed to leave them all mystified, when Very appeared once more. I sprang up and, as Marcus started to say, 'I think you have already met...' I greeted Very by kissing her quite fulsomely on each cheek, before offering her a seat. I was vaguely aware of an almost audible gasp behind me, but affected not to notice.

Very interrupted Marcus, 'Yes, yes, we had quite a long chat earlier, Marcus. And Marcus, I need to give you a dressing down...' here Marcus looked startled, not to say dismayed, '...you didn't tell me what a dish Ben is! Definitely film star looks!'

'Unfortunately, the film star in question being Lassie,' I cut in, to laughter all round. I was not used to such compliments.

'Well, I think so,' said Marcus and put a hand on my shoulder. There was a slightly awkward pause, as I felt my eyes beginning to fill, but then Very continued, 'But I'm afraid I'm going to have to drag Ben away now, Marcus. Time for the entertainment!'

'Entertainment?' Marcus sounded puzzled.

'Er, yes,' I explained, 'Very entered us for the karaoke competition. Didn't I mention it?'

It was an hour later when I finally made it back to our table. By a stroke of immense good luck, it turned out that not only was Very actually a more than competent singer — she had apparently given serious consideration to being a professional at one time — but also my recent hit with the lovely Janet, 'Baby, it's cold outside', was on the play list. A brief discussion with Very, who readily fell in with my suggestion of performing it as I had done at the CAOS Christmas concert, and we were away. Once again, there was a tremendous reception, and Very and I found ourselves the winners of the competition. Flushed with success, I looked for Marcus. I found him propping up the bar under the enormous artificial tree, downing what looked suspiciously like another Corpse Reviver.

'Oh, it's you,' Marcus growled after I'd tapped him on the shoulder. If I had been expecting an outpouring of enthusiastic admiration for my performance, I was sadly mistaken.

'Yes, well spotted,' I said dryly, 'well, what did you think?'

Marcus wiped a hand across his mouth to get rid of some of the liquor that I had noted with some alarm was dribbling down his chin. I also noticed the shirt buttons were undone almost to the navel... 'What did I think?' he started somewhat bibulously, 'what I thought was, what the f--- do you think you're doing? These are my colleagues and bosses here tonight, not your little band of am-dram queens.'

I was stunned. I started to respond, stammering, 'But I thought you would be pleased I was getting on so well with Very...'

'Yeah, sure,' Marcus scoffed, 'She's my boss. You've gone over my head, behind my back...'

'Quite the contortionist, aren't I?' I retorted, stung by his comments. Marcus looked as though he was going to carry on the argument, but at that moment friend Zak appeared.

'Just had to come and congratulate you in person, Ben,' he said, 'it was a fantastic performance. You must be very proud, eh Marcus?' He gave Marcus a playful punch on the shoulder, but Marcus, unsmiling, just shrugged and said, 'Yeah, sure.' Muttering something about getting another drink, he lurched off.

'What's biting him?' Zak asked, puzzled.

It was my turn to shrug. 'Just tired and emotional, I guess,' I said lightly.

Zak gave me a thoughtful look, but obviously decided not to pursue the matter. 'Is Very around?' he asked, 'I wanted to congratulate the pair of you and get you a glass of fizz to celebrate.'

'I'm not sure where she's got to,' I replied, 'as soon as we'd finished, she said she had a bit of business to attend to, but I don't know what that would be at this time of day.'

'Let me get you a drink to celebrate, Ben. Bolly?'

'Why not?'

Zak summoned the barman in a manner reminiscent of my old pal Tom in the hallowed portals of Et Alia and procured two glasses of champagne in what seemed like a microsecond. 'Salud!' he cried, and we chinked glasses. The talk of Very reminded me of her conversation with me earlier, and I seized the opportunity to do a little probing.

'So, you've not been with the firm long, Zak?' I began. He confirmed that this was the case. 'But you're already their super-salesman?' I added, with a smile.

Zak, being American, did not suffer from an English sense of false modesty. 'I guess so,' he stated, matter-of-factly.

'That must be good for your pay-packet?' I suggested, 'presumably you get a percentage of the sales?'

'Uh-huh.' He sounded non-committal.

'So, what's the secret of your success?' I asked playfully.

Zak's eyes narrowed slightly. 'If I told you that, you might give it away to my rivals.'

'No, no, you can trust me — I'm an accountant!' I was still in playful mode. 'Anyway, so who are your rivals?'

'You've already met one of them.'

'I have?'

'Yes. You remember Dalia, don't you?'

I thought for a second. 'Ah yes. The veggie eco-warrior, as I recall. She's in sales? Somehow, she doesn't look the type.'

'Not sure that there is a type, but she's certainly done well.' Zak finished his drink. 'But this is boring stuff, let's talk about something interesting.' There was something unnerving about the way that he suddenly looked at me with his brilliant blue eyes, but before I could respond, Gloria swept up to us saying, 'C'mon boys, get on the dance-floor,' and taking us by the hand, pulled us both across the room into a swaying mass of people. The heavy beat of the music and the swirling lights, on top of several glasses of champagne, soon began to take their toll, and I manoeuvred my way across the floor in search of somewhere to sit. I found a small table and chairs at one end of the room, flopped down and closed my eyes.

'Pace too much for you, eh?' The voice in my ear made me come to with a start. I opened my eyes to find Very looming over me. She dropped down into the chair alongside.

'I owe you big time, Ben Jonson-without-the-h!' she began.

'What?'

'Yep, I went back to the office just now and did what you suggested. And you were right.'

It all came back to me. 'Oh, the super salesman thing you mean? So you've got your man have you?'

'Sure thing!'

'Are you going to fire them?'

Very gave a mirthless laugh. 'Oh, I think that's inevitable, don't you? But not tonight. I don't want to spoil a great party, eh?'

245

'Perhaps not. Can I ask who the culprit is?'

'You can ask, Ben without-the-h, but I'm not saying. It wouldn't be fair.'

'No, I suppose so.'

'Time I went,' said Very, 'and looks as though the same goes for you. Can I give you a ride?'

'No thanks — I need to find Marcus. He seems to be in a bit of a mood about something, so I better not go without him.'

Very looked at me for a moment, then suddenly leaned forward and kissed me. 'Pity we didn't meet sooner,' she said softly, and with that she was gone, leaving me wondering what she had meant...

I stood up after a minute or so, and decided I'd better look for the elusive Marcus. I wandered about the hall for a while, then fought my way across the still crowded dance floor to the bar in the middle, where I had an inkling that I might locate him. Sure enough, perched on a stool with his broad back to me, there he was, one hand clasped firmly around what looked suspiciously like yet another Corpse Reviver, and the other equally firmly around Zak. They were talking in low voices, so I could not catch everything they were saying, but I caught a few words: 'You ought to say to him, Marcus,' Zak was saying, 'it's only fair.'

I froze for a second. What was this? The 'him' I took to be me. What ought Marcus tell me? That he had had a fling with the winsome Zak? Or worse, that he *was* having a fling with him? Steeling myself, I move forward and tapped Marcus on the shoulder. His other hand withdrew swiftly from his companion as he swung around to face me.

'Ben! I wondered where you were.'

'Can we go now? I'm knackered!'

Marcus pulled a face. 'Not sure, actually. I think I ought to stay on a bit longer.'

'Right, well, OK, I'll make my own way, should I?'

Zak intervened. 'I can see Ben gets back to your hotel safely. Time I was going anyway.'

'Don't bother, I can find my own way. I'm a big boy now!' I retorted, rather rudely, 'I'll leave you to carry on…your conversation!'

Zak looked startled, and Marcus tight-lipped as I turned on my heels and stalked off.

Remembering to collect my overcoat, I sailed out of the building looking up and down the street for a cab. There were none in sight, and as I stood wondering whether I should start walking, a dark saloon pulled up beside me and a window rolled down. 'You want a ride after all?' said a familiar voice.

I bent down to the open window. 'Well, yes, Very, thanks very much.' I winced at this unintentional play on her name. I added, 'if it's not too much trouble.'

She didn't reply, but the door swung open, and I climbed in. 'It's not far,' I started, 'Just down here a little way.'

'Marcus not with you?' she asked.

'Apparently not,' I replied.

Very shot me a look. 'Not had a row, I hope?'

I shook my head. 'No, he just seemed a bit tied up. Mainly with Zak.'

'Ah,' said Very, 'well, I wouldn't read too much into that. They worked closely together in Brussels.'

'Perhaps a bit *too* closely.' I was aware I was starting to sound a little hysterical.

Very put a hand on my leg. 'Don't go there, Ben. It's not wise.'

We pulled up at my hotel. I opened the door and started to

say my thank yous. On impulse I added, 'Do you want to come in for a coffee or something?'

Very gave me an amused smile. 'Well, the "something" sounds interesting, but no, thank you, Ben. Too complicated.'

I shrugged. 'Well, OK, if you say so. I'll say good night then. Hope to see you again.'

Very smiled. 'I hope so too, Ben. Now I must go.'

The car pulled away, and I stood watching as it disappeared into the traffic. I may have been mistaken, but I think I saw Very turn and look at me as the car sped away...

I must have fallen asleep as soon as my head touched the pillow: the time difference tends to catch up with you later in the day. I stirred vaguely when Marcus came crashing into our room sometime later, then he lay down and quickly started snoring. I went back to sleep and came to some hours later. I could see a sickly grey light around the edge of the blinds, as I rolled out of bed and headed for the shower. When I came back, Marcus was sitting up, rubbing his eyes.

'Awake at last! You OK?' I asked.

'Yeah. Bit of a head.'

'Not surprised, judging by the way you were knocking back those Corpse Reviver things!'

Marcus ignored this jibe. 'Why did you storm off in a huff?'

I bridled. 'I did not storm off in a huff, as you so quaintly put it! I was getting tired, and you wanted to party on, so I quietly left you to it and made my way back here.'

Marcus looked sceptical. 'Sure. But I just wanted to say...'

I did not get to find out what he just wanted to say, because at that moment, his mobile "pinged" loudly. Snatching it up from its perch on a low table, Marcus scanned it. 'Oh-ho!' he exclaimed, 'I wonder what's up. Just been summoned to a meeting with your new best friend!'

I looked blank. 'Veronica, of course!' he cried, 'I'd better get a shift on.' He leapt out of bed and disappeared into the bathroom. A few minutes later, he reappeared, hair wet and sticking up, and started rummaging around looking for clothes. 'I'll message you when I know what's going on,' he said, pulling a shirt over his head, 'I need to talk to you.'

'Talk? About what?'

'Later. Must dash.' He ruffled my hair as he dived out of the room. 'See you,' he called over his shoulder.

'Yeah. Sure thing. See you later,' I said moodily to his retreating back.

I ordered some breakfast, and sat absent-mindedly eating it, watching as the sun came up on a clear, brilliant, New York morning. Was I reading too much into the Zak thing? Perhaps I had behaved rather badly by leaving the party as I did. On the other hand, Marcus had been distinctly "off" with me earlier in the evening. What was it he had said after the karaoke? *What the f--- do you think you're doing? These are my colleagues and bosses here tonight, not your little band of am-dram queens.* Hardly conducive to the peace of nations. But perhaps there was something in what he said, or was trying to say. Perhaps I had been a bit too eager to show off, although to be fair, I was aided, abetted, not to say encouraged, by the enigmatic Veronica. I thought Marcus enjoyed our amateur operatics, but perhaps he just regarded them with amused disdain, something to keep me occupied and out of the way whilst...

The "ping" of my phone shook me out of my reverie. Glancing at it, I saw it was a message from Marcus. *Meet me in Central Park at eleven. By the skating rink.*

I made my way to Central Park at the appointed hour, and stood at the entrance to the rink, rubbing my gloved hands together against the intense cold. A tap on my shoulder after a few moments made me jump, and I turned to find Marcus standing behind me. 'Come on!' he said, 'let's literally get our skates on!'

'If I must,' I muttered under my breath. I have only been ice-skating a couple of times before and neither occasion proved to be a great success. The last time was with Julia in Austria, when the kids were much younger. They had all been really good at it, but I had struggled and spent more time spread-eagled on the ice than skating, much to the amusement of the rest of my family.

As we sat side by side on the bench, putting on our skates, Marcus turned to me and said, 'Look, I wanted to say sorry about last night. It was stupid what I said about the karaoke thing, and I shouldn't have done it. Can you forgive me? Please?'

My head was bent down as I did up the fastenings, and it was with some surprise that I felt a tear roll down my cheek and fall unbidden onto the frozen ground. Looking up at Marcus, I said, 'Well, I was pretty short with you later, and I'm sorry too. I didn't mean to mess up your evening.'

'Truce then?'

'Truce!' Marcus looked relieved. 'Just one thing,' I added, 'tell me honestly: in Brussels, when you were there such a lot, did you and Zak…?'

Marcus scoffed. 'Is that what you were so uptight about? Anyway,' he went on, stabbing my chest with a finger, 'I thought you had me down for a fling there with Alan Lowe. You must think I have plenty of stamina! But, no, honestly, nothing happened between Zak and me.'

I was tempted to add, 'Did you want it to?' but some questions are better not posed…

Instead, I asked, 'So what was the big pow-wow with the great white chief, aka Veronica, all about?'

'Ah yes! I was coming to that!' Marcus began, 'come on, let's get skating; it's freezing sitting here.' We moved off onto the ice proper, with me staying within a hand's grasp of the rail, and

Marcus nonchalantly gliding over the rink as if he had been born to it.

'So, go on, what happened?' I prompted as we completed a circuit without undue drama.

'Well, first of all, Very was very complimentary about you, old sport!' Marcus began, 'she told us all about the cosy chat you two had last night, and how she'd slipped back to the office late on and done a little checking. And of course, she found out that it was just as you said — all the credit notes, manipulation of work-in-progress, expenses and all the rest of it. And that naturally, first thing this morning, she had a meeting with the person involved and fired them.'

'OK, right, but do you mean Zak?'

'You thought it was Zak she was talking about?' Marcus sounded surprised, 'why would you think that?'

'Well, he fitted the description, or rather the sketchy outline that Very gave me, in that he was a new kid on the block, his sales were apparently very high and oh, I don't know, perhaps he was trying a bit too hard with the charm.'

Marcus gave a snort. 'I don't know he was trying with the charm, I think he's just like that. Anyway, you couldn't have been more wrong!'

'Well, who then?' I asked exasperated.

'It was in fact, that girl Dalia!' Marcus announced triumphantly.

'Dalia? You mean the veggie girl with the sense of humour bypass? Well, stone me!' I almost stumbled in surprise. Steadying myself, I went on in a thoughtful tone, 'Though now I think of it, I did express surprise that she was a good salesperson when Zak mentioned it last night.'

'Clearly you were right after all,' Marcus pointed out, 'since she seems to have been fiddling the books. Anyway, she's toast, as they say. But you, on the other hand, are the toast of the town, at least as far as Very is concerned. I think you've made a bit of a conquest there!' He gave me a playful nudge as he said this, which nearly sent me careering into the barrier. Regaining my balance, I mused on the events of the previous evening and the memory of Very turning round to look at me as her car drove away…

'Watch it!' Marcus brought me back into the present with a start. 'Now listen, Ben, I want you just to wait there for a second.'

'OK, but why?'

'Just want to have a quick circuit or two at speed without you getting in the way!'

'Oh well, fine, please don't try to spare my feelings, will you?' I protested.

Marcus grinned, and zoomed off. I watched him as he soared across the ice, a tall, muscular figure with an easy athletic grace. My mind went back to the previous evening when I had also studied him from afar, though that had been when he had been in deep conversation with the tantalising Zak. What was it that Zak had urged Marcus to say to me?

All at once, Marcus changed direction, and instead of going in a wide circle around the perimeter of the rink, he headed straight towards me. A few yards away, he dropped down, then pirouetting in a tight circle came to a halt, kneeling down on one knee in front of me. He held a small box in one hand, and I suddenly realised the answer to my question…